BLAST FROM THE PAST

ALSO BY DAMIEN BOYD

DI NICK DIXON

As the Crow Flies

Head in the Sand

Kickback

Swansong

Dead Level

Death Sentence

Heads or Tails

Dead Lock

Beyond the Point

Down Among the Dead

Dying Inside

Carnival Blues

Death Message

From the Ashes

Blue Blood

DI BOB WILLIS

Deceived by the Light

A DI BOB WILLIS NOVEL

BLAST FROM THE PAST

THE THREE MILLION COPY BESTSELLING AUTHOR

DAMIEN BOYD

THOMAS & MERCER

This is a work of fiction. Names, characters, organizations, places, events, and incidents are either products of the author's imagination or used fictitiously. Any resemblance to actual persons, living or dead, or actual events is purely coincidental.

Published by Thomas & Mercer, Seattle
www.apub.com

EU Product Safety contact:
Amazon Publishing, Amazon Media EU S.à r.l.
38, avenue John F. Kennedy, L-1855 Luxembourg
amazonpublishing-gpsr@amazon.com

ISBN-13: 9781662524721
eISBN: 9781662524714

Cover design by @blacksheep-uk.com
Cover image: © Rob Fuller © AlexanderBee / Shutterstock;
© Juliet Lehair / Getty Images

Printed in the United States of America

For Ken

Prologue

Tuesday 28th August 1962

It was a sobering thought.

Nine years old and he hardly knew the boy at all.

He was sitting opposite his son in the railway carriage, wondering who he was – who he was going to grow up to be.

Hardly a chip off the old block, that much was obvious.

There was a price to be paid for a career in the Navy, a life at sea. Perhaps this was it – or part of it?

Not exactly compatible with family life.

A son he hardly knew.

A son he didn't know at all, come to think of it.

The boy's younger sister was sitting next to him, banging her heels against the heater under the seat. Her feet didn't reach the floor, but then she was only six. And he'd only been at home for two of her Christmases.

Then there was his wife, at home with their youngest; eighteen months old.

He knew he shouldn't, but he'd done the maths and had been on shore leave at the relevant time. Give or take.

He had a family. A family life. But he'd missed most of it.

'Take them for a day at the beach, John,' his wife had said. 'You can go on the steam train. It'll be your last chance; the line closes in a week or two.'

It had seemed like a good idea at the time.

'Don't let them near the donkeys, though. They're riddled with fleas.'

Boarding school had been his idea. Not one of his best, as it turned out. He thought it might give the boy a bit of backbone; toughen him up.

It had worked – up to a point. The constant crying had stopped, but not the bed wetting. And rather than coming out of his shell, his son seemed to have retreated into it still further.

'He's never the same when you're around.' More pearls of wisdom from his wife. 'He's terrified of you.' Then she'd brought the Navy into it. Again. 'He's not one of your bloody crew. Barking orders at him all the time.'

It was about discipline.

And the boy had none.

'You don't treat the girls like that.'

A fair point. Possibly.

He'd bought them ice creams at Evercreech Junction, while they waited for the steam train. The platform had been busy, the queue long.

Everyone seemed to have at least one bucket and spade. Rachel hadn't wanted to bring hers. He'd asked her why she didn't want to build sandcastles like the other children – after all, he'd done it as a child – wasn't surprised by her answer. Disappointed, but not surprised.

'There's no point, Daddy. Paul will just kick them over.'

He'd been watching the crowds further along the platform when he heard her scream, turned to find her trying to pick her melting ice cream up off the concrete.

'I'll buy you another one when we get to the beach, Rachel,' he said, noticing his son smirking.

Sick to the pit of his stomach, but he decided to let it go. Was he allowed to admit he didn't much like his own son?

There was no one he could tell, least of all his wife.

The boy was standing on tiptoe now, leaning out of the window, looking towards the front of the train, the wind blowing his hair. Not a good idea on a steam locomotive.

'Get back in, Paul,' he said. 'You'll get a face full of soot.'

Then his son yelped, ducking back into the compartment, rubbing his eyes furiously.

'I warned you, didn't I?'

He'd have been smacked across the backs of his legs for being so stupid, but he decided to spare his son the public humiliation.

'Look, why don't you go and play with those boys in the corridor? They seem to be having fun.'

Running up and down, lurching from side to side, trying to stay on their feet as the carriage rocked, howls of delight filling the awkward silences in the compartment.

He stood up, slid open the door to let his son out, watched the boy running up and down, always a few paces behind the others.

He turned back to the window, peat fields flashing by on the far side of the canal.

The train slowed, the brakes squealing in protest, before it stopped at Ashcott, clouds of steam venting from the locomotive.

Standing room only now in the few carriages that had pulled in adjacent to the short platform. No space for children to run up and down the corridor, no sound carrying over the noise of the engine crawling out of the station.

Freight wagons in a siding, more peat fields, the train picking up speed again.

No sign of Paul.

Stupid boy.

'Rachel, go and see if you can find your brother.'

He looked at the woman sitting opposite him, rolled his eyes, the gesture returned with a knowing smile.

'He's not here, Daddy.'

'What?' He stood up, sat the girl down in his seat. 'Stay here.'

Elbows out, pushing his way through the families lining the corridor, checking in each compartment.

'Have you seen my son?' he demanded, panic rising in his voice. 'He's nine. About so high, fair hair.'

Shaking heads.

A cold sweat in the small of his back, his shirt clinging to his skin. People saw him coming, saw the look on his face, quickly getting out of his way.

'Paul! Where are you?'

He banged on the doors of the toilets, despite the 'engaged' signs.

'Paul, are you in there?'

Then it hit him. The boy must've got off the train at Ashcott.

He reached up for the communication cord, pulled the chain sharply.

PENALTY FOR IMPROPER USE £5

To hell with that.

Chapter One

Wednesday 12th February 1986

'Who does that to a nine-year-old boy?'

I thought it was a fair question. Took the good doctor by surprise though. That and the photographs. A small bundle – black and white.

Crime scene photos are colour these days, not that it makes them any more stomach churning. You'd think it would, but black and white seems to pack more of a punch somehow. Don't ask me why.

It was a dirty trick all the same and I felt a bit guilty, really.

She's sitting there, ashen faced, flicking through the album.

'Lunch? That would be lovely, thank you,' she'd said. 'Where?'

'How about the Crown at Catcott?'

'Not a Little Chef?'

'I'm offering to buy you lunch.'

'Catcott's a bit of a drive from Exeter. Isn't there somewhere closer?'

'It's lovely. Well worth it.'

'All right then. I'll take your word for it.'

I felt a bit guilty about that too. Don't get me wrong, it's a lovely pub. Close to where we need to be.

Close to the crime scene.

A nice lunch first, then we'll go for a stroll.

I should tell you about the good doctor, shouldn't I? Caroline Mellanby is her name, lots of letters after it too. She's my chartered clinical psychologist. That's right. Mine. Avon and Somerset Police insisted that I complete the course of ten sessions, and I did. If I'm honest, it didn't help much. I was already over it . . . over *what happened*, but that's another story. Caroline still insists on asking me how I *feel* about it every time she sees me, but then I suppose that's her job.

She was kind enough to write a decent report at the end of the sessions and Superintendent Sharp turned out to be as good as his word, so here I am working on the new Cold Case Unit. It's my first case, a pretty bloody hopeless one too, they said, but we have to be seen to be looking at it again, apparently.

'Don't waste too much time on it, mate.'

Now we're not doctor and patient, the only thing Caroline and I have really got in common is cricket, but there's not much of that going on in the depths of winter. Still, the photos will give us plenty to talk about. Perhaps not over lunch, though.

She snapped the album shut, slid it behind her handbag on the seat next to her. 'Have you got the post mortem report?' she asked, taking a large swig from her gin and tonic.

'Not on me,' I replied.

'So, let me make sure I understand this correctly. Someone snatched this boy, locked him in there and left him to die?'

'His body was found six weeks later,' I said. 'He'd been dead about four.'

'No food or water?'

'There must have been some water in the kettle and that kept him going for a while. He tried drinking from the chemical toilet and there were traces of vomit with the blue dye in it.'

'What was his name?'

'Paul Bromfield.'

'And you want to know what sort of person would do that to a child?'

'Sorry.'

'You bloody well should be, Bob. Springing it on me like this.' She took another swig of gin and tonic. I could see she was softening, the colour slowly returning to her cheeks. Thinking about poor little Paul Bromfield, rather than how angry she was with me. Hopefully.

She looked up, someone walking towards us with a plate of food in each hand. 'Where was this?' she asked, her voice hushed.

'Chilton Polden,' I replied, gesturing over my shoulder. 'It's a couple of hundred yards south of the A39, in the corner of a field.'

'Which explains why we're here?'

A shrug was the best I had to offer.

'We'll continue this when we've eaten,' she said, firmly.

Lunch in front of a roaring fire; I had thought it might make up for it. Scampi for her, in one of those nice plastic baskets. A twist of lemon, tartare sauce. What more could she ask for?

'I didn't bring my wellies.'

'The ground was frozen when we came in,' I said, through a mouthful of lasagne. 'And I borrowed Shirley's. They're in the back of my car.'

'Thought of everything, haven't you,' she muttered. 'This is going to cost you more than a pub lunch.'

I was ahead of her there. 'How about two tickets to the opening day of the first test against India?' I asked. 'June fifth at Lord's.'

'Sold.' She smiled. 'There'll be no fast bowling from Bob, sadly. I see your namesake has decided to hang up his boots. Commentating for the Beeb, by all accounts.'

Sharing the same surname had been enough. I've often wondered how many people there are out there nicknamed 'Bob' just because their surname is Willis and they like cricket. Must happen to anyone called Dylan too. 'Hello, my name is Mungo Dylan, but everyone calls me Bob.'

Could be worse, I suppose.

'When was this?' Caroline asked when our empty plates had been cleared away, the dessert menu left on the corner of the table; one of those small blackboards with the choices for the day chalked on it.

I turned it to face her. '1962,' I replied.

'Stone cold then.'

'Not for the family.' That felt a bit sharp, and I could see it had taken her by surprise. Her face reddened and she turned to the dessert menu to hide her embarrassment. Best to keep the conversation moving. 'He was on one of the last excursion trains from Evercreech Junction to Burnham-on-Sea at the end of August 1962. The line closed the following month. We've got Dr Beeching to thank for that.'

'Do you remember the case?' she asked.

'I was still in uniform, based at Ilminster. We were bussed over pretty much every day to help with the search. Found nothing.' I took a swig of beer. 'What I remember most of all was finding out later he'd been alive for a couple of weeks. I've been on plenty of other searches, a body is found and they were dead all along. Not Paul Bromfield. That stayed with me. There was even a psychic doing the rounds, telling everyone who'd listen – usually tabloid newspapers – that Paul was alive. She could *feel* it. Turned out she was right.'

Caroline looked up at the barman standing by our table. 'Just a coffee for me, please.'

'You talking about Paul Bromfield?' he asked. 'I haven't heard that name for a very long time.'

'You were around here back then?' I asked.

'I was at school in the village. Used to walk to and from. Not after that.' The barman shook his head. 'They never did find who did it. Case is long closed now, I expect.'

'Sad,' I said. 'Just a coffee for me as well, please.'

'Why didn't you tell him?' asked Caroline when he'd gone.

'It'll be public knowledge soon enough.'

'Do the family know you're looking at it again?'

'Not yet. I've only just started; a couple of days reading the file, that's it so far.'

'Where was he from?'

'Wincanton. It was supposed to be a day out at the seaside. A last ride on the steam train before it closed for good. It was a carriage with compartments, and he'd been running up and down the corridor. They'd got as far as Shapwick before anyone realised he'd gone.' I was watching the barman making the coffee, checking he wasn't listening. 'Paul's father pulled the communication cord, stopped the train just outside the station there. They searched it, but he must've got off, or been taken off, at Ashcott. He was definitely on the train at Glastonbury because his father took him to the loo.'

'And he starved to death?'

'Thirst would've got him before the hunger. Your organs shut down—'

Caroline had heard enough, waved her hand. 'It's why I became a psychologist, not a surgeon,' she said, with a grimace. 'Perhaps he was kidnapped, and then the kidnapper died?'

'They looked at that, ruled it out, but I'll be looking at it again,' I said. 'The thinking was it was deliberate. He was *deliberately* left down there to die.'

'Doesn't bear thinking about. Have you spoken to the investigating officers?'

'Not yet. The SIO is dead, anyway. That just leaves his bagman. Crime scene first, and I wanted your opinion on it.'

We waited while the barman left a tray of coffee on the corner of the table. I returned his quizzical look with a cold smile.

'Trauma. There's going to be some major trauma in your killer's past.' Caroline was stirring her coffee, although most of it was ending up in the saucer. 'Then, triggered by some event, either internal or external, it manifested itself in this behaviour.'

'Is that it?'

'What more d'you want?'

'A name?'

'Very funny. Look, there's not a lot to go on, is there?' She took a sip of coffee. 'Nothing sexual?'

'No,' I replied. 'There was no evidence of physical or sexual violence. He was just kidnapped and left down there to die.'

'Then I'm not sure what else I can tell you, Bob. Offender profiling is big in America, and I've read some interesting stuff in the journals, but there's no sexual violence here. The nature and degree of that can tell you a lot. Physical injuries too, but this poor lad's been left to waste away. That will be relevant, of course.' Caroline frowned her distaste. 'The slowness of it will be part of it. It'll be someone who's been confronted with that in their past, perhaps. Either themselves or a loved one. And, if you think about it, the war ended only seventeen years before.'

'What about age and gender?'

'I'd just be guessing.' She unwrapped the little chocolate that had come with her coffee, dropped the wrapper in the ashtray. 'There's going to be some significance in what happened to the little boy. You can be sure of that. Either the manner of his death, or the place. That said, it could just be a coincidence. The killer might have left the boy down there, intending to return, lost his nerve and not gone back.' She fixed me with a steely glare. 'You keep saying *down* there, Bob. It's not underground, is it?'

'Afraid so.'

She shuddered. 'Perhaps if we went and had a look at this place?'

'I've got the keys.'

'I thought it was some sort of shed, or a garage.' She reached over to pick up the photo album again; thought better of it. 'What exactly is it?'

'A nuclear bunker.'

◆ ◆ ◆

We left Caroline's car at the pub, and a few minutes later I squeezed my Volvo estate into the field gateway near the entrance to the public footpath. Traffic was racing past on the A39 and it felt like an age staring in my wing mirror before I could open the driver's door.

'Hardly remote, is it?' she mumbled, leaning on the car, sliding her feet into Shirley's welly boots, one eye on the traffic flashing past.

'Do they fit?' I asked.

'They're a bit big, but they'll be fine.' Caroline straightened up. 'How is Shirley?' she asked.

'Getting there.'

'Not many ex-wives would be so understanding.'

'I know.'

We picked our way along the verge, thick clumps of wet grass waiting to trip us up, send us pitching forward into the traffic.

'Actually, it is pretty remote when you think about it,' said Caroline. 'Lots of people, but no one's going to stop, are they?'

'No one to hear you scream,' I said, turning to watch a red Golf GTI race past, music thumping over the noise of the engine.

'What about the footpath? Does that get used much?'

'You'll see.'

The stile was easy enough to find, although it wouldn't be long before it was hidden in the vegetation, the first buds of spring just visible in the bramble hedge, along with the cans and crisp packets.

'No one's been over this in ages,' she said, gesturing to the lichen growing on the tread.

'There's nowhere to park, apart from that gateway.' I was holding her hand, trying to steady her as she climbed over the wobbly stile. 'Hardly going to be a dog walking paradise either, is it? Not with the beach a few miles away.'

'There's the view.' Standing with her hands on her hips now, looking out through the bare branches of the copse in front of her. 'Would you look at that.'

The Somerset Levels stretched away to the south, criss-crossed by electricity pylons and the railway line, the motorway off to our right, rivers and rhynes glistening in the afternoon sun.

'We're on the top of the Polden Hills,' I said. 'The perfect place for an Observer Corps bunker.'

Caroline spun round. 'They were still in use in 1962, surely?'

'Some still are, even now. This one is.'

'How did the killer know Paul wouldn't be found, in that case?'

'Maybe he was hoping he would be?'

Another stile on the south side of the copse, then we were out into an open field, following the hedge. There was no path, just a line of electric fence posts at jaunty angles, the tape trodden into the mud under hoof prints. Horses then, rather than cows, safely stabled for the winter no doubt.

We walked around a patch of bare earth in front of a frozen cattle trough, heading towards a gate in the far corner of the field.

'You're not expecting me to climb over that, are you?'

'The bloke said it opens, so you'll be fine.'

'What bloke?'

'He runs the pub over at Burtle. He's the Chief Observer, in charge of the post.'

'It really is still in use?'

'Some have been abandoned, returned to the landowner, and the Observer Corps is winding down. They spend most of their time in the boozer, apparently.'

'Nice work if you can get it.'

'They're all volunteers,' I said, lifting the chain off the gatepost. The gate swung open, a small compound visible in the far corner of the next field. Concrete fence posts and barbed wire enclosing an area the size of a squash court.

'What are those green things?' asked Caroline.

'The bigger one is the entrance,' I replied. 'The other two are vents.'

A small gate meant we didn't have to negotiate the barbed wire, although I sensed that Caroline might baulk at the ladder. I hadn't mentioned that.

'This is it,' I said, with a reassuring smile, gesturing to a square concrete block that had been painted bright green. It stood about three feet high, and she was watching me undo the padlocks, one either side of the steel hatch.

'There's a ladder, isn't there,' she said, gritting her teeth. 'How else do we get down there?'

'You'll be fine.'

'I know I will be, but what about you?'

It was a fair question and one that had crossed my mind, if I'm honest. It was nearly eighteen months ago now, a car hit me out on the A303, smashed my left elbow and knee. They're a lot better these days but still ache in the cold. 'The bloke said to lean back, brace yourself against the wall as you climb down, then you can't fall.' I lifted the steel hatch, peered down into the gloom.

'You are joking.'

'Here,' I said, handing her a head torch. 'He lent me these. One each, saves us switching on the generator.'

'You did say two tickets to the test match?' Caroline was tightening the elasticated strap around her head.

'One for you and one for your husband.'

A steel ladder, fixed to the concrete with heavy bolts, disappeared into the darkness below.

'Thank God I wore trousers today.' She sat down on the edge of the entrance chamber, turned to allow her legs to dangle over the shaft. Then she reached forward and took a firm hold of the top rung of the ladder with both hands; she shuffled nearer, feeling for it with her feet, looking down to illuminate the way with the beam of her head torch.

Climbing down now, muttering something.

I waited for her to get clear of the bottom of the ladder.

'God, it's cramped down here.' Her voice echoed strangely, the shaft plunged into darkness again as she stepped off the bottom rung and into the bunker itself. 'How many men would be down here at one time?'

I leaned over, shouted my reply down the ladder. 'Two, sometimes three.'

She appeared again at the bottom of the entrance shaft, opened a door. 'That's the chemical toilet,' she said, quickly slamming it shut. She looked up. 'Are you coming down, or what?'

I led with my bad leg and was soon down the ladder. Two bunk beds against the far wall, a single to my right, so three could stay down here, although the thin mattresses felt damp to the touch. There was a table to my left, one of those folding director's chairs in front of it, wood with a canvas seat. A wooden cupboard bolted to the wall, the door hanging open.

'It's just teabags and some of that UHT milk.' Caroline was shining her torch at the kettle. 'That must be a new one.'

There was a light above my head, a cord dangling down, so I reached up and pulled it. It gave a soft click, but no light came on. Next to it on the ceiling was a strange-looking chrome plate, perhaps an air filter; it corresponded with where the air vent had been at ground level.

'1962,' said Caroline, softly. 'That makes it twenty-four years ago. It's no place for a nine-year-old boy to die alone. I'm guessing the generator wasn't switched on?'

'No.'

'In the darkness then.' She shook her head, her torch beam flickering on the far wall. 'Poor little lad must've been scared out of his wits.'

'Cold too,' I said. 'Even in August.'

'You said six weeks, so he was found in the October?'

'The sixteenth,' I replied. I was looking along the shelf fixed to the wall above the table: a loo roll, a can of three-in-one oil, an open packet of doughnuts, salt and pepper shakers. 'The ROC got the shout that all observation posts had to be manned immediately, round the clock. The first lot to get down here found him.'

'October 1962.'

'The Cuban missile crisis.'

'Of course.' Caroline nodded behind me. I could tell from her torch beam.

I slid the album of crime scene photographs out of my coat pocket, opened it at the first one, taken from the bottom of the ladder. Paul's body lay on the single bed behind me, curled into the foetal position. I resisted the urge to turn and look. The table and chair against the wall in front of me looked much the same in the photo: clutter on the shelf, a folded newspaper; a transistor radio, not that there'd be any reception down here.

I'd wondered if the killer had intended to take a picture of Paul holding the paper, use it for a ransom demand, possibly. Another theory ruled out by the original investigating team; the killer never made contact with the family.

I turned to the next photograph, a close-up of a Bunsen burner on the table; it looked out of place, the rubber tube dangling uselessly, no sign of a gas bottle and no gas supply to the bunker anyway. None of the Observer Corps volunteers knew what it had been doing there, either. It'll have spent the last twenty years in a box in the evidence store somewhere, and be on its way to me by now, hopefully. My request went in the day before yesterday.

'Seen enough?' I asked.

I left Caroline to climb the ladder, sat down on the director's chair, the wood creaking. I switched off my torch, tried to imagine what it must have been like for Paul, all alone in the darkness. The only light came from the bottom of the entrance shaft, the hatch open at the top. Close that and it would be pitch black. No light from anywhere; you wouldn't even be able to see your hand in front of your face.

Torch back on, I headed for the bottom of the ladder. I held my breath, opened the door to the toilet cubicle. Tiny, just enough room for a chemical toilet, not cleaned out since the last time the bunker had been occupied either. Paul must've crawled in here, in the darkness, looking for water. Caroline was right, it didn't bear thinking about.

I slammed the door, turned for the ladder and started climbing into the light, filling my lungs with clear, cold air as I neared the top, grateful to be out of the stale, damp atmosphere of the bunker.

Caroline had switched off her torch and was holding it by the elastic band, running her fingers through her hair. She was standing in the long grass by the entrance, watching me as I climbed out, closed the hatch and locked it.

'What have we learned?' she asked.

'A lot about what that poor little bugger must have gone through before he died. That I'm going to find whoever did it, and God help them if they're still alive.'

'You have to face that possibility, Bob,' said Caroline. 'You might find the killer is dead after all these years.'

'I'll cross that bridge when I get to it.' I pulled off my head torch, took a step forward.

'Watch where you're treading.' Caroline was pointing at my feet. 'Those are crocuses coming through.'

I looked down, the first buds of purple flowers emerging around the edge of the concrete plinth.

'There are primroses too. And those look like bluebells on their way. Might be daffs. Hark at me,' she said, handing me the torch. 'Anyone would think I knew what I was talking about.'

'Would they self-seed or has someone planted them?' I asked.

'Crocuses and bluebells self-seed. The pods get dropped by birds, then once they've got themselves established, the bulbs divide and away you go. Primroses too, although they're not bulbs.'

I stood there for a moment, staring at the flowers, some I'd trodden on, but then Shirley always said I'm a clumsy oaf.

'Spring is just around the corner,' said Caroline, rubbing her hands together.

'Yeah.'

We trudged back to the car in silence. The sun had gone behind the clouds, and it was noticeably colder, the thin copse along the roadside offering little shelter from the biting east wind that was picking up.

'What's next?' she asked, anxiously looking over her shoulder as I waited for a gap in the traffic large enough for a three-point turn.

'The evidence store. There's lots of stuff.'

'You will let me know how you get on. And if you find anything you think I can help with, please do say so. I feel sort of responsible for the little lad now.' She sighed. 'I expect you feel the same.'

'Something like that.'

Chapter Two

The good doctor was right. Not many ex-wives would be so understanding.

Shirley's second husband, Alan, was murdered. Mistaken identity – his body was found in my flat – followed by a feeble attempt to set me up for it: killed him, realised it wasn't me, tried to make it look like I'd done it. Fooled the police for a while, but not Shirley, thank God. Anyway, by the end of it I was able to tell her that Alan's killer was dead and that was enough for her.

They'd been letting me live rent free in the flat above their post office in Blagdon. Alan was stocktaking, must've heard them breaking in, went upstairs to investigate and you can guess the rest.

The most remarkable bit about the whole episode is that Shirley never blamed me for it. Not once. Our daughters did. *You just couldn't let that A303 thing go, could you?* Not Shirley. She knew the score. It had to stop, and no one else was going to do it.

She even gave me Alan's fishing tackle; said he'd have wanted me to have it.

I'm still living in the flat; paying Shirley rent now. I've been fishing on the lake a few times too, taken a boat out; always steer clear of Rainbow Point though. I checked last time out, and my tyre tracks down to the water's edge have gone, so I might give it a go next season.

What can I tell you about my divorce? Sad, if I had to sum it up in one word. Shirley was sad about it, and so was I. Neither of us had met anyone else. It wasn't anything like that. She blamed the job and perhaps that was it. Divorce is an occupational hazard for police officers. Doesn't make it any easier, mind you.

Two daughters. Christine and Joanne. They're speaking to me again, and I've got Shirley to thank for that as well. I was even invited to go with them to Longleat. Fancy that. Sitting in the back of the car with my grandson, laughing at the monkeys, roaring at the lions. He's a bit young to go fishing or take to the cricket, but maybe one day.

Shirley still runs the post office and shop. She's downstairs most days, nips in and does my washing up, leaves food in the cupboard, milk in the fridge. She always said I'd last five minutes without her and she's right.

I had a breakdown, but you probably guessed that from my friendship with the good doctor. The divorce played a part in it, of course it did, but it was more about . . . *what happened.*

I suppose I should tell you what did happen. Well, basically we were after a killer operating along the A303 between Ilminster and Wincanton. He was killing young women who'd broken down at the roadside late at night, so my partner and I lay in wait for him, Lizzie standing by her car in a lay-by, hazard lights flashing, me waiting in the bushes. Only, that night, I was in the pub and she went on her own.

That was Lizzie.

I got there too late, was hit by a car.

I was in hospital for months, stopped paying my rent, ended up sleeping in my Volvo. That's when Shirley found me, brought me here.

Got him in the end though, so I can sleep at night again.

I haven't slept in my car since then either, even though I bought the estate version specially.

I've got myself a telly from Radio Rentals at long last, although I'm sitting in the dark, thinking about all sorts of things, but mainly poor little Paul Bromfield, stuck down in that bunker.

It feels as if Avon and Somerset Police are going through the motions, to be honest, anxious to be seen to be looking at the case again but not wanting to waste any real resources on it. That's where I come in. After all, I'm hardly much of a *resource*, am I?

It's still not public knowledge, but it will be soon enough, when I start talking to witnesses, ruffling feathers. There's going to be a press conference at some point too, the chief constable announcing the creation of the Cold Case Unit to great fanfare, no doubt. Mind you, I'm not sure he'll be revealing that the only one looking at Paul Bromfield's case is little old me.

The good doctor said that joining the Cold Case Unit would give me something else to worry about. And it has.

I've got a few days, so it's the evidence store first thing in the morning. Then Paul's family. They're still living at Wincanton, wondering who killed their little boy. And why. They need to know their son's case is being looked at again, before they read it in the newspapers. It's not a meeting I'm looking forward to. There'll be awkward questions.

'How many officers are on your team?'

'Er, it's just me.'

It's not all bad, though. I haven't been down that way for a while. A short run along the A303 afterwards and I'll be in the Little Chef at Camel Hill. An All Day Breakfast with a side order of beans, followed by a Jubilee Pancake.

Now, that is something to look forward to.

That's the only real problem with this flat, to be honest. The nearest Little Chef is miles away. A new one has opened on the A37 at Farrington Gurney, but that's still the best part of twelve miles from here. It was different when I was up and down the A303 every day, there are plenty of them; here they're few and far between. That said, it's not too much of a problem tonight, because I've had a decent lunch.

Sad, isn't it – that the only thing I've had to worry about lately is the proximity of my nearest Little Chef.

Well, not anymore.

Now I've got Paul Bromfield.

Poor little bugger.

◆ ◆ ◆

I never spent much time at Avon and Somerset Police headquarters. My thirty years were up last month, and I must've been here a handful of times, usually for some training course or other. It's at a place called Portishead, which is on the coast. I did go for a drive round last time I was here, mainly because I got lost trying to find my way out to the M5. A dreary seaside town in winter. They all look the same.

I have a feeling I've been along the seafront before, perhaps in the early sixties when the mods and rockers clashed here rather than at Weston? I'd have had other things on my mind in that case, such as not getting the shit kicked out of me.

The HQ is an odd place too; looks more like a university campus, really. Red brick buildings dotted about a large open space.

I hope the bloke who cuts the grass has one of those mowers you sit on.

There's a canteen, of course there is, but the breakfast isn't up to much.

The Cold Case Unit is in a building round the back. Small, two storeys with a flat roof; used for storage, possibly, judging by the marks on the floor. It's been cleared out to make way for us. Well, I say 'us', there's only me at the moment. More are on the way, I'm told, but I'm the first. I was given a list of cases, have no real idea why I picked this one to start with, although I remembered the name so that might've been it.

There's a retired superintendent taking overall charge, but I'm not sure when he's due. On holiday, apparently. Until then it's just me, and I'm hoping someone will be along in a minute to fix the heating. The radiators are stone cold, a bit like the cases.

We're consultants, paid a daily rate. My pension's kicked in too, so I'm doing all right. Still had to argue with Shirley to get her to accept any rent for the flat, though.

No power of arrest, which is a shame and might become a problem later, depending on how close I get. We'll see.

I picked the largest of the rooms on the first floor, mainly because there was a gas fire, and I've rearranged the tables. It looks like there's a snooker table in the middle of the room now, covered in files and boxes, the Bromfield case papers. Took a while, but I've got them in some semblance of order. There are two lockable filing cabinets for anything confidential, a kettle on top and one mug.

Don't say it.

Standing in the bunker has given me a new sense of purpose. That's the best way I can explain it.

'Where d'you want this lot?'

I turned around to see a figure standing in the open doorway. He was leaning on a sack truck loaded with three boxes, each marked *Evidence PB* followed by a number. I'd heard it being dragged up the stairs, one step at a time, so knew someone was coming.

'Fuck me, it's Mungo Willis, isn't it?' The bloke laughed out loud. 'I felt sure you'd be dead by now.'

I must've looked at him blankly, because he clearly felt the need to explain himself.

'It's me. Mike Hardy. I didn't have the beard back then. For fuck's sake, mate, we were dragging that rhyne over at Shapwick when we got word they'd found this little lad,' he said, gesturing to the boxes on the sack truck in front of him. 'Mike. I was based at Bridgwater.'

'I remember. Sorry,' I lied.

'I got invalided out not long after that. Broke both my legs, can't run, so they gave me a job in the archive.' He took a piece of paper out of his pocket, unfolded it. 'Of all the cases you could've picked. Now I see it's you I understand why. The request says *Bob* Willis.'

'Just a nickname,' I replied.

'On these tables, is it?' He was wheeling the sack truck towards two tables against the back wall that I'd left empty.

'Thanks.'

'Mind if I call you Bob?'

'Everyone does.'

He left the boxes on the table, stopped at the top of the stairs, turned. 'Find the fucker, Bob,' he said. 'And if he's dead, let me know and I'll piss on his grave.' Then he picked up the sack truck and started hobbling down the stairs.

It took me a few minutes to summon up the courage, sitting in front of the fire with a mug of coffee, the only sound that comforting hiss you get. I had one of these fires in my old flat, used to sit listening to it for hours until the gas ran out. The case felt personal after yesterday's visit to the bunker and it was about to get more so. One of those boxes had Paul's clothes in it. The bedding.

Start with box 1; archived 20th April 1964. It was the same day BBC2 started broadcasting; it came up at that pub quiz Shirley dragged me to a couple of weeks ago.

I slit the tape with my door key, opened the box. Everything was in separate bags inside; brown paper with the contents of each bag scribbled on the label.

Gloves on, I lifted one bag at a time, Paul's clothes coming out first. No need to open those.

Shirt.

Shorts. Yes, he was wearing shorts. How cold must he have been down in that bunker?

Underpants.

Socks (grey).

Sandals.

Teddy bear (small), ear torn.

All of the bags were dated 16th October 1962 and signed by the officer who had sealed them. Detective Sergeant Jack Welshman.

The next box contained larger bags, bulging: the bed linen from the single bed and the bunks. No need to open them either. Far better to keep them sealed. They'd be going for forensic testing. Things have moved on a bit since the sixties.

Let's see how far.

The third box was heavier, the contents loose, not in sealed bags. I recognised some of the items from the crime scene photographs. The original salt and pepper shakers, damp and clogged, the inevitable loo roll, the newspaper – the *Daily Telegraph* as it turned out. I checked the date: Tuesday, 28th August 1962. The same day Paul was taken. It was folded open, but none of the articles or headlines seemed remotely relevant. Maybe the killer had been reading it on the train? Hiding behind it, even?

I slid the paper into an evidence bag, sealed it, signed and dated it. You never know, Forensics might be able to get something off it, even after all this time.

The date was telling. Either the killer left poor little Paul down in the bunker the same day he snatched him, or he went back later and left the newspaper down there. Ask yourself which is more likely. In my experience, old newspapers go in the bin, or around fish and chips, possibly.

I reached into the box, lifted out the Bunsen burner and placed it on the table, the rubber tube dangling over the side, just as it did in the crime scene photographs. It looked brand new, no scorch marks, residues. Nothing.

I remembered the witness statements. None of the Observer Corps volunteers had seen it before and no one knew what it was doing down there. Extensive enquiries had been made of the manufacturer, the investigating team had even been able to trace the supplier, but it got them precisely nowhere.

A dead end.

It was the same with the transistor radio. I took it out, set it on the table in front of me. A Bush TR82, according to the label on the box. Long wave and medium wave, but no reception down in the bunker anyway, that had been checked. No battery either.

I was careful not to touch the tuning dial. The original investigation team had checked, of course, and it didn't appear to have been tuned to any particular station, although the likelihood was that Paul had fiddled with it in the darkness, trying to switch it on.

I was still sitting there, staring at the radio, when I heard footsteps on the stairs.

'Er, sorry. I was told to collect some boxes to go off to Forensics.'

I dropped the evidence bag with the newspaper in it into the top of the clothing box, resealed it. 'These two,' I said. 'Thank you.'

I waited until he'd gone, then resealed the third box and locked it in the bottom drawer of a filing cabinet.

Time to go and meet Paul's parents.

◆ ◆ ◆

I turned into the drive off Bayford Hill, on the edge of Wincanton, looked up at the house.

I feel a bit guilty, to be honest. They probably know someone's here because of the gravel under my tyres. That and the dog barking in the front window; a golden retriever with its paws up on the windowsill. But they've got no idea what's coming. No idea what memories are about to be brought roaring back; what nightmares.

It was a grand house. Steps up to a white-painted front door, entrance porch with pillars, bay trees in pots. I thought I saw a curtain twitch, so they'd just be waiting for the doorbell to ring.

I climbed out of the car, admired the view across the vale to the south. I can't see them, but I can hear cars out on the A303.

An internal door slammed, then the front door opened. John Bromfield was a small man, a thick head of grey hair, dark horn-rimmed glasses. He was standing on the doorstep, hands on his hips. He had the bearing of a military man, but then I was looking for it. Captain, Royal Navy Retired to give him his full title. Born in 1920, so sixty-six.

'Who are you?' he asked. He was on the bottom step now.

'My name is Mungo Willis,' I replied. 'Everybody calls me Bob.' I was standing on the far side of my car, not that I'm a coward, you understand. 'I'm a retired detective inspector with Avon and Somerset Police, working on the Cold Case Unit.'

His legs went from under him and he collapsed on to the stone steps, one hand on the pillar. He sat there, staring at me, his mouth hanging open.

'I'm sorry, that must've been a bit of a shock,' I said. 'Here, let me help you up.' I was walking around the front of my car.

'I'll be fine.' He waved my hand away. 'Couldn't you have rung?'

'Would it have been any easier?'

'Not really.' He stood up, still holding on to the pillar. 'Can you give me a minute to speak to my wife?'

'Yes, of course.'

'Wait here,' he said, disappearing back inside the house, leaving the front door ajar.

I was standing on the top step, listening – if I'm honest. Heard the scream. It came from the back of the house, was followed by sobbing.

I'd thought a lot about how people might react, finding out their loved one's murder was going to be looked at again after all these years, although I'd learned long ago that different people react in different ways. The most important thing, it seemed to me, was to avoid giving them false hope. There could be nothing worse than that in a situation like this.

No expense spared.

No stone unturned.

We'll find him this time.

No. No. No.

Some families had been putting pressure on, demanding that their cases be looked at again, but the Bromfield family hadn't done that. That their son's case was being looked at again was my decision, not that they needed to know that.

'We're through here.'

I pushed open the front door, followed the voice along the corridor to the kitchen. Eleanor Bromfield was sitting at the kitchen table, her husband standing behind her with his hands on her shoulders. I took out a business card, left it on the table in front of them.

'Why haven't we heard about this Cold Case Unit before?' asked John, picking up the card.

'It's new,' I replied. 'Paul's is the first case we're going to be looking at.'

There was a clock on the wall opposite the cooker. Only one framed photograph underneath. Eleanor was looking up at it, her eyes welling up again. 'We've got a picture of him in every room,' she said.

'Tell me about your daughters. Rachel and Kim, isn't it?'

'Rachel's thirty now, married and living in Stroud,' replied John. 'Kim is twenty-five and in London.'

'Paul would've been thirty-three this year.' Eleanor stood up, took a deep breath. 'Take Mr Willis through to the living room, John. I'll make us some tea.'

Chapter Three

'Why does everyone call you Bob?'

Small talk, while we waited for Eleanor to make the tea. We were sitting in the front room; bright, with a large bay window making the most of the view. Two armchairs, a three-seater sofa. Nice floorboards with a rug, a smaller rug in front of the fire. Nothing on the mantelpiece, apart from a framed photograph of Paul. No television either. That said, the house was big enough to have a separate room for that.

'It's a nickname,' I replied. 'After the cricketer.'

'I was at Headingley in 1981, watched Bob rip into the Aussies. What a day that was,' said John, his eyes glazing over when he remembered why I was there. 'Paul loved his cricket. I took him to Lord's for the Ashes test in '61.'

I turned, listening to the sound of scratching at the inside of the door on the other side of the hall.

'That's Buster,' offered John. 'He can be a bit exuberant, so we shut him in there when we have visitors.'

Eleanor bustled in carrying a tray of tea. Cups and saucers, a teapot. She set the tray down on a small table to the side of one of the armchairs.

'Shall I do the honours?' she asked.

'White with one, thank you,' I said. I wondered how much longer they'd keep the small talk going, or whether I should get straight to the point. Perhaps give them a bit of time to work up to it.

'Rachel's pregnant.' Eleanor leaned over, handed me a cup of tea. 'She said if it's a boy, they're going to call him Paul.'

She was doing her best to keep her composure, but there was a tremble in her voice. Hardly surprising, really.

'Have you been down in the bunker?' asked John.

'I went down there yesterday.'

John glanced up at Eleanor.

'I've never been down there,' she said. 'They asked me if I wanted to go, but I didn't. I couldn't bear it.'

'I went,' said John, a tremble in his voice. 'Not long after they found him.' A sharp intake of breath, blown out through his nose. 'I just sat there, in the dark, trying to imagine what he must've gone through. How frightened he would've been. He was just a child.'

'Have you got children, Mr Willis?' asked Eleanor.

'Two, and one grandson,' I replied. 'And do call me Bob, please.'

'What d'you think happened?' John was stirring his tea. 'Did someone leave him down there deliberately or did something happen to his kidnapper? We never got a ransom demand.'

'I don't know yet.'

'Detective Chief Superintendent Hall was never able to answer that question,' said Eleanor.

'He was never able to answer any bloody question.' John was staring at the picture on the mantelpiece: Paul in his school uniform. 'Eric never found any answers.'

'Poor man,' said Eleanor. 'I think the investigation broke him. He retired the following year, died two years later.'

'We don't blame him. Not really. He did what he could with what he had.'

'Tell me about the day Paul went missing,' I said, looking at John. I'd read the statements, knew Eleanor wasn't there.

'I was at home with Kim,' she said. 'She was only eighteen months old.'

'I took Paul and Rachel on the steam train. We were going to the beach at Burnham for a ride on the donkeys, you know how it is.' He shrugged. 'The line was closing for good a week or so later, so I thought it'd be a nice day out. Paul was boarding at Caterham School and we'd got a week or so left before term started. I was on leave and it was the Tuesday after the August bank holiday. The twenty-eighth.'

'You must remember the case, Bob,' said Eleanor.

'I was in uniform at the time, based over at Ilminster. We were bussed over every day to help with the search.'

Eleanor leaned forward with a plate of biscuits. Custard creams. Nice. I took one, balanced it on the edge of my saucer. 'I was dragging a rhyne over at Shapwick when we heard he'd been found.' Actually, I'd forgotten that detail until Mike Hardy mentioned it that morning. I looked back to John, hoping he'd continue.

'We caught the 0936 from Evercreech Junction. I drove there, left the car.' He stood up, placed his cup and saucer on the mantelpiece, started pacing up and down on the rug in front of the fire. 'It was an excursion train and they'd laid on extra carriages; there was even a locomotive at the back. The platform was crowded with parents and children going for a day out at the seaside, just like us. Children were running up and down the platform. I remember feeling a bit awful, if I'm honest. Paul didn't know any of the local children, so he just stood there watching them playing. I tried to get him to go and join in. Rachel did, but he wouldn't.'

'We made sure Rachel and Kim went to school locally after that,' said Eleanor, her voice taut. 'So they'd have some friends. And we didn't want to let them out of our sight.'

'Boarding school was my decision,' said John. 'Eleanor never agreed with it.'

'No, I didn't.'

'Did you see anybody behaving oddly on the platform, anything unusual?'

'God, d'you know how many times I've been asked that question? How many times I've asked myself that question over the years.' John shook his head. 'No, I saw nothing that gave me even the slightest concern. Nothing and no one looked out of place. We weren't there long anyway, perhaps ten minutes, then the train pulled in, steam and smoke everywhere. There wasn't much wind, so it seemed to hang in the air, much to everyone's excitement. Kids were screaming and shouting, train doors were slamming all along the platform. We got on, found some seats in a compartment and waited for the off. Rachel had the window seat next to me and Paul the one opposite her.' He was gesturing with his hands. 'Paul was facing the direction of travel.' He slumped into his chair, deflated, his face ashen. 'You'll have to forgive me,' he said. 'Not a day goes by when I don't think about him, but I haven't thought about that day in a long time.'

Eleanor reached over and took his hand, squeezed.

'Anyway,' he said. 'We were just outside Glastonbury when he said he needed the loo. The one at that end of the carriage was engaged, so we got off at the station there. I stood on the platform where I could see him go into the loo and Rachel sitting in the compartment. I was also making sure the train door stayed open so it wouldn't leave without him, but the guard saw me and made sure we were back on board before he waved his flag.'

'What happened after that?'

'We were off again, Paul leaning out of the window, but he must've got some soot in his eye. He ducked back in, rubbing it furiously. Then he spotted some children his age running up and down the corridor. I think they may have been kids he recognised from the local primary school; he went there before we sent him to Caterham. Mr Hall traced them and spoke to their parents. Nothing.' Another shrug. 'They were still running up and down when the train was at Ashcott station, but they had to stop when more people got on. I don't recall seeing Paul after that. It was a moment before I realised he wasn't there, so I asked Rachel to go and see if she could see him, but she couldn't. I told her to stay where she was and went to look for him myself. I looked up and down the carriage, checked every compartment. I even looked out of the window, back down the track, in case he'd fallen out, but I couldn't see anything. It was then I pulled the communication cord.'

John's breathing had quickened, the panic roaring back. He opened a cabinet next to his armchair, took out a bottle of whisky. 'Anyone else?' he asked.

'I'll have one,' replied Eleanor.

'Not for me, thanks,' I said. No exceptions. Not since that night I left Lizzie to die.

'We stopped just outside Shapwick, so it must've been Ashcott where he was taken off. Either that or he got off and was snatched by someone on the platform. We searched the train, found nothing.' A swig of Scotch. 'The guard radioed ahead and the police were waiting for us when the train crept into Shapwick. They collected the names and addresses of all the passengers, then they were allowed off and it was searched again. Some officers even went back down the track. Ashcott station was searched as well.'

Eleanor was sitting on the edge of her chair, staring into the tumbler she was holding in both hands. 'John came home with Rachel, told me what had happened. He didn't want me to hear it from anyone else.'

'It was my fault, wasn't it?'

'It was the fault of the person who took him,' I said. 'The person who left him down in that bunker.'

'That's what I keep telling him.' Eleanor sighed. 'The guilt nearly killed him. He took compassionate leave, ended up having to retire from the Navy. We had to keep going though, for Rachel and Kim's sake. We had to give them as normal an upbringing as we could.'

'One day at a time,' muttered John. 'Still is, to be honest. Then you come knocking on our door.'

'Look, I can't tell you anything you don't already know, can't give you any guarantees, don't want to give you any false hope. All I can say is that Paul's case is being looked at again and I wanted you to hear that from me before you saw it on the news.'

'Thank you.'

'Forensic science has moved on a bit in the last twenty-plus years and everything we've got went off to the lab this morning, so we'll see what comes of that. In the meantime, I'm going to be interviewing the witnesses again, starting afresh as if it happened yesterday.'

'Believe me,' said Eleanor, draining her glass. 'It feels like it did.'

I stood up, headed for the front door. 'I'll be in touch.'

'Even if there's no news.' Eleanor looked up, blinked, releasing tears that ran down her cheeks. 'Please.'

'Of course.'

John followed me out, closing the living room door behind him. 'She's upset. We both are.'

'I understand. And I'm sorry for bringing it all back.'

'It's never gone away.'

I hadn't really noticed the hall on the way in. Black and white tiled floor, much like a chessboard. A large shell casing with umbrellas and walking sticks in it. The inevitable telephone table.

Above that was a black and white framed photograph of a ship at sea. A destroyer or a frigate, possibly.

'That's my ship,' said John. 'She was a River class frigate; built for convoy escort. I joined her as a lieutenant when she was commissioned in 1943, left her as a lieutenant commander when she was decommissioned in 1952. Ship's captain by then, but that was my only command; always an executive officer after that, on bigger ships.' He was still looking at the picture. 'I was based ashore at Plymouth after Paul was taken, did the weekly commute; managed to get promoted to captain before I had to call it a day. Did you serve, Bob?'

'I did my national service – square-bashing for two years – joined the police when I came out.' I hadn't noticed the stained-glass windows in the front door either. They cast a strange glow on the tiled floor. 'I should warn you there's likely to be some press attention when the chief constable announces the creation of the Cold Case Unit. I'll ask him to avoid mentioning Paul's case, but it won't be long before it becomes public knowledge anyway, of course, when I start talking to witnesses again.'

'You do what you have to do, Bob. We'll deal with it. It's not as if we haven't been through it before.' John opened the front door, then shook my hand. 'I've got a good feeling this time. I think you're really on our side.'

Actually, I'm not. I'm on Paul's side, but I didn't think I'd tell him that.

There's a time and place for everything.

Chapter Four

There was a time I hid my car behind the restaurant, skulked at the table in the back corner. Not anymore. These days I sit in the window, watching the world speed by on the A303.

Camel Hill, off the Sparkford roundabout. Thursday evening, just before five; the traffic will start to build soon. It's Valentine's Day tomorrow, so there'll be a bit more heading west for the weekend. It might be the start of half-term too. That's always good for a traffic jam.

'Hello, Bob. Not seen you for a while. Usual, is it?'

There can't be many people greeted like that in a Little Chef. Although Shirley would tell me it's not something I should be proud of.

She has a point.

I was unfurling my spoon and fork from the napkin, laying them out neatly on the table in front of me, ready for my Jubilee Pancake, when I saw it out of the corner of my eye. I should have known, really.

A little red Allegro.

There are a few of them about, of course there are, but I recognised the driver of this one, leaning across the passenger seat to look up, see if I was there. She even gave me a wave; more of an 'I've seen you, don't try to hide' sort of a wave than a cheery greeting.

I hadn't seen her for a few weeks, not since before Christmas. Lizzie's younger sister, Angela. She tells everyone she's a journalist, but remind her that she's actually the social and events editor at the *Chard and Ilminster News* and you'll learn new words.

Basically, it's coffee mornings, fetes and agricultural shows.

That said, she was very helpful in the hunt for Lizzie's killers; got me out of a scrape or two along the way as well.

Yes, I think we're friends.

Even though I killed her sister.

Everybody tells me it wasn't my fault, more times than I care to mention. Shirley, the good doctor, Lizzie's parents. Angela.

Everyone.

Still feels like it, though.

If I had to guess, I'd say Ray Keenan, the crime reporter at the *County Gazette*, has had a tip off about the Cold Case Unit and Angela's been sent to see what she can find out. He covers crime for both papers and knows we're friends.

We'll see.

She slid on to the bench seat opposite me. Her hair was a bit longer, had a run-in with a bottle of peroxide by the looks of things too. She was wriggling out of her coat.

'What's this I hear about a Cold Case Unit?' she said.

Straight to the point.

'Fine, thanks,' I replied. 'You?'

'Yeah.'

'Did you have a nice Christmas?'

'Not really. I was stuck at home with my parents. Again.' She rolled up her coat, left it on the seat next to her.

'There'll come a time—'

'I know all that.' She was admiring the pancake that had been placed on the table in front of me, a wisp of steam rising from the cherry sauce. 'Can I have one of those, please?'

I looked up, nodded to the waiter. 'On my tab,' I said.

'And a Coke, in that case.' Angela smirked. 'So, you were going to tell me about the Cold Case Unit.'

'It's not really a social event, is it?' I braced myself for the barrage of expletives.

'I'm not social events editor anymore.' She folded her arms, leaned back on the bench seat, a smug look on her face. 'You are looking at the new trainee crime reporter for the *County Gazette*.'

'Congratulations,' I said. I was still waiting for the cherry sauce on my pancake to cool a bit; bloody stuff is like molten lava.

'It's thanks to you, really. Ray Keenan was impressed with me, apparently. Thinks I've got what it takes.'

'And what does it take?' I knew the answer to that one, although police officers tend to have a fairly low opinion of crime reporters.

'An enquiring mind.'

'Sounds like you're applying to join the police,' I said. 'We're after the same information, only you want to print it in a newspaper.'

She was stirring her Coke with the straw.

'When was this?' I asked.

'I started in the new year.'

At least that meant it wasn't a cynical ploy to get to me, that she wasn't being used by Ray Keenan. 'You understand what "off the record" means?'

'You told me stuff last time,' she said, defensively.

'We were trying to find your sister's killers. And, actually, I told you bugger all.'

'Ray couldn't print what he did know; said he'd been slapped with a D-Notice. I didn't know what that was, had to look it up.'

'We made a good team last time, and we can do that again, provided everything is off the—'

'I understand what "off the record" means, but what's in it for me? If you tell me stuff and I can't use it, what's the point?'

'There's a deal, and the deal is that if you don't print anything I tell you, then if and when the time comes to make the arrest, I tip you off, you can be there with a photographer and get the scoop.'

Scoop is the magic word with journalists. I learned that long ago.

'I can't print anything at all?'

'Anything I tell you. Generic stuff is fine. There's going to be a press conference and you can report on that.' I took a mouthful of pancake, a bit too soon as it turned out.

'So, there is a Cold Case Unit?'

'Do we have a deal?'

'Yes,' she said, over a loud sigh.

'In that case, there is a new Cold Case Unit and I'm working on it.'

'Paul Bromfield?'

I waited while the waiter placed a plate in front of Angela. 'You'll need to give it a minute,' I said.

'Ray remembers the Bromfield case,' she said, blowing on the cherry sauce. 'It was before I was born.'

'I worked on it at the time. Searching the fields.'

'How far have you got with it?'

'Read the case papers, been down the bunker, visited the family. I've only been on it three days.'

'What's the plan for tomorrow?'

'Don't know yet.'

'Can I come?'

'I tell you what, you get me a complete set of all the *County Gazette* articles written about the case and a copy of every single photograph taken, not just those that were printed, and I'll think about it.'

◆ ◆ ◆

I should tell you about my spare bedroom.

There's a lock on the door, nothing inside except a deckchair facing the back wall. It was my incident room when I was after Lizzie's killers. Photographs stuck on the wallpaper with Sellotape, a blackboard, arrows pointing here, there and everywhere. I'm sure you can picture it.

I'd spend hours sitting there, staring at it.

Shirley must've had a key, because she knew about it. I'd changed the lock too; still not worked out how she did that.

It took a while to clear out after it was all over. The Sellotape came off the wallpaper, but there are still a few pinholes, if you look closely.

It's a good space, only side windows, so I've got the whole back wall of the flat.

The blackboard's still there, the Bromfield family tree chalked top right. I've been at the Sellotape again and there are photographs of the crime scene, of Paul. One of Ashcott railway station from 1962.

No arrows yet.

Give me time.

I'm having trouble sleeping again too. I was all right before, apart from the odd pee in the middle of the night; gentlemen of a certain age, and all that. It started on Wednesday, after my trip down the bunker. Last night as well. The same dream, a stubborn bugger it is. I wake up, roll over, go back to sleep and I'm straight into it again.

It's dark and I'm sitting in my car. I can feel the panic, my breathing shallow and quick just telling you about it. I wind down the window, climb out and I'm in the bunker, fumbling about in the blackness. I lie down on the single bed, curl up . . .

I wonder what the good doctor would make of that.

I can tell you exactly what she'd make of it, actually. It's my brain conflating two experiences into one. It's a good word, *conflating*. She used it once before and I had to look it up.

Anyway, I'm not having another breakdown. I wouldn't want you to think that. And to be honest, it would be odd not to be affected by what happened to Paul. Not when you've been down in the bunker.

Felt it.

So, that was last night – once I'd shaken off Angela – and made a start on my incident room. I've got the office at Portishead this time, of course I have, but it's miles away, and the less time I spend there the better, particularly when this retired super gets back from his holiday and starts throwing his weight about. I'm not daft. I know how these things work, and my reputation will have preceded me, you can be sure of that.

What reputation is that?

Quite.

I've left my car in the car park at the Railway Inn, and I'm standing in the middle of the road, on what was once the level crossing at Ashcott. I'm looking west towards Shapwick. The tracks have all gone now, but I can see where they ran, parallel to the South Drain. The line is a gravel road now, used by the peat cutters, probably. Old cars and a caravan have been dumped in what was the old siding.

Behind me, the station house is still there, a small garden at the side, trapped between the old railway line and the drain. There's a light on inside, so I might knock on the door.

The platform makes a sad sight, the white line along the edge fading, brambles overtaking the railings. There's even one of those old glazed noticeboards that would have had the timetable in it, the doors hanging off, glass smashed.

I've got some old photographs in my pocket, so I take them out, hold them up. The old gates on the level crossing are long gone. The signal box too. It looks like there was a waiting room and ticket office as well – demolished.

I'm trying to imagine what it looked like in 1962. We arrived by coach for the search, but I must've been on the steam train as a kid. Everyone had.

Smoke rising from the smokestack on the locomotive, steam hissing, passengers milling about on the platform, children with their buckets and spades, carriage doors opening and closing, the guard's whistle.

I wonder what Dr Beeching would make of it, now it's all gone; can't ask him, though. He died last year.

I ignore the 'Keep Out' sign, walk along the platform, hands thrust deep into my pockets.

My feeling is that Paul must have got off the train here. Trying to snatch him off a crowded train would have been far too dangerous, far too risky. Snatching him off the platform with a train at the station would've been risky too. All those passengers sitting there, staring out of the windows, would've seen it.

If that's right, then it means that Paul got off, the train left without him and then he was snatched. I'm not reinventing the wheel here, the original investigation arrived at the same conclusion.

I've walked down the ramp at the end of the platform and am standing on the edge of the undergrowth, looking down at the South Drain, although I seem to recall it's called the Glastonbury Canal this side of the bridge. Perhaps Paul went down to the water's edge? He'd have been out of sight of the station house and ticket office down there.

Easy prey.

I'll tell you another thought that occurred to me in the night. How does John Bromfield live with himself after what happened?

How does he get through the day? The easy answer, I suppose, is to ask what's the alternative. He has a wife and two daughters to consider.

It's been raining hard lately, and the canal looks like milky coffee. They must have the sluices open too, because it's flowing west, towards the sea, branches and clumps of dead reeds being swept along.

It would've looked very different in the summer of 1962, as it does every summer. Lily pads along the margins, fish swimming about in gin clear water, ducks and swans feeding. Swallows flitting about. That's how I remember it – ignoring the divers stirring up the mud. The Royal Navy started at Shapwick on the South Drain, the British Sub-Aqua Club here, and they met in the middle.

Found nothing.

Now we've got our own dive team, of course; not back then.

I mentioned how important it will be to avoid giving anyone false hope, didn't I? And I wouldn't say this to anyone else, but somewhere out there is a person who knows exactly what happened to poor little Paul Bromfield.

Someone who knows what happened because they did it.

They've moved on.

They're living a normal life.

Trying to forget what they did.

Enjoy it while it lasts, you bastard.

Chapter Five

The station house is where the stationmaster used to live. I wonder if he still does, I thought, ringing on the doorbell.

Red brick, built on the sliver of land between the railway tracks and the drain. Raised beds in the garden at the side, bamboo canes and the rotting remains of last year's runner beans. A gravel drive beyond that, an old Ford Escort and two Anglias rusting away.

A figure loomed up behind the frosted glass of the inner door, called out without bothering to open it. 'Who is it?'

'Police.'

The door opened slowly, nervously. A shout of 'police' tends to have that effect. The man was old, in his eighties, possibly. A check shirt with food down the front, baggy trousers, open at the fly. He was wearing an old dressing gown over the top, the cord tied loosely around his waist.

'I'm looking for the stationmaster,' I said. 'James Bucknall.'

'You've found him.' He opened the outer door. 'What d'you want?'

'To talk to you about Paul Bromfield.'

The old man's eyes glazed over, and it must've been at least thirty seconds before he took a breath. I wasn't counting, obviously, but it felt like it. He nodded to himself, remembering. It's a name that does that to people. I learned that in the pub on Wednesday night.

'You'd better come in,' he said, disappearing back inside. I followed, closing the doors behind me.

'In there.' He gestured to the living room, overlooking the Glastonbury Canal. 'I've got some soup going on the stove. I'll just switch it off.'

Most of the bottles on the drinks cabinet were empty, the framed photographs black and white. One of a wedding; if I had to guess I'd say he'd survived his wife. Another of a young man in Somerset and Dorset Railway uniform standing on the level crossing, exactly on the spot where I'd stood twenty minutes earlier.

'Sorry about that.' Bucknall shuffled in and sat down in the armchair. 'Just move those,' he said, gesturing to the pile of newspapers on the sofa. 'Now, Paul Bromfield.'

'You remember the name?'

'How can I forget it?' He picked up a pipe from the ashtray, started sucking and blowing on it, then he tapped it out in the hearth. 'You don't forget something like that, particularly when your son is arrested for it.'

Not our finest hour, but I'll let it pass for the moment. 'How long did you work on the railway?'

'Man and boy. I started in 1919 at the age of seventeen, and they closed me down with the line in 1962.' He was stuffing tobacco into his pipe, picking the loose bits off his dressing gown. 'It stayed open for a while after that for freight, peat mainly, but you don't need a stationmaster for that. They gave me a gold watch and told me I could stay here until I snuffed it. I'm not sure they thought it'd be this long, though.'

'Rent free?'

'God, no. I mustn't grumble, though. It's a good deal cheaper than the market rate. Edgar Lamb, over at Burtle, had the local pub named after him. I got this dump.'

'Is that your wedding photo?' I asked, turning to look over my shoulder.

'Twenty-fourth of August 1926. I was twenty-four. The happiest day of my life. Fifty-two years, then the silly old bugger went and died on me, didn't she. I told her, if you die, I'll never speak to you again.'

It was obviously a line the old boy trotted out with monotonous regularity, probably to hide his sadness; the good old British stiff upper lip and all that.

'What can you remember about the day Paul went missing?'

He'd filled his pipe and was lighting it, huge clouds of sickly smoke billowing into the room as he spoke. 'It was a sad enough time as it was. The last excursion train to Burnham went on the eighth of September and we closed the day after that. There were plenty of families and kids on their way for a day at the beach, so they were happy enough. We were all breaking our hearts.'

'Who's *we*?'

'I was stationmaster. There was Max Samways in the signal box; he looked after the level crossing as well. I can't remember who was driving the train, or the fireman, but the guard was old Arnie Wood. They're both still around.'

'They're on my list,' I said.

'Max lives over Woolavington way. Arnie moved to Watchet to be near his sister. Haven't seen them for yonks.'

I pretended to write something in my notebook. I had their addresses anyway. 'That day?'

'It was just a normal stop on the excursion train. Six carriages, so longer than usual; three at the platform, but it didn't matter because passengers were getting on, not off. I don't remember anyone getting off at all, then Arnie blew his whistle, waved his flag, hopped on and off they went. The next thing I knew the station was swarming with police.' He frowned. 'I did give a statement at the time.'

'I've read it.'

'You've got to remember what it was like when a steam train was in a station. And this one was a top-and-tail, a locomotive at both ends. The steam, smoke, and when they were getting ready to leave it was worse. The phrase *getting up a head of steam* exists for a reason.'

'So, you saw nothing unusual?'

'I saw nothing at all. You couldn't. On a windy day it wasn't too bad, but that day there wasn't a breath of wind to carry it away. I know they thought at the time the lad got off the train at the far end of the platform, and he might've done. I couldn't say one way or the other.' His pipe must've gone out and he was lighting it again. 'They were here for days, searching. There were divers in the drain, lines of officers in the fields.'

'I was one of them,' I said. 'I was dragging a rhyne over at Shapwick when we got word he'd been found.'

'The line had closed by then.' Bucknall shook his head. 'And I'd *been* retired. I was sitting here, this very chair, heard it on the evening news.'

'Had you seen anyone hanging around the station before the train pulled in?'

'There were some passengers waiting. Marge used to work in the ticket office, and she'd sold quite a few tickets. She's dead now, though. Those last few excursions were the busiest.'

'What about anglers?'

'On the canal?' A dismissive wave of his pipe. 'It's not wide enough here, they go further up. I've seen a couple, maybe, in the entire time I've been here.'

'So, you saw nothing,' I said. Not that I'd expected anything else really. It explains why it's a cold case.

'Nothing at all.'

'What about Andrew?'

'He's not all there, if you know what I mean?'

Bucknall looked at me for reassurance, so I nodded. Thought I should.

'He wasn't quite right as a boy, never was. My wife worried about him all the time. Got him through school, but he couldn't hold down a job. Then he's arrested for Paul Bromfield's murder, and we've got your lot here turning the place upside down.'

'I've read the interviews.'

'Six weeks it took, before they saw sense and let him go.'

'He confessed, so they had to look at him.'

'I understand that.'

'Where will I find him?'

The old man looked crestfallen. 'You're not going to arrest him again, are you?'

'I just need to speak to him. I need to speak to everybody.'

'He uses this address, but he lives in a caravan in the old siding, the other side of the road.'

◆ ◆ ◆

I've worked on a few cases that have *gone* cold over my long and unremarkable career, but this is the first time I've picked one up that's been cold for over twenty years.

Stone cold, you might say.

I've got a horrible feeling I know what's going to happen too. I'll speak to all the witnesses, one by one, and they'll all say exactly the same as they did in 1962.

'I didn't see anything, what with the smoke and steam on the station.'

'I did give a statement at the time.'

Of course they did. I've read them all. The train driver, the fireman, the guard. I must've spent over an hour with the stationmaster and learned nothing new.

Then there are all the passengers on the train. None of them saw anything either, most too busy with their children, the excitement of being on the steam train, a day at the beach. It was a recurring theme, almost as if it had been fed to them by the officer taking their statements. I can hear it now.

'I didn't see anything, I'm afraid.'

'Too busy looking after your children?'

'Yes.'

'Excited at being on the train, I expect?'

'Yes.'

'A day at the beach?'

'Yes.'

You can guess what the witness statements say, almost without exception.

That said, the original investigation was thorough. I wouldn't want you to think it wasn't. Everything that could have been done – should have been done – was done. The simple fact of the matter is that no one saw anything, and that's why the case went cold.

What I have got, though, is a detailed map of the passenger compartments showing where each person was sitting. There were six carriages, all full, and a statement was taken from each of the adults on board.

It's Friday afternoon now and the press conference is fixed for Monday morning, apparently. I don't have to be there for it, mercifully, but what it does do is give me a couple of days before it becomes public knowledge the case is being looked at again.

Before *he* finds out we're coming for him.

I had an idea in the night – *thinking outside the box* they call it these days. If I'm going to find new evidence, it's going to come from witnesses who weren't spoken to in 1962.

No statements were taken from the children on the train, because they were all too young. Their parents were given the task of seeing if any of them saw anything, and there's a line in each of their statements to that effect.

'I spoke to my seven-year-old son/daughter, fill in name here, and he/she saw nothing either.'

Too young they may have been, but they're bloody well old enough now.

Chapter Six

I'm going to do this methodically, starting with the older children first, and those on the carriages in the middle of the train. They'd have stopped adjacent to the short platform at Ashcott and been furthest from the locomotives. I'm guessing – hoping – the steam and smoke might've thinned out a bit, hoping they might remember seeing something.

There's Paul's sister, Rachel, as well. She was on the train, sitting in the compartment with her father, although she was only six at the time. Anyway, I'm going to leave that carriage to last, if only because John Bromfield would probably have seen anything untoward happening to his son.

Sounds a bit thin that, but I'm going to speak to them all, so it hardly matters in what order I do it.

Some have been easier to track down than others. Some are dead, sadly.

First up is Justine Paterson.

Justine was nine at the time. She'd been at a sleepover with her friend, Jenny, and was on the train with Jenny and her mother. Teaches at the primary school now, over at Catcott. It'll be her lunch hour too.

Her father spoke to her at the request of the police and confirmed, in a short statement, that she remembered seeing nothing.

We'll see.

I parked in the lane opposite the school. One of those old school buildings that are disappearing fast, sadly. A new one is built, the old one sold off for housing; seems to be happening everywhere these days. They'll tell you it's about capacity.

There were kids running around the playground. I could hear screams, one crying; fallen over, probably. A teacher standing with his back to the railings, didn't seem unduly concerned by the tears.

'Excuse me,' I said. 'I'm looking for Justine Paterson.'

'She's in the staffroom.' He glanced over his shoulder at the child still crying. 'Could you ring the bell on the front door, someone will come. I've got to deal with this.'

I did as I was told.

There's something about teachers. They have a way of making you feel like a child, even when you're in your fifties. I nearly said 'please, sir'.

An older woman answered the front door. The head, probably. She wasn't impressed with my business card.

'Don't police officers usually carry warrant cards?'

'I'm a consultant, working on the Cold Case Unit.'

'You'd better come in,' she said, stepping back. 'Wait in there. I'll let her know you're here.'

A classroom, the desks and chairs tiny. I looked at the paintings all around the walls, remembered the pictures my daughters used to bring home from school. I never seemed to have much time for them, back then, but Shirley kept them all. She even got them out at Christmas, gave me a second chance.

I wondered if John and Eleanor Bromfield had kept Paul's artwork.

'Can I help you?'

Taller than me, but then most people are. Trousers and a red pullover, covered in paint, the lot of a primary school teacher, perhaps. I introduced myself, explained that I was looking again at the Paul Bromfield case.

'I remember it.' She perched on the large table at the front of the classroom, folded her arms. 'I found out years later I'd been on that train. Jenny told me.'

'You're still friends with Jenny?'

'She works in a solicitor's office in Bridgwater; was my bridesmaid when I got married last year.'

'Congratulations,' I said. It's something you say, isn't it? 'What can you remember about the day Paul went missing?'

'I'd stayed over at Jenny's the night before. Her parents lived in Glastonbury. We walked down to the station, had an ice cream, got on the train.'

'Which carriage were you in?' I know the answer to that one, but I'm just seeing how much she actually remembers.

'We were right at the back, the last compartment of the rear carriage. We'd been told to get on the carriages at the back, and we'd walked along the platform a bit, but had to run because the train was longer than Jenny's mum had expected. She'd done a picnic, and I'd got a bucket and spade.'

'Where did you sit in the compartment?' I asked.

'I had the window seat looking forwards; Jenny and her mum were sitting opposite me. I remember our feet didn't reach the floor and we got told off for banging our heels on the heater. There was this metal grille thing under the seat.'

'Can you remember any of the stops along the way?'

'Not really. The stations were crowded, the train too, people standing in the corridor. Families mainly, off to the beach like we were.'

'Where did you get off?'

'Shapwick, I think it must have been. I seem to remember coaches taking us to the beach and not knowing why.'

'What I'd like you to do is imagine yourself sitting in that carriage,' I said. 'Kicking your heels against the seat. You got on the train at Glastonbury and off at Shapwick, which means the only stop on the line was Ashcott, and that was where Paul must have been taken. Did you see anything when the train pulled into the station?'

'Not really. Our carriage stopped outside the station, didn't get to the platform. I could see along a bit, though, and there was a man there in railway uniform. The stationmaster, I suppose. They used to have them back in those days.'

'What about when the train pulled out? You'd have been looking at the platform. The last person on the train to see it.'

'I was probably mucking about with Jenny.'

'I know lots of people got on the train, but did you see anyone get off?'

'No.'

'Anyone left on the platform when the train pulled out?'

'There was someone waiting to open the level crossing.'

'Any cars waiting at the barrier?'

'Not that I . . .' She was staring at the floor at her feet, her eyes glazed over. 'There might have been a tractor out that side,' she said, waving her left arm. 'I can't be sure, there were people standing in the corridor, so I only got a glimpse. It could have been in a field that side.'

'What colour was the tractor?'

'Red.'

'Can you remember the driver?'

'No.'

'Do you remember the siding? It would've been on your right as you pulled out of Ashcott, between you and the South Drain.'

'There were a couple of empty freight wagons, possibly. I remember we watched a swan take off. Then it wasn't long before the train screeched to a halt. Jenny fell out of her seat, ended up on the floor in front of me.'

'And you saw nothing out of the window between Ashcott and where the train stopped?'

'No, just miles and miles of fields.' She took a deep breath. 'I do remember the search though. It was frightening. Police everywhere. We weren't allowed to walk to school, go out anywhere. We used to be out on our bikes all the time, playing. Not after that.'

I was looking along the art on the wall, beach scenes, some of a steam train, although it was more likely to be Thomas the Tank Engine.

'You said you found out years later that you'd been on that train.'

'It was the twentieth anniversary of the boy's disappearance, and the family was doing an appeal for information, trying to keep his memory alive, and you can't blame them for that. I was over at Jenny's place, and she just came out with it. "We were on that train," she said. It had never occurred to me until then.'

Something didn't sound right to me. How could she not have known? 'When Paul's body was found and it became a murder investigation, all the parents of children on the train were told to ask them if they remembered seeing anything. Your father gave a short statement to say that he'd asked you and you remembered nothing.'

'No, he didn't. He never asked me.'

'Why not?'

'You'd need to ask him that, only you can't. He died six years ago.' Justine shrugged. 'Maybe he didn't want to upset me, or perhaps he was trying to protect me. Whatever it was, he never asked me if I remembered anything. Never mentioned he gave a statement to the police, either.'

◆ ◆ ◆

I'm standing on the doorstep of the schoolhouse in Catcott. Justine has just closed the door behind me, promised to let me know if she remembers anything else.

You can imagine what I'm thinking, though, can't you?

How many other children are there out there who were never asked whether they remembered anything?

Shielded from the horror of it all by their parents, the vital piece of the puzzle buried.

Maybe.

Time for a chat with Detective Chief Superintendent Hall's bagman before I go any further. See what he remembers.

Chapter Seven

I know the type. Early promotion to detective sergeant, then stuck at that rank for the rest of their career, unfulfilled and bitter with it. I only avoided the same fate thanks to Shirley pushing me onwards and upwards, although I can hardly claim that twenty years on CID at Ilminster left me fulfilled. No, any sense of satisfaction came later, after catching Lizzie's killers. That made it all worthwhile.

I'm sitting in my car outside a converted warehouse in Langport, letting my prejudices run amok. He'll be divorced, his flat rented. There'll be an empty bottle of whisky on a coffee table in the living room, in amongst the takeaway cartons. The curtains will be drawn, even though it's mid-afternoon.

Don't ask me how I know.

Stereotypes exist for a reason.

Detective Sergeant Jack Welshman. Can't say I know the name, but then he was based at Taunton, and retired before I joined CID, so our paths wouldn't have crossed. I do remember seeing DCS Hall during the search for Paul. He was on the far side of a field, a group of plain-clothes officers standing with him, so Welshman would've been one of them, almost certainly.

No Entryphone, so I was soon knocking on the door of his ground floor flat. I heard a groan, then footsteps.

He was younger than I'd expected. Neatly dressed in corduroys and a check shirt – sleeves rolled up – and one of those tank tops that Frank Spencer wears, with a diamond pattern; golfers wear them too. Thick glasses with a magnifier on a stick a few inches in front of the right lens. Combed grey hair, no smell of alcohol. He looked at me, then stared at the business card I held up in front of him.

'You'd better come in.'

I knew he'd retired in 1965, so it must've been early retirement. He couldn't be more than about sixty-five or so. I should've checked, really.

He led me along a corridor, past an open door. The room was brightly lit, a raised desk covered in tools, lamps, and bits of a grandfather clock.

'I repair clocks for local antique dealers,' he said, watching me from the end of the corridor, his hands on his hips. He looked at his watch. 'One minute to four. Come in and have a seat. I apologise for the noise.'

There must've been eight in his workshop, five more on the wall in the corridor, and I counted two grandfather clocks and three cuckoo clocks in the living room, one on the wall right behind my head. We waited patiently for the din to subside.

'Sorry about that,' he said. 'How can I help?'

'I'm working on a new Cold Case Unit, and we're looking at the Paul Brom—'

He raised his hand, silencing me before I could say anything else. He was just sitting there, staring into space. Then he took off his glasses, replaced them with another pair from the bookshelves beside him. 'I need a cup of tea.' He stood up, walked across to the kitchen door. 'You?'

'White with one,' I replied. 'Thank you.'

He was buying himself some time, which was fine. If ever a bloke looked as though he'd had the stuffing knocked out of him it was Jack Welshman, and all it had taken was mention of Paul's name.

I can't say I was surprised. I remembered the case from the times I'd been involved in the search, but to have worked it, been closely involved in the hunt for Paul, then the murder investigation? We like to think we're professional, and we are, but some cases still get through, stay with you. I was listening to the kettle boiling, wondering how I'd have reacted if it had been my case back in the day.

I glanced around the room, looking for the alcohol, but couldn't see any. Plenty of books, all non-fiction and most of them about clocks. There was a drinks cabinet, empty probably.

He placed a coaster on the coffee table, left a mug of tea on it, handed me a packet of biscuits. 'Sorry about that,' he said, sitting down in a leather armchair by the fireplace. 'Some names . . . You know how it is.'

'I do.'

'That was the end, for me, that case. I got out. It killed Eric Hall, did you know that?'

'John Bromfield told me.'

'The stress of it.' He was stirring his tea, watching it going round and round in the mug. 'It got to everyone.' He looked up sharply, fixed me in a steely glare. 'You must remember it, surely?'

'Uniform, out of Ilminster,' I replied. 'We were bussed over to help with the search. I was out on the Levels near Shapwick when we heard he'd been found.'

'You've seen the crime scene photographs, Mungo?'

'Haunting.'

'That they are. Can I call you Mungo?'

'Everyone calls me Bob, after the cricketer.' It raised a smile, albeit a fleeting one.

'I was the first one to go down in the bunker,' he said. 'A lad from the Observer Corps found him, but he didn't even step off the bottom of the ladder; wondered what the smell was, shone his torch in and was on his toes out as quickly as he could. Then uniform arrived and secured the scene. No one went down till we got there, apart from a doctor, who confirmed it was a boy, approximately nine years of age. Dead. I had to go in, make sure it was Paul. He was just lying there, curled up on the bed. I switched the generator on, so the light came on, and there he was. Poor little bugger.' He rested his mug on his knee. 'And the smell, you can imagine the smell down there, can't you?'

It was a rhetorical question.

'I'll tell you what upset me the most.' His eyes had glazed over now. 'His hands were covered in blood and there was blood smeared on the inside of the hatch, so he must've climbed the ladder in the dark and tried to get out, hanging there on the top rung, banging for all he was worth, scrabbling until his hands bled. He was nine years old, for heaven's sake. I still have nightmares about that. And people will try to tell you there's a God.'

I wasn't sure how to answer that, either. So thought it best not to try.

'How many are there on the case?' he asked. He'd sat up, was trying to recover his composure.

'Just me at the moment. The CCU is new. There's going to be a press conference on Monday.'

'I hope it's not just a box-ticking PR exercise, doing it because they need to be seen to be doing it.'

'Not as far as I'm concerned.'

'Pleased to hear it.' He took a sip of tea, left his mug on the bookshelf next to him. 'Have you seen the family?'

'Yesterday,' I replied. 'I wanted them to know what's going on before they saw it on the telly.'

'How were they?'

How the fuck do I answer that?

'Expecting their first grandchild,' I said.

'And how did they react to news the case was being looked at again?'

'Relieved, I think.'

'John was a good father, wanted to be doing something the whole time, so he was out searching, organising local volunteers who wanted to help as well. I remember going to see him with Eric to tell him we'd found Paul's body. He was up to his waist in a rhyne near Godney. There'd been a sighting – there were loads of those – and we took him to one side, but he knew from the looks on our faces. His first instinct was to go home and tell his wife. We offered, but he wanted to do it himself. We took him home; never said a word in the car.'

Time to get him talking about specifics.

'What did you make of the Bunsen burner?' I asked.

'We never found out what that was doing down there. None of the Observer Corps lads had seen it before. There wasn't even any gas. It was just sitting there on the table with the tube hanging over the edge. It can only have been taken down there by the killer, but we can't be sure exactly where he left it because Paul might have moved it fumbling around in the dark. We had it dusted for prints, asked everyone we could, and . . . nothing.'

'I've sent it for forensic testing,' I said. 'Things have moved on a bit.'

'We traced where it was originally bought, even traced the buyer, but how many times it changed hands after that, who knows. You think there's some significance to it?'

'There has to be. Even if it's only in the mind of the killer. He took it down there for a reason.'

'So, what's your plan?' asked Welshman.

'From what I can see, the original investigation did everything humanly possible—'

'Thank you.' Welshman looked relieved it wasn't going to descend into a blame game. And it wasn't. Not on my watch.

'It'll be about finding new evidence,' I said. 'And whatever significance there might be in existing evidence.'

'Like the Bunsen burner.'

'Exactly.'

'New evidence will be hard to find.'

'There are the children on the train,' I said. 'Adults now.'

'We spoke to anyone aged eleven or over, from memory. With their parents present, of course. The younger ones we asked the parents to speak to them and took a short statement. There were quite a few in the six to nine bracket. Lots even younger too.'

'I spoke to one of them today. She was nine at the time, in the last compartment of the rear carriage, sitting facing the direction of travel. She said her father never asked her, never spoke to her about it at all, but there's a statement from him on the file saying he had, and she saw nothing. She thinks he was shielding her from it, trying to protect her.'

'Either that or he just didn't want to get involved.' Welshman grimaced. 'I wonder how many others there are.'

'I'm going to speak to them all, one by one, and I don't care how long it takes.'

'Good for you. Let's hope you find something.' Welshman had picked up his mug, raised it, took a swig.

'When was the last time you went down in the bunker?' I asked.

'That first day when we found him. I never went down there again. Why?'

'How about above ground?'

'I went once, if you must know. Left some flowers.'

'When was that?'

'1972, ten years to the day we found him.'

'Same time of year then. Autumn.'

'Is that relevant?'

'I went there the day before yesterday and there were crocuses, primroses and bluebells, Spring flowers coming through. Does that mean anything to you?'

'Why would it?'

'I've no idea.'

'You'd expect wildflowers out there, surely?' asked Welshman.

'I suppose you would.' I drained my tea, set my mug down on the coaster. 'Were you still working on the case when it was closed?'

A sad nod. 'Two years we'd worked on it, the team gradually getting smaller. John Bromfield never made a fuss, never caused a scene. We went to see him, me and Eric, sat in the front room of the family home over at Wincanton, told him the case was being closed. We gave him the usual platitudes – *we've exhausted every line of enquiry, if anything new comes to light it will be looked at.* Then, the next day, the files were boxed up and off to storage. Eric had a heart attack a couple of weeks after that, the first of several until the last one, the whopper; dead before he hit the floor. My papers went in not long after that, and my hobby became my job,' he said, a sad glance at the cuckoo clock next to the mantelpiece.

'So,' I said, standing up. 'What d'you think happened to Paul?'

'There were two schools of thought on that,' replied Welshman. 'Eric thought Paul had been left down there deliberately. I thought the killer left him down there intending to return but never did, for whatever reason. Either he lost his nerve, or died.'

'There is a third possibility,' I said, turning for the door. 'What if the killer left him down there intending that he *would* be found?'

◆ ◆ ◆

We looked at it, but Eric dismissed it; never really pursued it as a serious line of enquiry.

That's what Welshman said. But it makes sense, if you think about it. When the killer left Paul in the bunker, there's no way he could possibly have known how long it would be until the observers next went down there. It might have been one week, it might have been three. As it turned out, it was six, and they only went down then thanks to the Cubans.

Most Observer Corps bunkers were manned intermittently, even in the sixties. Now it's even less than that. Training sessions take place at the pub, by all accounts, and it's more of a social thing, if anything.

I need to speak to the observers, find out exactly how often the bunker was occupied in 1962, and, more importantly, who knew. There's a statement from the Chief Observer on the file, of course there is, a copy of the rota too, not that anyone seems to have stuck to it.

We all make assumptions, don't we? And just about all of mine about Jack Welshman were wrong. He was kind enough to offer to help me too, and I'm going to need some help, but it must be fresh eyes. No one involved in the original investigation.

Even I know that.

I may not be finding new evidence, but I'm asking new questions, which is a start.

Chapter Eight

I was sitting in the back corner of the Edgar Lamb. The pub had been open for an hour or so, but was still quiet. Some of the tables had been laid for dinner, a single red rose in a little vase in the middle – it was Valentine's Day after all.

There were love songs playing over the music system, quietly though, so you could still hear yourself think.

I was waiting for the right moment. A small group at the bar had popped in for a beer after work by the looks of things, and I was hoping they'd be on their way before too many more people turned up.

It needed to be a quiet chat.

I knew he'd seen me. He kept glancing in my direction, expecting me to wave him over. Fred Hicks. The pub landlord and Chief Observer. He probably wanted his keys back. I'd still got them, needed to hang on to them for a while too. I might have to go down in the bunker again.

He looked a bit younger than me, maybe fifty or so. In his twenties in 1962. I knew he was an observer back then; there was a statement from him on the file.

I heard empty beer glasses being slammed down, watched Hicks putting them in a dishwasher under the bar as the group left; a cheery wave and a shout of 'Good luck, lads!'

Actually, they looked more like a darts or skittles team, come to think of it; off to an away match. They'll make a detective of me yet.

Hicks was walking in my direction now, casually, checking the tables. Then he stopped in front of me.

'Finished with the keys yet?' he asked.

Tall, slim, obviously didn't drink his own beer. Thinning blond hair, greying at the sideburns.

'Have you got a minute?' I asked, gesturing to the empty chair in front of me.

'Er, yeah.' He looked over his shoulder, checked someone else was behind the bar. 'Sue's here now. As long as you need.'

'Drink?'

'No, thanks.'

'I'll need to hang on to the keys, if that's all right.'

'Fine.' He sat down, brushing crumbs off the table with the back of his hand. 'You never said why you needed them, but I'm guessing it's Paul Bromfield.'

'It is.'

'I'll never forget that as long as I live. We got the shout, all bunkers to be manned round the clock. I remember thinking the bloody balloon was going up. It was terrifying. Our job was to monitor radiation levels, so that's what we all thought. This is it. Then the first lads down the ladder found him and the bunker was sealed off by your lot. I ended up helping out over at Langport and Puriton, filling in like, you know.'

'Are most of the lads still around?' I asked. Might save me a bit of time tracking them all down.

'Tom Carmichael is dead. He was Chief Obs back then. I went to his funeral. 1978, something like that.'

'Anyone else?'

'Derek Slater. He was first down the ladder, found the little lad. Drug overdose. The coroner said it was accidental, but we all knew. . .' He stood up. 'Perhaps I will have that drink.'

I watched him walk across to the bar, wait while Sue pushed a tumbler up underneath a whisky optic. Twice.

'So, what,' said Hicks, sitting back down. 'Are you looking at the case again?'

'There's a new unit.'

'Good,' he said.

'What about the rest of the team?'

'Adam moved to Edinburgh. The rest are still around, although only a couple of us are still observers.'

It took a few minutes to go through my list, ticking them off one by one.

'The corps is winding down, to be honest. I wouldn't be surprised if it shuts down altogether at some point. There isn't the same need for it, and you can't get people to volunteer. Everyone's too busy these days.' He shrugged. 'Puriton's closed, the bunker handed back to the landowner. The rest will go the same way, I expect.'

'Why do you do it?'

'Civic duty.' Indignant. Then he softened. 'And it was a bloody good piss-up, to be honest. A social, although that side of it was never the same after Paul was found down in our bunker. It was ages before any of us went down there again as well. No one could face it.'

'How often was the bunker occupied in 1962?'

'It varied. There was a rota, but that was just to keep the higher-ups happy, really. It was more about who was on call, rather than who would actually be going down there. We'd meet for a beer, do the training days, and there'd be an exercise once or twice a year, but that was it, really.'

'Where did you meet?'

'Here, although the pub was called the Station Hotel back then.' He gestured over his shoulder with his thumb. 'We used the room at the back, met once a month for a few beers, a game of skittles. We even had a team that used to go round the local pubs, compete in the league, you know.'

'And where was the rota kept?'

'On the noticeboard in the back room. We don't bother with a rota anymore. We meet here on the last Thursday of every month. Keeps it simple.'

'Who had access to the back room?'

'Anyone. It was open. Still is. There were a couple of other local clubs that used the noticeboard back then as well; darts, the fishing club used it for their matches, team sheets and what have you. The cricket club.'

'So, if I looked at the rota on the noticeboard in 1962 it would tell me that the bunker was occupied every weekend, is that right?'

'Yeah, I suppose it would.'

'But it wasn't?'

'No.'

'Was that common knowledge that the bunker wasn't actually occupied?'

'No, I don't think so. Our friends and family knew, obviously, but I wouldn't think anyone else did. It wasn't something we broadcast.'

'When was the last time it was occupied before Paul Bromfield was found down there?'

Hicks took a sip of whisky. 'There'd been an exercise, from memory, mid-August, but apart from that probably not for months, what with people being away on summer holidays and what have you.'

'And when would it have been occupied again, had it not been for the missile crisis?'

'Tom might have gone down to check on it; he did that from time to time, usually when it rained heavily, so that might not have been until the November, possibly.'

'He said in his witness statement the bunker had been occupied . . .' I flicked through the pages of my notebook, 'on the weekend of the eighteenth and nineteenth of August 1962.'

'That was the exercise. We thought it was a bit strange at the time, because it all seemed so sudden. We'd usually get more notice of a training exercise, they were booked months in advance sometimes. Maybe they were just keeping us on our toes, because of what was going on in Cuba?' He turned at the sound of chatter, a large group at the bar, ordering drinks. 'I was down there for the exercise, did my shifts, but apart from that it would've been Easter. Look, I wouldn't want you to think we were unique in this. Most teams rarely went down in their bunkers. They weren't supposed to be manned all day, every day, but when the shout came, down we went, as happened in the Cuban thing.' He drained his glass. 'People forget how close we came to nuclear war. Scary it was, for those of us who knew what was going on.'

'You must have talked about it with the other team members at the time, had theories about what happened to Paul.'

'The general consensus was that he'd been left down there; the kidnapper intended to come back but never did.' Hicks was staring at me. 'You don't buy that?'

'No.'

'Why not?'

'The original investigation checked everyone who died for miles around in the six week period Paul was missing, ruled them all out. So, let's say the killer – and let's be clear about this, a *killer* he is – lost his nerve instead, why not make an anonymous phone call? Walk into a remote phone box – they're dotted all over the countryside – dial 999, wear gloves. Easy.'

'You think the killer deliberately left him to die.' Hicks curled his lip. 'Some of the lads thought that.'

'No, I don't think that either. Someone looked at the noticeboard in the back room there and thought Paul would be found within a few days. He was snatched on the Tuesday after the bank holiday, and if the rota was correct, he should've been found alive and well on the Friday night.'

'So it was our fault?' Hicks stood up.

'It was the fault of whoever snatched him and left him down there. No one else.'

'In that case, you're right.' Hicks was glancing over his shoulder at the bar again, the queue longer now, Sue looking flustered. 'Why didn't he make your anonymous call from a remote phone box when the search dragged on and on and Paul still hadn't been found?'

'I don't know. Yet.'

◆ ◆ ◆

I left my empty glass on the corner of the bar – orange and lemonade, in case you were wondering – and I'm standing in front of the noticeboard in the back room. There's a small bar, the shutter down, a skittle alley too, but I can't see the far end in the darkness.

The noticeboard is one of those green felt ones, criss-crossed with black tape and a collection of drawing pins in the bottom corner.

There's an Edgar Lamb Golf Society outing to Burnham and Berrow coming up in April. A WI coffee morning in the Edington village hall. A list of fishing matches on the River Brue, two left before the season closes. A couple of business cards from local taxi firms.

I had hoped I might have been getting somewhere, that I might have narrowed it down a bit. If someone really did leave Paul down there intending him to be found, then it must've been someone who knew he'd be found. Then I find this bloody rota, pinned on a noticeboard in a busy pub, would've given anyone and everyone the impression the bunker was occupied when it wasn't.

One step forward, two steps back.

There's a word for that.

Bollocks.

Chapter Nine

Weekends drag in the winter months. There's no decent sport to watch. No Ashes tour Down Under this year to keep tabs on, so that just leaves the Five Nations rugby.

This weekend is different, though. I have Paul Bromfield to keep me company. And work to do.

It's Saturday afternoon now and I'm on my way to see Jenny Pugh in Bridgwater. I slept well last night, oddly enough, and spent the morning at Portishead, tracking down the children on the train in the six to eleven bracket. I've found quite a few. It's easy when their parents are still living at the same address. That got me fourteen.

Another twenty-seven to find.

Not all of them will be alive, of course.

That was a sad phone call. I felt awful, but the father understood I couldn't possibly have known.

It's one of those clear, crisp winter days, with a blue sky. Cold, unless you're in direct sunlight.

These are the children too young to have been interviewed by the police in 1962. Instead, their parents were asked to see if they had noticed anything unusual. All well and good, in principle, but as we know from Justine Paterson, not all parents did as they were asked. Perhaps he was protecting his daughter, or simply didn't want to get his family involved. Either way, Justine's father gave a false statement in a murder investigation. Unless he did ask, and Justine's just forgotten.

Anyway, we've moved on now. They're all adults and I'm going to be asking the questions this time.

Jenny Pugh is Justine's friend. Justine had been having a sleepover at Jenny's house, and they were on the train to Burnham the next day.

I'm driving slowly along Durleigh Road, looking for a large semi-detached house. She'll be there, babysitting for her sister, she said. Her red Mini Metro in the drive.

I parked behind it, got out, looked up at the house. There was a young woman standing in the front window, patting a baby that was lying over her shoulder.

In my experience that usually leads to vomit all down your back.

Happy days, although I hadn't appreciated it at the time.

She was standing in the open front door now, looking down at me. 'I was half expecting the cricketer,' she said, smiling.

I used that line to break the ice on the phone. Always works.

'Bob's just a nickname,' I said. 'But that's what people call me.'

'Come in then, Bob,' she said. 'Justine rang me last night, so I know what you're here about.'

Saves me the trouble of explaining it.

'I won't take up much of your time,' I said, when she closed the front door behind me.

'What is it you want to know?'

I followed her into the living room. 'Your mother gave a statement, said she'd asked you and you didn't see anything that day.'

'Justine said her father lied, told the police he'd asked her when he hadn't.'

'I'm wondering how many other parents tried to protect their children in the same way, tried to keep them out of it.'

'My mother asked me. I remember it clearly.' She was sitting on the window seat, still rubbing the baby gently on the back.

'I think she's gone to sleep.'

'Really?' Jenny craned her neck to look, breathed a sigh of relief, then placed the baby in a carrycot on the sofa. 'My niece,' she said. 'Only four months old.'

'I read your mother's statement,' I said, my voice hushed. 'She said you didn't see anything.'

'That's what I told her.'

There was something about the way she said it.

'It wasn't strictly true.'

'Go on.'

'Look, I don't know, after all this time.' She hesitated.

'Don't know what?'

'I don't know whether it's real or I imagined it, whether it's a picture I've seen somewhere; whether it's something I wanted to see, after we found out what happened to that little boy. I've just got this image in my head. I think it's from that day, but I can't be sure now, not after all this time.'

'Describe this image to me.'

'I'm on a train, and it's moving slowly, and I'm looking along a platform, I'm not even sure if it's Ashcott. There's steam and smoke; and a figure standing there, at the top of the ramp. I can't see his face, just a hooded coat. It's green, like one of those parkas.'

'What else can you remember?'

'We got on at Glastonbury. The train was long when it came in, and we'd walked down the platform, but not far enough, so we had to run. We were the last group to get on that last carriage. My mother lifted Justine up, then climbed in herself. We found some seats and then when it stopped at the next station, which was Ashcott, we weren't anywhere near the platform, so no one could get off, not that anyone wanted to; we were all off to the seaside. It was when we were pulling away again, that's when I saw him . . . *think* I saw him.'

'A man?'

'I thought it was a man, from the size.'

'Was there anyone else with him?'

'That boy, you mean?'

'Anyone.'

'No.'

'What did this man do then?'

'He just turned away, disappeared into the steam and smoke. To be honest, I can't be sure it's not a dream, something I saw on the television even. I couldn't swear to it.'

'Would it help to go back to Ashcott?' I asked. 'The line is closed but the platform is still there.'

'I can do that.' She gave a nervous smile. 'Anything.'

I followed her into the kitchen, watched her make a cup of tea.

I can picture what she means. Some of my earliest memories are just still images now, pictures, and I don't really know if they're real or I've imagined them. At best, it's an unconfirmed sighting by an unreliable witness.

Better than nothing, but not much.

◆ ◆ ◆

'You had a visitor.'

It was dark when I got home, but the shop was still open, so I popped in to see Shirley, pick up some milk.

'Who was it?' I asked.

'Some girl, said she was a journalist with the *Gazette*,' she replied. 'She's waiting for you in the Seymour.' She picked up a piece of paper from the till. 'There was a phone call for you as well.

You're to be at Portishead for nine on Monday. Any problems ring the admin office.'

'I really must get a phone line put in upstairs.'

'And what good would that do? You're never there.'

I picked up a carton of milk.

'You don't need that. I put one in your fridge earlier on.'

'Thanks.'

Tell people you live above the post office in Blagdon and they go there looking for you, even when I tell them I've got a separate entrance round the side. They might try the flat first, I suppose. Hardly my fault. The phone calls are, though. I give out the post office number, tell people they can leave a message for me. Shameless, really.

Shirley's looking better. The colour has returned to her cheeks and she's starting to smile occasionally.

When she forgets.

The black clothes have gone, put on a bit of makeup as well. I think she must've had her hair done, although I've never been very good at noticing that sort of thing. She divorced me on the grounds of unreasonable behaviour, had plenty of ammunition for that; failing to notice her appearance didn't even make the list. I ought to make an effort, really.

'You're looking well,' I said.

'Thank you.' Her face reddened. 'We've been here before, haven't we, Bob? I've got food in for two, invite you for supper, but you're distracted by whatever it is that girl wants, don't turn up. The food goes in the bin and I end up drinking a whole bottle of wine. Alone.'

'Sorry.'

That same old look of resignation. I've not seen it for a while.

'I'm used to it now. You know where I'll be and there's lasagne if you want it. No matter if you don't. What case are you working on?'

She knows about the Cold Case Unit, thinks it'll be good for me.

'Paul Bromfield,' I said, solemnly.

'You'd better go, see what she wants. It might be important.' Shirley remembered the name, the horror of it all unfolding on the television news. The whisky I got through after a day on the Levels, searching. The anger we all felt when we found out Paul had been alive for days, weeks.

Shirley had lived through it, been on the receiving end of it.

'Who picked that one?' she asked.

'I did.'

She'd been pregnant with Joanne at the time, Christine had been two, or three possibly. I forget. Being parents ourselves made it . . . closer to home, somehow. The good doctor would have a better word to describe it, but you get the picture.

Shirley put a packet of Silk Cut in her pocket, pulled the shutter down over the tobacco display, locked it, then flicked off the lights behind the counter. 'You'd better go,' she said. 'I'm locking up. You know where I am.'

'Thanks, Shirl.' I turned the sign in the front door to 'Closed', dropped the latch and let it slam behind me.

Chapter Ten

Angela was sitting in the corner of the pub, hiding, a glass of something dark and fizzy on the table in front of her. I spotted her through the window, watching both doors like a spectator at a tennis match. I tapped on the glass, gave her a cheery wave; watched her snatch a box off the bench seat next to her, head for the exit.

No time for a drink then.

'Glad to be out of there,' she said, pushing through the swing doors with her backside. 'Those two idiots at the bar kept pestering me. I'd already told them to piss off twice.'

'How long were you waiting?'

'Half an hour or so. I tried the Little Chef first, but they said you hadn't been in today.'

'Portishead, then Bridgwater.'

'Where's your car?'

'Outside my flat.'

She thrust the box into my arms. 'Here, you can carry this.'

'Photographs?'

'Everything we've got. I've had all the negatives developed as well, so there are loads of them.'

'Have you looked through them?' I asked, as we walked down through the village.

'I had a quick flick through. Couldn't see anything, but then I don't know what I'm looking for, do I?'

I do, and so do you.

People always say that criminals return to the scene of the crime. I've lost count how many times I've heard that over the years. So, we'll see, won't we.

'Have you eaten?' I asked.

'No.'

'There's a chippy over at Churchill.'

'Haven't you got anything in the fridge?'

'Some cheese, there's some bread and a packet of biscuits.'

'That'll do.'

I was holding the box in one hand, balancing it on the railings at the top of the metal staircase, fumbling in my pocket for my keys with the other.

Angela hesitated in the open front door. 'Is this where Alan was found?' she asked, staring at the new carpet in the hall.

'Yes.'

She hesitated, then stepped over it anyway, made straight for the kitchen. 'How about cheese on toast? They taught us how to make that in home ec.'

'Lovely,' I said. I'd closed the front door behind us and was unlocking the door to my incident room.

Shirley had put a shade on the ceiling light, but I'd taken it off again. The more light, the better. I'd got one of those angle lamps too, sitting on the floor and pointing up at the blackboard on the wall. There still wasn't a lot on the blackboard. A few names, a couple of crime scene photographs of the inside of the bunker. Angela hadn't seen those before, but then she was a trainee crime reporter, needed to get used to seeing such things.

Not that you ever really get *used to it*. I wouldn't want you to think that.

I was sitting in the deckchair, slitting open the tape on the top of the box with my door key, when she appeared, staring at the picture of Paul lying dead on the single bed. She had her back to me, wiped her eyes, then turned for the door. 'Cheese on toast won't be long,' she said, a tremble in her voice.

The box was full of black and white photographs. Different sizes, some in a shoebox, so I decided to start with those.

'They're the ones I got developed from the negatives. They look like duplicates to me, or they're very similar to some of the others anyway, probably not worth bothering with at the time.'

I flicked through them one by one; all of the same scene, police cars lined up along the A39: a couple of Morris Minors, an old Austin 1100, an unmarked Rover in regulation black, blue light on the roof. There was even a marked Bedford van. Parked on both sides of the road, wheels on the grass verge. A cordon was visible in the distance, traffic stopped by more patrol cars blocking the road. An ambulance too.

A small group of officers was visible adjacent to the stile the good doctor and I had climbed over only the other day. Their shoulders were hunched, the mood clearly sombre.

The day they found Paul. Must be.

Most of the photographs had been taken looking west along the A39, but some looked to the east, where a small crowd had gathered at a police cordon set up much nearer the stile. Local people, probably, those caught by the road closure, who'd got out of their cars and gone to have a look. News would have travelled fast too, so some may have come specially to gawp.

I hoped so anyway.

I stood up, picked up the magnifying glass from the windowsill and looked at the crowd. Too far away for any faces to be discernible, so identifying any of these people would be impossible; some were peering over parked patrol cars, others were standing on the grass verge, trying to get a better view.

I separated the pictures into two piles, one looking west, the other east; left them on the floor beside the deckchair. Then I turned to the rest in the box, picked out a few at random, before upending the box on the carpet.

No shortcuts here. One by one, it would have to be.

It was going to be a long night.

The smell of burning toast was getting stronger when Angela appeared with a plate in each hand, knives and forks sticking out of her pocket.

'There's no tomato sauce,' she said. 'How can you eat cheese on toast without tomato sauce?'

'Shop's shut, I'm afraid. Isn't there a real tomato in the door of the fridge?'

'That's not the same.'

We ate in silence, Angela glancing up at the picture of Paul when she thought I wasn't looking.

'I spoke to one of the children on the train today,' I said. 'She was nine at the time, so never gave a formal witness statement. None of the young children did.' Angela gave me a knife and fork, but I was using my fingers.

Who eats cheese on toast with a knife and fork, for heaven's sake?

'She thinks she saw a man on the platform at Ashcott, which is the station where we believe Paul was taken. She's got an image in her head of a figure in the smoke and steam wearing a hooded coat, possibly green.'

'An image in her head?' asked Angela, spraying crumbs on the carpet in front of her. She was sitting on the floor, her back to the wall.

'What can you remember when you were nine?'

'Quite a lot.'

'It was only a few years ago for you, though, wasn't it,' I said. 'Think about your earliest memories. What can you actually remember? I just see blurred faces now. Pictures in my mind of being on holiday with my parents. We're at Dawlish, on the beach; I think I can remember being there, but I can't see their faces anymore. I get that detail from photographs. Maybe I'm getting the whole memory from the photographs?'

'I can remember being at primary school. And on my seventh birthday we went to see the dolphins at Brighton, but you're right, I just see pictures of it in my head now. Lizzie being splashed when they jumped out of the water; Mum caught that on camera.'

I leaned forward in the deckchair, left my plate on the carpet next to me, and picked up a handful of photographs.

'So, we're looking for a bloke in a green coat.' She looked up at me, squinting at a picture through the magnifying glass. 'Have you got another one of those?' she asked.

'No, sorry.'

The original photographs were date stamped on the back, so we kept them in separate piles. Some showed a line of uniformed officers in a field. I remembered it well, walking slowly, responsible only for the ground directly in front of you, looking for anything, anything at all. Finding nothing.

I had to look twice, three times even, and there I was. Thirty or so, I'd have been then. I know it was me, because I was a good deal shorter than the officers either side of me. I recognised both of them, played in the second row of the police rugby team, but the names had gone. I set the photo to one side, carried on looking.

'What's that one?' asked Angela.

I handed it to her, and she held it under the lamp, squinting at it. 'Is that you? In the middle there.'

'Yes.'

'You never said you'd worked the case.'

'You can hardly call it *working the case*. I was just a pair of boots on the ground. That's it.'

'What was it like?'

'Upsetting.'

Angela knew not to press the point.

We sorted them by date. The photographer from the *Gazette* had been busy, out and about most days, it seemed. He'd photographed Ashcott railway station, the siding and the line between there and Shapwick, the station at Shapwick with the train being searched, the doors open, officers standing on the platform.

Divers in rivers and drains, rhynes being dragged.

The largest pile was taken the day Paul had been found, and I'd Sellotaped five of the images on the wall, to the left of the blackboard. Angela was standing up, examining them through the magnifying glass.

'The first four are date stamped,' I said. 'The last one came from the shoebox. The foreground is blurred, so that's probably why it wasn't developed at the time.' She'd stopped in front of it, tipping her head, moving the magnifying glass up and down. 'There's a figure on the extreme right, standing on the grass verge behind a patrol car.'

'A hooded coat. Fuck. Yes.'

Chapter Eleven

Sunday is an odd day; in my experience anyway.

I managed to get rid of Angela mid-morning, but not before Shirley had got completely the wrong idea.

'For God's sake, Bob, you're old enough to be her grandfather.'

'I slept on the sofa, Shirl.' I must've looked suitably dishevelled, because she believed me; knows me better than that too.

Giving her something to do seems to be the key to keeping Angela happy. This time her task was to check with the various news agencies for any other photographs and negatives from the 1962 investigation. We'd been through the box, but that was just the *Gazette* photographer. There would be more out there, and who knows what we might find?

Off she went, happy as Larry.

Cost me a breakfast in the new Little Chef at Farrington Gurney, though.

I've got a few calls to make, so I'm spending the afternoon in the office at Portishead, working my way through them, trying to set up interviews with the remaining children on the train. The shop shuts at midday on a Sunday, but I didn't think Shirley would let me use the phone all afternoon.

Actually, she probably would, I just didn't want to ask.

The other thing I want to do is have a proper look at that Bunsen burner, read all the statements again. It was left down in the bunker for a reason. Everybody knew that in 1962, knew it was sending a message; just never found out what message.

Nice and quiet on a Sunday afternoon; had the place to myself, but I expect that'll be the last time.

I've got to be here at nine o'clock in the morning and I'm guessing the retired superintendent taking over the unit is back from holiday. There'll be the press conference too, and they're best avoided.

I've always kept a low profile, and old habits die hard.

◆ ◆ ◆

I decided to go for a stroll. The sun was shining, and I thought it would be nice out on the Levels, might even see one of those murmurations everyone bangs on about.

Park at Ashcott, follow the old railway line to Shapwick.

Got my timings wrong, unfortunately, and I'm standing on the end of the platform at Ashcott in the dark. It is February, after all.

There's moonlight reflecting on the water of the Glastonbury Canal, and I can see lights on in the old station house. Occasionally a car rattles over the bridge, then bounces over the old level crossing.

I'm standing just about where nine-year-old Jenny Pugh saw the figure in the hooded coat disappear into the swirling smoke and steam.

Let's assume Paul got off the train, and this person enticed him off the end of the platform and down the bank towards the water. Maybe they went further along the tracks, or even across them, but where did they go then?

To get to Station Road they'd have to have gone back past the station house, the ticket office, signal box.

Unless they went out into the peat fields.

The working theory at the time was that Paul got off the train, maybe went down to the water's edge – he loved his fishing – and the train left without him. So, a man in a hooded coat approached him, told him he's got a car and he'll give him a lift. I can hear it now.

'We'll soon catch up with the train at Shapwick or Edington, then you can jump back on and your father need never know.'

A lamb to the slaughter.

Poor little bugger.

◆ ◆ ◆

'Crikey, you're in early, Bob.'

I know the bloke on the gate at Portishead. He worked at Clevedon police station back in the day and our paths crossed on Weston seafront, trying to separate the mods and rockers.

'Couldn't sleep,' I replied.

'You're on the new Cold Case Unit?'

'Paul Bromfield.'

He nodded. 'I remember it.'

We all do.

'Get the fucker,' he shouted, as he lifted the barrier.

The small car park round the back was empty when I arrived, so I'd have the place to myself again, for a while, at least.

Eric Hall had known the significance of the peat fields and there was a statement on file from every single employee of Petfu Peat Holdings, even former employees. No one had seen anything, of course they hadn't, but people lie.

You have to understand the landscape, really. Peat cutting leaves deep scars on the ground, trenches, gullies, tracks in between them. It's a maze at the best of times, and in heavy rain it all floods.

Parts of it were flooded in the summer of 1962. There'd been lots of rain, lots of abandoned cricket matches.

The peat fields had become an impenetrable wasteland.

Unless you knew the way.

The peat was taken out on freight trains that used the same railway line. Petfu even had their own siding a half-mile or so east of Ashcott.

The witness statements from the Petfu employees had been kept in a separate box and I'd put them in the top drawer of the filing cabinet, sorted into alphabetical order. It seemed a good place to start.

I'd read some of them, but not all, not by any means. One after another, all saying the same thing.

'I work for Petfu Peat Holdings.'

'I was at work as usual on Tuesday 28th August 1962.'

'I didn't see anything.'

They'd all need to be spoken to again, but if they'd lied before, they'd do it now.

I had the sudden feeling this case was going to drag on for months. On a purely selfish level that wouldn't be the end of the world, because I'm being paid by the day, but tracing witnesses, speaking to them one by one, listening to them saying exactly the same as they said last time, was going to be soul-destroying.

I heard the door slam at the bottom of the stairs, footsteps.

Detective Superintendent Clive Ash, retired. I knew the name, the reputation. What was more worrying was that he'd probably know mine.

'You'll be Bob Willis.'

'Yes, sir,' I replied.

'Call me Clive. We're all retired now, aren't we?' He took off his coat, hung it over the back of a chair, glancing around the table at the papers I'd sorted into various piles. 'You've made a start on the Bromfield case, I'm told. You should've waited until I arrived.'

'I've been here a week, didn't want to waste the time twiddling my thumbs.'

He was tall, a tweed sports jacket buttoned tightly over a beer belly.

We call them beer bellies, don't we? Might not be beer at all. Mine isn't. Not anymore.

'Who decided on the Bromfield case?'

'I did.'

He slid on a pair of reading glasses and leaned over the table.

'The evidence has already gone off to Forensics,' I said. 'There wasn't a lot; the Bunsen burner, radio, stuff you see in the crime scene pho—'

He raised his hand, silencing me mid-sentence.

'You still drinking, Bob?' he asked, without looking up.

'No.'

'How long?'

'Six months.'

He straightened up, his eyes narrowing as he looked me up and down. 'You don't look much like a fast bowler,' he said, no hint of a smile. 'I'll be honest with you, Bob, when the ACC asked me to set up this Cold Case Unit, you weren't my first choice. You're here as a personal favour to DCS Sharp, something to do with what happened out on the A303.'

'It's a long story.'

'Isn't it always?' He walked over to the window and looked out, a mixture of engines and voices in the car park below. 'Well, the cavalry's here.'

'How many?'

'Six to begin with,' he replied. 'Tell me, why the Bromfield case?'

'I remembered it, was out in the fields as part of the search effort, remember the day he was found.'

'A good choice,' Ash said, over the footsteps in the stairwell.

◆ ◆ ◆

The introductions didn't take long.

They all knew each other, probably handpicked by Ash. I didn't know any of them, but they'd all heard of me; frowned when they said it too. I was the odd one out, felt as if I'd gate-crashed a party and they were just waiting for me to go home.

I can live with that, all the same. After all, it's not about me, is it? It's about little Paul Bromfield.

At least they all remembered the case, were familiar with the basic details.

'Well,' said Ash, 'Bob's been on it a week already, so perhaps you'd kindly fill us in on how far you've got?'

I looked around the table, counted two smirks. It was a question designed to make me look like the idiot they probably thought I was. Reputations precede, and all that.

'I've started by tracking down the children on the train. Statements weren't taken from the younger ones, but they're adults now. The first two have been interesting. Justine Paterson was nine at the time. Her father said he'd spoken to her, and she saw nothing, but she told me he'd never asked her about it. The second one, Jenny Pugh, said that she recalls seeing a figure in a hooded coat standing at the end of the platform. She describes it as an image in her head.'

Ash looked surprised, to be fair to him.

'I've got meetings set up with eleven others, names and addresses for six more who live in other parts of the country,' I continued. 'If what Jenny says about the man in the hooded coat is right, then we need to speak to the peat cutters again, ask them specifically about that. His only way out would've been across the peat fields.'

'That's good work, Bob,' said Ash.

'I've also got hold of all the photographs taken by the *County Gazette* photographer and had the negatives developed. There's a photo taken the day Paul's body was found – never been developed before. It's looking east along the A39 towards a crowd of onlookers, and there's a figure in a hooded coat standing on the grass verge.'

'Where are these photographs?'

'The box is in my car,' I replied.

Between you and me, I'd had to go back for it. Glad I did now. There was a duplicate of the important photo too, so Ash need never know about my spare room.

'I've also spoken to the stationmaster, who's still living in the station house. The current Chief Observer, who was on the team at the time. He's the landlord at the Edgar Lamb.'

'You have been busy.' Ash was staring at me.

I'm hoping he thinks he misjudged me, but I might be wrong.

'Right,' he said. 'Give the details of those meetings you've arranged to Nick and Maggie and they'll interview the witnesses. Gary and Vic can make a start revisiting the peat cutters.'

Nice. Ash obviously doesn't trust me; doesn't know me, I suppose. You'd think I'd be pissed off, but it leaves me free to focus on the Bunsen burner, doesn't it?

'It would be useful to have this photo up on the board so we can all see it,' he continued, 'and copied so we can show it to potential witnesses.' Ash checked his watch. 'I'd like a copy for the press conference at eleven too.'

'I can organise that, guv,' said the officer to my left. A retired DS, I forget her name.

'I spoke to Eric Hall's bagman, Jack Welshman,' I said. 'He's keen to help in any way he can. I've also spoken to Paul's parents, so they know about today's announcement.'

Ash nodded. 'I'll speak to them myself later on today.'

I'd been watching the bloke sitting opposite me, shaking his head and sighing with monotonous regularity. Ash's old bagman, if I had to guess, along for the ride and the daily rate. He was working up to something and my gut told me I wasn't going to like it.

'Seems a lot of fuss for one dead kid,' he said. 'Surely there are more important cases we should be looking at first?'

I stood up sharply, sending my chair crashing into the filing cabinet behind me. I slid the keys out of my pocket, dropped them in the middle of the table. 'Those are the keys to the bunker,' I said. 'I suggest anyone who thinks that, takes them and goes down there, see for yourself how that nine-year-old boy died.'

'Quite,' said Ash.

'I'll go and get the photos from my car.' I let the door slam behind me.

Fuck them.

I'm not here to make friends, am I?

Chapter Twelve

I've never liked press conferences, but then I never really had to worry about them; never reached a high enough rank. I occasionally gave a quote to the local rag outside court, but that was about it.

Despite my best efforts, I found myself sitting behind a table in the press suite at Portishead; one side of the assistant chief constable, Ash the other. He thought I ought to be on hand in case there were any detailed questions.

'Shall I stand at the back?'

'No, up at the front with us.'

I'd read the file, hadn't I?

Ray Keenan was there, the crime reporter from the *Gazette*, and he had Angela in tow. I was just hoping she remembered our deal.

There were TV cameras too. Glad I put on a clean shirt.

The ACC read the statement prepared for him by the press office and, thankfully, I managed to stifle a chuckle when he said the CCU was to be staffed by the 'brightest and best' from among our retired officers. I thought I saw Ash glance at me out of the corner of his eye then.

After that there was a lot about advances in forensic science.

Then he moved on to Paul Bromfield, the first of the cases to be looked at by the new unit. Ash took over at that point; delighted to announce early progress, he put the photograph of the hooded man up on the overhead projector.

Two things sprang to mind. Firstly, we were going to be inundated with the bereaved wanting the cases of their murdered loved ones investigated next. Fair enough, can't blame them for that. And, secondly, if he didn't know already, the hooded man sure as hell knew we were coming for him now.

I'm sure I even heard Ash say that no stone would be left unturned.

'I think Detective Inspector Willis is probably best placed to answer that,' said Ash.

Bollocks.

Not listening in class again. I'd drifted off, didn't even know they'd moved on to questions.

'Perhaps you could repeat the question?' I asked.

'Why wasn't that photograph uncovered by the original investigation?' Someone at the front, holding a Dictaphone at arm's length.

'It was taken by a press photographer and never developed. There's a sequence of five, all of them blurred in the foreground.'

'What can you see in this sequence?'

'The hooded man is seen turning away and walking east along the grass verge of the A39.'

'Can they be enhanced?'

'We'll certainly be looking at that,' replied Ash. 'But I would ask anyone who recognises this person to come forward, or the person himself even, so we can eliminate you from our enquiries.'

The ACC stepped in, shut it down after that, a couple of questions shouted from the back.

'Will you be speaking to Andrew Bucknall again?'

'What about Andrew Bucknall?'

◆ ◆ ◆

Once in the corridor behind the press suite, the ACC turned, practically pinned me to the wall.

'Look, it's Bob, isn't it?'

'Yes, sir.'

'Have you spoken to Andrew Bucknall yet?'

'Not yet, sir.'

'Sorry, who's Andrew Bucknall?' asked Ash.

'He's the stationmaster's son,' I replied. 'He confessed at the time, but it turned out he had an alibi, so he was released. I read his interviews, there's nothing there. He couldn't even describe the inside of the bunker when asked.'

'Maybe he'd put Paul down there in the dark?'

I shrugged. 'He knew nothing about the Bunsen burner either.'

'Bring him in anyway,' said the ACC. 'We've got to be seen to be—'

'Is that what this is about?' I snapped. 'Being *seen* to be doing it.'

'Leave it with me, sir,' said Ash, moving the ACC along the corridor, away from me. 'Bob's done a sterling job getting things going. It was him who found the photo of the hooded man, and a witness who says she saw him on the platform.'

The ACC looked over his shoulder at me, making no effort to hide his disapproval. 'Just keep an eye on him,' he said to Ash. 'You know he drinks.'

◆ ◆ ◆

So much for focusing on the Bunsen burner; turns out I'm to be Ash's bagman – for this afternoon anyway. He did surprise me, though. He lobbed the keys to one of the others before we left the office, told them to go down in the bunker and see it for themselves before they did anything else.

All of them. No exceptions.

I'm driving his Rover and we're on our way to Ashcott to speak to Andrew Bucknall. Utterly pointless, but we have to be seen to be doing it, apparently. The poor bloke's going to shit himself. Again.

'You're not going down in the bunker?' I asked, casually.

'No need.' Ash was sitting in the front passenger seat, reading Andrew's original interviews, and spoke without looking up. 'I'm ex-RAF.'

Two pensions. Nice.

'You?'

'I did my national service,' I said. 'Then joined the police.'

He nodded. 'Where will we find this Andrew Bucknall then?'

'He gives the station house as his address, but he lives in a caravan in what was the old railway siding on the other side of the bridge.'

'He was a regular visitor to the bunker in the months after Paul was found.' Ash looked up. 'How does he explain that, I wonder?'

'It wasn't him,' I said, firmly. 'He hasn't got the capacity for it. I doubt he'd have been able to pick the padlocks on the hatch for a start. Whoever did it picked them; Forensics found the telltale scratches inside the barrels. There's no way Andrew could've done that.'

'He has issues then.'

'He does.'

'He confessed.'

'And what would the Police and Criminal Evidence Act make of that confession, I wonder?'

'A good point.' Ash turned in his seat, dropped the papers in the rear passenger footwell. 'The glory days when we could lean on people and get away with it.'

'He should've had his father there when he was interviewed, or a responsible adult. He should do now, probably.'

'We're just going for a chat, Bob. I want to see for myself, see if we really can rule him out.'

Twenty minutes later I parked the big Rover across the gate at the entrance to the old siding. Ash got out of the car, looked over at the platform.

'This was the level crossing,' I said. 'Shapwick is that way.' I pointed to the west, over the bonnet of the car. 'There's his caravan.'

It was covered in green algae and lichen, a path to it through undergrowth that was beginning to swamp it. Behind it the bank dropped down to the South Drain.

'So, that dirt track is the old railway line,' said Ash, nodding to himself. 'Let's go and stand on the platform. You can tell me what this new witness says.'

It didn't take long, standing on the spot where a nine-year-old Jenny Pugh would have seen the figure in the green coat that fateful day.

'Was all that vegetation there in 1962?' asked Ash, looking at the trees and bushes lining the old track on the far side of the line.

'Some, but not that much. It's grown up in the years since. You'd have seen over it from the train, a clear view across the peat fields.'

Ash walked slowly to the end of the platform and down the ramp. I followed.

'He went this way, then.' He grimaced. 'Bastard.'

'He must've taken Paul back along the line to the old peat siding, or over the tracks and gone across the peat fields.'

'How deep is the drain?'

'Six to eight feet in the middle.'

Ash took a deep breath. 'Just do me a favour, Bob. However long this investigation takes, stay off the booze.'

◆ ◆ ◆

I turned sideways, squeezed through the gap in the brambles, and knocked on the door of the caravan.

Blankets had been pinned at the windows and there was a bag of rubbish on the ground by the steps. I looked round the side, wished I hadn't bothered.

'What's round there?' asked Ash.

'A bucket.'

'Say no more.'

I knocked again.

'Go away.' The voice was faint, tight.

Ash leaned forward, thumped on the door. 'Police, Andrew. We need to speak to you.' He looked at me, his eyes wide. 'What the hell's he living here for?'

'His father said he likes it. There's a room for him in the stationhouse, but he prefers it here.'

'What do you want?'

I thought I saw the blanket in the window twitch.

'To speak to you about Paul Bromfield,' replied Ash.

Soft footsteps, then the door opened slowly.

Forty-four years of age, but then I knew that. A full growth of beard, hair matted. He was wearing one of those green parkas with the fur lined hood, jeans and trainers. He wiped his nose on his sleeve. 'What about Paul Bromfield?' he asked.

'You remember the name,' said Ash.

'Of course I do.'

'Can we come in, Andrew?' I asked.

The only light inside came from the skylight, which was covered in algae, giving everything in the caravan a green tinge. There was a sleeping bag on the bed in the front window. No curtain, but then the front of the caravan was buried in the thick vegetation, so no light was getting through anyway. Tins of this and that on the sink, some of them opened, the contents eaten from the can, a spoon still sticking out of one of them. Beans and Spam mainly. A tin of peaches too.

'Why did you confess to locking Paul in the bunker?' Ash asked. He looked as if he was about to throw up, so probably wanted to get straight to the point and get out of there.

'Mr Hall said I could go home if I did.'

'Why were you arrested in the first place?'

'I don't know.' Andrew sat down on the edge of his bed; arms folded tightly across his chest. 'Some people said they'd seen me hanging around the bunker.'

'And had you been hanging around the bunker?'

'I suppose.'

'Why?'

'I don't know.'

'Yes, you do.' There was a sharpness to Ash's voice. Impatience, or trying to intimidate Andrew, possibly.

'I went on my bike to place some flowers.'

'Did you know the bunker was there before Paul was taken?'

'Everybody knew.'

'Did you go there before Paul was taken?'

'Sometimes. There's a footpath.'

'And where were you the day he went missing?'

'I went on the train to Burnham, but we only got as far as Shapwick. I got free train travel because of my dad; used to go all the time, hang around down by the amusements. Still do sometimes, but I have to catch the bus now.'

Ash tapped me on the shoulder, gestured to the door.

We make judgements about people. I may have mentioned that before. We all do it. It takes some of us longer than others, but we get there in the end. I'd arrived at my judgement of Andrew by speaking to his father, reading his interviews and looking at where he lived. It had taken Ash a bit longer to arrive at the same conclusion. Being thorough, I'll give him that, which might explain why he retired a superintendent and me a lowly DI.

A rusting bicycle was leaning up against the brambles, probably the same bike Andrew had ridden over to the bunker all those years ago.

'There's his bike,' I said, when we were back out in the fresh air. 'Hall was clutching at straws by the time he picked him up. It was nearly a year after Paul had gone missing, for a start. And when they checked, witnesses came forward to say they'd seen him on the train and the coach to Burnham.'

'A shambolic episode in an otherwise exemplary investigation,' muttered Ash. 'Let's hope.'

'A measure of the pressure they were under,' I offered.

Andrew had come out of his caravan, shut the door behind him and was shuffling along the old siding towards the stationhouse, a few paces behind us. I recognised the sound of jeans that were too long, dragging on the ground behind his shoes.

We were following the line of the tracks, the gravel still visible in the wispy grass.

I stopped, turned. 'Andrew,' I said. 'How often do you visit the bunker?'

'Quite a lot.'

'And what do you do when you're there?'

'Just sit, looking at the view. It's peaceful.'

'When did the crocuses and primroses appear?' I asked.

'The following spring. After Paul . . .' His voice tailed off.

'There are shoots coming up. What are they?'

'Bluebells. There are loads of them now.'

'Were they there before Paul was found in the bunker?'

'No.'

'You can go.'

'What the hell was that all about?' asked Ash, when Andrew was finally out of earshot.

'I really don't know.'

◆ ◆ ◆

I spent an hour on the photocopier when we got back to Portishead, tucked the bundle of papers under my arm, and made my escape before Ash had a chance to stop me.

'I'm going to focus on the Bunsen burner,' I said, when I was already halfway out of the door.

'Er, Bob—'

'Cheerio.'

'Right. Keep in touch.' Ash was shouting down the stairwell by the time I reached the bottom. 'I want to know what you're doing.'

I think he's on my side, actually.

'Don't confuse high rank with ability, Bob,' he'd said in the car on the way back to Portishead. 'More often than not it's about ambition rather than talent.'

I've never been blessed with much of either, to be honest. Shirley tried to instil a bit of ambition in me, with moderate success; detective inspector isn't to be sniffed at, after all.

Now, I'm standing in my spare room, staring at the photographs on the wall. I've read the statements dealing with the Bunsen burner twice and am none the wiser.

There's the transistor radio too. What was that doing down there? There wasn't even any reception.

The original seller of the radio and the burner were traced, as was the person who'd first bought the radio. It had been a gift for an elderly neighbour, who died, then it went off to a house clearance sale.

I arrived at some conclusions today. I've had a lot of time to think, driving to and from Portishead, as well as acting as Ash's chauffeur, giving him a guided tour of Ashcott station. This case isn't going to be solved by speaking to all of the witnesses again, even with the photograph of the mysterious man in the hooded coat to show them.

No, it's going to be solved by understanding the significance of the Bunsen burner and the radio; clues deliberately left behind by the killer.

I'm starting to wonder whether he actually wanted to be caught at the time, whether that's why he left those particular items for the police to find.

Whether it was part of some elaborate game.

The press conference made the national news, I saw it on the evening bulletin. The ACC's announcement, followed by some black and white footage of the original search. That means it'll be front and centre in tomorrow's papers.

I hope Ash remembered to ring Paul's father.

As for the killer, if he's alive, he knows.

The game's back on.

Chapter Thirteen

'Well, that's put paid to any peace and quiet.'

I was sitting in the window of the Little Chef at Farrington Gurney, just about to tuck in to an All Day Breakfast, when a red Allegro sped in to the car park and screeched to a halt behind my Volvo. Angela was out of the car and running towards the entrance, leaving the driver's door standing open in the rain.

Must be important to interrupt my breakfast.

Then she was standing over me, watching me bolt my food.

'What is it?' I asked, through a mouthful of crispy bacon and griddled tomato.

'A child's gone missing,' she replied. 'Are you just going to sit there?'

'And what would you have me do?'

'Well, I—'

'Sit,' I said, gesturing to the bench seat opposite me. 'Have you eaten?'

'I'm not hungry.'

'In that case, go and park your car properly.'

It bought me a minute or so to finish my breakfast.

The timing is interesting, coming the day after the press conference, the morning after the evening news. That might explain

Angela's hysteria, but children go missing all the time. More often than not they're found somewhere they shouldn't be, safe and well.

No, it's the timing.

Angela sat down opposite me, wiped the rain off her forehead.

'Where?' I asked.

'Watchet,' she replied. 'Ray got a tip off from a police contact and he's gone straight over there.'

'What do we know about the child?'

She raised her eyebrows. 'A nine-year-old boy. He was on his way to school in the town; didn't get there, so his father went to look for him, found his bicycle in the lane.'

A nine-year-old boy. Now, that is too much of a coincidence, I think we can agree on that.

And, if I'm right, that means it is a game.

'Get yourself a cup of tea or something,' I said, standing up.

'Where are you going?'

'Make a phone call.'

There was a payphone on the wall in the lobby and I had enough change.

'CCU.'

I recognised the voice, that twerp who thought we had better cases to be investigating. 'Is Clive there?' I asked.

'Who is it?'

'Bob Willis.'

'Hold on. That prick's on the phone, asking for you, guv.' It was muffled, so he'd made an effort.

'Where the hell are you, Bob?' asked Ash, coming on the line.

'Out and about,' I replied. 'Have you heard the news this morning?'

'No, what?'

'A nine-year-old boy is missing over at Watchet. Never made it to school. They found his bike abandoned in a lane.'

'Look, we're dealing with a cold case. Something that happened nearly twenty-four years ago.'

'A nine-year-old boy, the morning after the press conference. It can't be a coincid—'

'Yes, it can, but if it isn't, in the unlikely event it is connected, then no doubt we'll be asked to liaise with the investigating team in due course.'

'We need to—'

'We don't need to do anything except focus on the Paul Bromfield case, Bob. Let this lad over at Watchet go through the normal channels. They'll probably find him, but if they don't then it'll be a different kettle of fish, and we can feed into the investigation what intel we have.'

'I think I ought to—'

'Stay out of it, Bob. That's what you ought to do. You said you were going to focus on the Bunsen burner, so do that. Nothing else.'

He rang off abruptly. Slammed the phone down on me would probably be a better description of it, actually, not that there'd been anything more to say.

'Come on,' I said. 'You haven't got time for that.'

Angela was pouring herself a cup of tea. 'Oh, right. Where are we going?'

'Watchet.'

◆ ◆ ◆

'Ray said he'd be outside the school,' said Angela. 'Reckoned everywhere else would be off limits.'

It had taken us an hour or so to get across to Watchet. We'd left her car in the car park at the Little Chef; they know me well enough in there now, said it would be fine.

I'm sure I've been here before but can't for the life of me remember when. It's a nice little harbour town on the north coast, just along from Hinkley Point. Come to think of it, it might have been an anti-nuclear demo when they were building the power station in the early sixties. Something like that anyway.

We parked down by the harbour, asked the way to the school; found the crime reporter from the *County Gazette* sitting in his car.

He wound down the window, releasing the smoke that was filling the passenger compartment. 'They're not saying much. The lad lives on a farm the other side of St Decumans. Uniformed officers are swarming all over the place, but I've not seen any sign of CID yet.'

'Have you been out there?' I asked.

'The lane's closed. You can't get anywhere near the scene.'

Angela frowned. 'Scene? Scene of what?'

Keenan glanced at me, shook his head. 'Oh, to be young again,' he said. 'When you've been at this a while, you know, you just know. His bike's in a ditch by the side of the road and he's gone. You work it out.'

'What's his name?' I asked.

'Simon Horsey,' replied Keenan.

'Take us up there, as far as we can go anyway.'

The lane climbed out of Watchet, high hedges on both sides, sweeping bends, great fun on a bicycle getting to school, not so much fun going home.

There were glimpses of the Severn Estuary through field gateways, trees leaning with the prevailing wind.

'There's a turn-off up here to the farm,' said Keenan. 'It's called Willow Grove Farm, but the lane's blocked.' He pulled into a passing place, a patrol car blocking the left turn about fifty yards ahead.

'Wait here,' I said, climbing out of the passenger seat.

'Can I come?' asked Angela.

'He won't get very far with one of us in tow, will he?' Keenan lit a cigarette, dropped the match out of the open driver's window.

The conversation with the uniformed officer on the roadblock was short and sweet, successful all the same.

'No warrant card?'

'We're all retired, working as consultants.'

'Nice work if you can get it.'

I smiled. Kept walking.

About five hundred yards, he'd said.

Several cars were parked in the lane where a farm track forked off to the right, uniformed officers beyond, looking at something in the ditch, a camera flash going off intermittently.

The fork in the road was an ideal place to lie in wait for someone, for a child on a bicycle; getting ahead of myself, though, God willing.

A uniformed sergeant was striding towards me, his arm raised. 'Who are you?' he demanded. 'How the bloody hell did you get past the cordon?'

Business card again.

'What cold case?'

'Paul Bromfield,' I replied.

The blood drained from his face. 'That was over twenty years ago.'

'1962.'

'And what makes you think there's a connection?'

'Just the timing. Did you see the news on the TV last night?'

'I did. It's in the paper too. I remember the search,' he said, curling his lip. 'Lines of us out on the Levels.' He was tall, so it could have been him standing next to me in that photo.

'Me too.'

'You were there?'

'Dragging a rhyne the day he was found.'

'Give me a minute.'

I watched him sit in the driver's seat of a patrol car and reach for the radio.

The photographer was still taking photos of the bicycle. It was upside down in the shallow ditch at the side of the lane, thrown there, possibly – probably. It was a small racing bike, no tape on the handlebars, no mudguards either. A hand-me-down, if he had older brothers.

'CID are sending someone from Minehead,' said the sergeant, slamming the car door.

'Can I speak to the family?' I asked, more in hope than expectation.

'DS Simpson is on the way. Better wait until she gets here.'

'Oh, come on. You know what'll happen. She'll tell me I'm wasting everyone's time and to sling my hook.'

'Perhaps you are. Have you thought of that?'

I spent the next twenty minutes standing in a field gateway, keeping out of the way. More uniformed officers arrived in minibuses, from Bridgwater and Minehead, although I noticed a Taunton call sign on the roof of one.

The search was widening, but then if Simon had gone missing on the way to school, that would've been eight-thirty or so, and it was nearly lunchtime now.

Officers were fanning out across the fields, more heading towards an area of woodland on the other side of the West Somerset Railway line. Others in waders heading for the river.

All the right things were being done, and I couldn't fault the response.

It was time CID got involved too.

A car pulled up in the lane, a woman sitting in the passenger seat, a younger man driving. My heart sank. I knew who they were, knew they were both too young to have been serving officers at the time of Paul's disappearance and murder. They might know the name, of course. Some people did, and there'd been that documentary on the TV a couple of years ago, around the time of the twentieth anniversary.

A two-piece suit, practical shoes. Late thirties, possibly; older than my daughters anyway. She had short dark hair, did all the talking too, the younger officer a DC caught in her slipstream, probably. The uniformed sergeant was pointing in my direction now.

Brace yourself, Bob.

'No.' She took my business card, slid it into her coat pocket without looking at it. 'You go in there talking about Paul Bromfield and the parents are going to shit themselves. That's the last thing we need at the moment.'

'You know the name?'

'My family lived in Moorlinch. I was twelve at the time.'

'This lad's the same age as Paul,' I said. 'And the Cold Case Unit was announced yesterday. It was on the news, and the lead story in today's *Gazette* is the reopening of the Bromfield investigation.'

'I get it, but it's too early for that connection to be made. The mother's hanging on by her fingertips as it is.'

'Have you spoken to the family?'

'Uniform have made the basic enquiries, and we're going down there now.'

'Let me come with you,' I said. 'I won't say a thing, I'll just listen. You have my word.'

She was breathing deeply through her nose, mulling it over. 'It's not connected to the Bromfield case. It can't be.'

'Yes,' I said. 'But what if it is?' I let that hang in the air for a moment. 'You can tell them I'm a retired DI, working as a consultant, an expert in missing children.'

'And are you?'

'I'm a retired DI, working as a consultant, yes.'

'No mention of Paul Bromfield?'

'None.'

She puffed out her cheeks, nodded her agreement, and I followed them back to their car.

I just have to hope the family didn't see the footage from the press conference on the TV news.

Chapter Fourteen

One dairy farm looks much the same as any other. Smells the same too.

It was at the end of the lane, a tired farmhouse behind a crumbling dry-stone wall. Slates on the roof had slipped; the windows were rotting in places. Traces of white paint still clung on to the crumbling grey render underneath the eaves.

A large German shepherd standing guard in the porch was the only sign of life, until a man appeared on the far side of the yard, hosing out the milking parlour, a trail of cow muck leading out on to a farm track beyond.

The cows still have to be milked, whether your son has been kidnapped or not.

The man looked us up and down, then carried on flushing the muck down a drain. A cowhand, probably.

Hopefully.

Simon's father had other things on his mind this morning.

There was a light on inside the farmhouse, the upstairs curtains drawn.

'Remember, I do the talking. Not a word about Paul Bromfield.' DS Simpson was using both hands to open the rickety gate, lifting it across the cracked paving stones of the front path.

A figure appeared in the front porch, clipped a lead on the dog and dragged it inside. Seconds later it appeared at the bay window on the right, watching us intently.

He was an older man. Simon's grandfather, probably. The boy's father would be out looking for his son.

The man opened the front door. 'Police?' he asked.

'Yes, sir,' she replied, holding up her warrant card. 'I'm DS Mary Simpson. This is Detective Constable Mitchell.' She stuck to the agreed line for me – retired DI acting as a consultant.

'I'm Simon's grandfather,' replied the man. 'My son is out looking for him, I'm afraid.'

'Is your daughter-in-law at home?' asked Simpson.

'She is.' He stepped aside. 'Come in.'

The next few minutes were difficult, but then they were always going to be. Simon's mother was distraught, as you might imagine, and didn't react well to being asked the same questions all over again.

'We've already been asked that by the uniformed officers who came this morning,' said the grandfather.

'We've already been asked that as well.'

They were the standard questions you have to ask.

'What time did you last see him?'

'What was he wearing?'

'What time does he usually leave for school?'

'How long does it take him to get there?'

'What time did the school ring to say he wasn't there?'

'Has he ever gone missing before?'

'Does he have any hiding places?'

'Had there been an argument or anything like that?'

'And you've checked everywhere you can think of? Phoned friends, family?'

The mother did her best to answer them all, despite her father-in-law's huffing and puffing.

'You should be out there looking for him.'

If I had a quid for every time I'd heard an anxious parent say that over the years . . .

Poor woman. She was sitting at the end of the kitchen table, a grubby coat over a drab dress, wellington boots. Been out looking for him as well, I shouldn't wonder.

I stuck to my side of the bargain with Simpson, kept quiet.

Farmhouse kitchens hadn't changed much over the years. No electric kettles and toasters here. No microwave ovens. Cold too, the back door standing open, washing on the line out in the rain that had started falling again.

'David will be back in a minute,' said the mother. She was staring at a piece of soggy toast on a plate. 'He was going to check the barns and down by the river. There's a water tank, as well.'

'Is there a slurry pit?' asked Simpson.

'Covered and locked.'

The boy's grandfather was watching me, his curiosity growing, judging by the frown etched on his forehead. Any minute now.

Simpson had spotted it too. 'Who runs the farm, Mr Horsey?' she asked.

'Er, it's run by my son these days. I've stepped back from it. We've got it set up as a limited company. I've got some shares, but when my wife died her shares went to David. Why d'you need to know that?'

'Just background, really.' Simpson was watching Mitchell scribbling in his notebook. 'And it's a dairy farm?'

'Dairy and beef. We've got some heifers in a barn round the back.'

He was a tall man; weathered, but then farmers tend to be, for obvious reasons. Brown brogues, corduroys and a check shirt, the sleeves rolled up to reveal several tattoos.

'I was off to the livestock market,' he said, when he noticed me looking. 'It's the social side, really. I was just on my way out when the school rang.'

'Was Simon having problems at school?' asked Simpson.

'No,' replied the mother.

'Being bullied, perhaps?'

'No.'

'So, there's no reason you can think of why he would have wanted to skip it?'

'He liked it.'

She stood up at the sound of a diesel engine outside. 'That's David. Has he got him?' She ran to the back door, the sound of wellington boots on the path.

'Have you found him?'

He took off his cap, hung it on a hook inside the back door. 'No.'

'These are detectives, David,' said his father.

Tired eyes, imploring, met with the usual platitudes from DS Simpson. But what else could she say? And I've come out with the same crap often enough.

'I'm going to have something to eat and then get back out there,' said David.

'I'll arrange for an officer to come, and as soon as there's any news, you'll get it. All right?'

'Thank you.' The grandfather was gesturing along the hall, back to the front door. I took the hint, even if Simpson was a little slow to get it.

He was watching us from the front porch as we walked down the garden path, Mitchell trying to drag the gate closed behind us. Then I heard the front door close, footsteps behind us.

'You.'

I turned, knowing somehow it was aimed at me.

'I didn't say anything in front of them, but I saw you on the news last night. You were at that press conference. You're in that new Cold Case Unit, investigating the Paul Bromfield murder, aren't you?'

I glanced at Simpson, who puffed out her cheeks.

He slid my business card out of the breast pocket of his shirt, read my name aloud. 'Mungo Willis.'

'Everybody calls me Bob.'

'You're here because you think my grandson's going to die like Paul Bromfield.'

'I'm just here to rule out any connection to the Bromfield case. That's all,' I said.

'What makes you think it might be connected?'

'The timing, and Simon's age.'

'That's it?'

'That's it.'

He cleared his throat. 'I won't say anything to them *yet*, but I hope to God you're wrong.'

◆ ◆ ◆

'For fuck's sake.' Simpson had managed to contain herself until we were back in the car. 'You never said you'd been at a televised press conference. The poor bloke's going to be beside himself now.'

'You need to check every single Royal Observer Corps bunker, and you need to do it now,' I said.

'You're off your fucking rocker, mate.'

We drove back down the lane in silence, arriving just in time to see Simon's bicycle being loaded into the back of a police van. Safely wrapped in plastic sheeting and off to Forensics.

Simpson waited until Mitchell got out of the car, turned in the passenger seat and glared at me. 'You still think the cases might be connected?'

'I almost hope they are, because if so, it tells me two things,' I said.

'What things?'

'Firstly, that Simon is still alive. And secondly, that knowing what we know now, we have a fighting chance of finding him.'

She was softening. 'All right, there's the timing and the boys' ages. What else? I'm going to need something more than that to get it past my DI.'

'Did you see the tattoos on the grandfather's forearms?'

'I saw he had some, but I didn't really notice what they were.'

'A white ensign and an anchor,' I said. 'He's ex-Navy.'

'So?'

'Paul Bromfield's father is ex-Navy.'

Chapter Fifteen

I thought I'd better make myself scarce after that, so I left Angela with Ray Keenan; he said he'd drop her back to her car, and it left me free to pay Arnold Wood a visit.

He was the guard on the train that fateful day in August 1962.

I'd got an address for his sister in Watchet, so my guess was that he'd moved in with her. Born in January 1901, so that made him eighty-five now.

It was a bungalow on the road out to Williton.

I parked in the drive behind a Fiesta, knocked on the door. Turned out they were expecting me at some point, after seeing the press conference on the TV the evening before.

The mention of Paul Bromfield's name had brought it all back.

It had that effect.

'He was very upset last night,' said his sister. 'So, I'm glad you've come so quickly.'

I thought it best not to mention the search for Simon Horsey.

'Is Mr Wood well?' I asked.

'Old and frail, but he's still got his marbles, if that's what you mean?'

It was, as it happened.

Arnold Wood was sitting in a chair in the living room, a blanket over his legs. He looked up at me with greying eyes. 'You're old enough to remember it,' he said.

I sat down on the sofa opposite him, told him what I could remember of the search for Paul. It's called establishing common ground with the witness, and you'll find it somewhere in the manual. I told him what was left at Ashcott too: the platform and the old station house, with the old stationmaster, James Bucknall, still living in it.

'He went through hell when your lot arrested his son,' said the old man, curling his lip.

'How long had you worked on the Somerset and Dorset Railway?' I asked.

'All my life, till they laid us all off at the end of that summer.'

'And what can you remember of the day Paul went missing?'

'Not a lot before, but afterwards. I remember police crawling all over the place. It was just a normal day before that, really. Large crowds, families going for a last ride on the steam train and a day at the beach. We had a couple of extra carriages and a locomotive behind,' he said, gesturing over his shoulder with his thumb.

'And you were the guard on the train?'

'Yes. I'd wait until everyone was on, close any doors left open, wave my flag for the lads up front to get going and then hop on.'

'What did you do then?'

'I was supposed to check tickets, but I wasn't bothering at that stage. Sod them, the buggers were making us all redundant anyway, so I sat in the guard's van, filled in my log and then read the paper.'

'We've got a statement from a new witness. She was a child at the time and describes being in the last carriage. They'd gone to the end of the platform at Glastonbury, but the train was too long for the platform at Ashcott and they were stuck out in the countryside.'

'Used to catch a few out, did that.' The old man chuckled. 'Didn't matter that day, though. Everyone was getting on. I don't remember anyone getting off.'

'When the train pulled away, she says she looked along the platform and saw a figure at the top of the ramp.'

'All I can say is I didn't see anything, not on the way into the station, or pulling out.' Wood shrugged. 'I'd have been standing middle of the platform, looking towards the front of the train, though. Wouldn't have seen this person. He'd have been behind me, wouldn't he? Don't remember the girl either, I'm afraid.'

'Was there a lot of steam and smoke?'

'There always was, when you first pulled in; venting steam. I'd get off, walk forwards into clouds of it sometimes, help people on to the train, help with their luggage. And we had the engine at the back this time, don't forget. By the time everyone was on it'd usually have cleared, at least so the lads up front could see me waving my flag. A lot depended on the wind.'

I was learning nothing new, so I made my excuses and left, promising to pass on his best wishes to the old stationmaster.

If nothing else, it was another box ticked.

And it was time to get back to Portishead and face the music.

◆ ◆ ◆

'Oh dear, Bob, what have you gone and done?' said Ash, when I walked into the CCU office.

It was dark, the car park full, which meant there'd be an audience for my earwigging.

'I've been to Watchet,' I said. 'Spoken to the guard on the train.'

'What *else* have you gone and done.'

It wasn't a question. Ash knew, and so did everyone else, judging by the looks on their faces: disapproval, contempt; backs quickly turned on me.

'The ACC was over here looking for you.' Ash glanced up at the clock on the wall – someone must've put new batteries in it. 'Said he'd be back at six. Right about now.' The front door slammed, a loud bang echoing up the stairwell. 'I told you to stay out of it, mate.'

'Is he back yet?' demanded a voice from out on the landing.

'Yes, sir,' replied Ash.

The ACC was standing in the doorway now, glaring at me, his face flushed, nostrils flaring. He was dressed in civvies – looked like he'd been playing golf – so probably called in from an afternoon off.

'Let's take this in here,' he said. He turned, and I followed him across the landing, into a room opposite. Ash came too.

It was a large room, still used for storage, but there was space just inside the door for the three of us.

'You're off the CCU, Willis,' said the ACC. 'You've stirred up a bloody hornets' nest over at Watchet. And what the hell did you think you were doing, telling the family their son's disappearance was connected to Paul Bromfield?'

'I didn't tell them that, sir,' I said.

'The grandfather recognised you from the press conference.'

'He said he wouldn't say anything.'

'Well he bloody well did.'

'I was just there to make sure it wasn't connected. It's the timing—'

'Sod the bloody timing! It's pure coincidence.' He'd taken off his glasses, was rubbing the bridge of his nose between his thumb and forefinger. 'The family are going mad, screaming at the SIO to check the bunkers, so I get called in to liaise with the RAF. Now we've got the whole Observer Corps on alert, pagers going off all over Somerset, Dorset, Devon and Cornwall. They're checking every single one. What've you got to say about that?'

'Good.' Not what he wanted to hear, probably, but sod it. No harm in doubling down now. 'If I was the SIO, I'd want them checked.'

'I bet you would.' He slid his glasses back on, thrust his hands into his pockets. 'You're not exactly renowned for your gut instincts though, are you?'

I'm not renowned for much, actually, but that's a different matter.

The ACC turned to Ash, standing with his back to the door. 'What d'you think, Clive?'

'I think Bob's got a point, sir,' he said.

Well, fuck me.

'If I was the SIO,' continued Ash, 'I'd be checking the bunkers. It's not just the timing, there's the age of the boy. I spoke to Mary Simpson and she told me the grandfather is ex-Navy as well. One coincidence is fine, two even, but there are three here. Circumstantial, possibly, but would you want to be the one telling the boy's mother we didn't check?'

Took the wind out of the ACC's sails, did that.

'It was Bob who found this new witness, don't forget, and he's got a week's head start on the rest of us.'

The ACC was stewing on it, so Ash turned to me. 'What did the guard say, Bob?'

'He was standing in the middle of the platform, looking towards the locomotive,' I replied, 'so wouldn't have seen this figure at the end of the platform. He'd have been behind him.'

'Makes sense.'

The ACC was looking me up and down now, barely hiding his disdain. 'No, I'm sorry, Clive,' he said. 'You've got the pick of retired officers and we really don't need his sort on the CCU. His selection was against my better judgement in the first place.'

A figure loomed in the small frosted window and there was a tentative knock at the door. Ash turned round, opened it.

'There's a telephone call for the ACC, guv.'

The ACC barged past me, stalked across the landing into the office opposite. Ash and I followed; no harm in listening to his end of the conversation.

'It's the phone on the desk, sir,' said a voice behind us.

The ACC picked up the handset. 'Saunders. Yes. Thank you.' The ACC turned to Ash, raised his eyebrows. 'All bunkers are clear, that's Avon, Somerset, Dorset, Devon and Cornwall. Thank you. No, that won't be necessary. That's very helpful and I apologise for the inconvenience.' He replaced the handset. 'That was the air commodore. Every single bunker in the South West operational area has been checked and there are no nine-year-old boys to be found anywhere.' He walked slowly to the door, stopped, turned. 'My decision is final, Clive,' he said. Then he was gone, his footsteps on the stairs ending with the slam of the front door.

'Sorry, Bob,' said Ash.

'At least we checked. We had to check.'

Chapter Sixteen

Shirley knew, just from the look on my face. 'You'd better come in,' she said.

I could hear the television in the living room. 'What are you watching?' I asked.

'It's an old film with Robert Mitchum. You eaten?'

'No.'

'There's some of last night's cottage pie left, if you fancy it. I had a salad.'

'There's been another child taken, Shirl.' I'd followed her into the kitchen, was leaning on the doorframe, watching her switch on the oven. 'A nine-year-old boy, just like Paul Bromfield.'

'Where?'

'Over at Watchet.'

'And you think it's connected?'

'Has to be.'

She took a sheet of silver foil off a dish, scrunched it up and dropped it in the bin. 'What are you going to do about it?'

'Nothing. I've been fired.'

'Already?'

Nothing surprises Shirley, not as far as I'm concerned. Not anymore.

It took me ten minutes to tell her what had happened. I started with the new witness, thought it might make it look like I'd achieved something, then filled her in on my visit to Watchet and the ACC's conversation with the air commodore.

'You did the right thing,' she said. 'Sounds to me like Saunders was just looking for an excuse to get rid of you.'

'There's still a kid out there, though, isn't there.'

'I did see something on the local news, didn't put two and two together.' She flicked on the kettle. 'I'll make us a cup of tea.'

How many times has she said that over the years?

'It feels like it's my fault this boy's been taken. If I hadn't picked the Bromfield case . . .' I let my voice get drowned out by the boiling water.

'Sit,' she said, gesturing to an empty chair at the kitchen table.

I ate in silence, Shirley leaning on the worktop watching me. She was sipping a glass of white wine, knew better than to offer me a glass.

I say watching me; *studying* me is more like it. There's a sad smile creeping across her face.

'I blame myself,' she said. 'You spent far too long stuck in the middle of nowhere. A life of pub fights and shoplifting in Ilminster. It never occurred to me at the time, but it must've been soul destroying. Hardly surprising you started drinking.'

'It's thanks to you I made DI.'

'We should have moved to Bristol, or London even. I see it now, but I liked Ilminster; liked working in that bloody florist. And it was a good place to bring up the girls.' She picked up my empty plate, left it in the washing up bowl. 'I'm sorry, Bob.'

'There's nothing to be sorry for.'

'Yes, there is. And now here you are, finally doing the sort of work you should've been doing all along.'

'Not anymore, I'm afraid.'

'Rubbish. They've checked the bunkers and there's no connection with the Bromfield case as far as they're concerned, which means it's down to you. What's his name, this boy who's missing?'

'Simon Horsey.'

'You'd better get out there and find him. Poor little sod.'

◆ ◆ ◆

I spotted it straightaway. A little red Allegro, parked on the pavement outside the post office.

I was driving down through Blagdon, and there she was.

God knows how long she'd been sitting there.

I stopped, wound down the window.

'What did they say when you got back to Portishead?' asked Angela.

'They fired me.'

'Oh, shit.'

'You can't leave that there,' I said. 'Park it round the back. I'll wait for you.'

'Where are we going?'

'The Edgar Lamb.'

She was about to ask why, but I pulled forward, parked at the top of the lane that leads down to the lake.

Shirley was right, of course. If there is a connection between Simon Horsey's disappearance and the Bromfield case, then no one else is going to be looking in the right places. They'll be looking, plenty of them, but in the wrong places, just like we were all those years ago – day after day, searching the fields, dragging the rhynes.

And I have to try, don't I? If nothing else, on a purely selfish level, I've got a point to prove now. That sounds awful, doesn't it? It's not about me, of course it isn't. It's about that little boy, and I've got half an idea where he might be.

Clutching at straws, possibly, but sometimes that's what you have to do when there's nothing else left.

The passenger door opened and Angela jumped in. 'The Seymour's open, if it's a drink you want?'

'It isn't.' I accelerated down through the narrows, headlights in the distance coming towards me. 'What's going on over at Watchet?' I asked, waving at the car that stopped to let us pass.

Bloody nuisance, these narrow lanes, particularly when you get stuck behind a bus or lorry.

'They're running around like headless chickens,' replied Angela. 'The senior investigating officer did a piece to camera at the scene about seven, an appeal for information, gave out a photograph of Simon. Ray's putting it on the front page tomorrow. He said in the light of the announcement about the Bromfield case being reopened, all operational nuclear bunkers in the South West area have been checked and are clear.'

'That's what they told me when they fired me.'

'There's a detective sergeant,' continued Angela. 'She seems to have her head screwed on. She got them searching anything underground: water tanks, cellars, there was even an abandoned air raid shelter.' A shake of the head. 'Nothing.'

'Is that it?'

'Plod were out in the fields, lines of them, but that got called off when it got dark. They're doing house to house now; every single house in the town.'

'Plod?' I asked, with a heavy sigh.

'That's what Ray calls them.'

It's a love-hate relationship, police and crime reporters. I may have mentioned that.

'Are you going to tell me what we're doing going to the Edgar Lamb at this time of night?'

'If I put my foot down, we should make it in time for last orders.'

Actually, it's quite simple, really. All *operational* nuclear bunkers is a good start.

But, what about the non-operational ones?

◆ ◆ ◆

I pushed open the front door of the pub just in time to hear that familiar shout from the barman.

'Time, please, ladies and gentlemen. Glasses, please.'

If I'd been after a drink, it would've been disappointing, to say the least. But I wasn't.

The barman was busy filling a dishwasher under the bar, people placing their empties on the tray in front of him and heading for the door.

'I'm looking for Fred,' I said.

'It's his night off,' he replied, slamming the dishwasher shut.

'Where can I find him?'

'He'll be upstairs, but—'

I'd kept my business cards, before you ask. Just in case.

'Lisa.' He was calling across the bar to a woman emptying ashtrays and wiping tables. 'Go and see if Fred's up, will you? Tell him it's the police to see him.'

Impersonating a police officer, although I hadn't, not really. It's not as if I'd shown him a fake warrant card. Angela seemed to be enjoying the subterfuge, anyway.

'Who's this Fred?' she asked.

'Runs this place,' I replied. 'He's also Chief Observer. Told me last time I spoke to him that the ROC bunker at Puriton was closed, handed back to the landowner.'

'Which means it's *non*-operational.' Angela grinned. 'You crafty sod.'

'We'll see.'

The door at the end of the bar opened, Fred Hicks appearing in his pyjamas and dressing gown, the rope belt tied tightly around his waist.

'Oh, it's you.' Hicks glared at the barman. 'He's not police. He's a consultant. What d'you want?'

'Another child's gone missing,' I said.

'I saw it on the news.'

'You said the bunker over at Puriton was closed.'

'It closed in 1968. Why?'

'I need to know where it is.'

'You don't think . . . ?' His voice tailed off.

'I need to check.'

'Of course you do.' He snatched a piece of paper off the till, started drawing a map. 'It's not in Puriton at all, so why it was called ROC Puriton I'll never know. It's actually the other side of Pawlett. Take the first left off the main road, then left again into Gaunt's Road. About a mile along there you'll see a farm track. Follow that across two fields, then it's in the far corner.' He drew an 'x' in the corner of a field on his map, went over it a few times, then handed me the piece of paper.

'You said it had been returned to the landowner?'

'Gaunt's Farm. Just follow the lane, and when it drops down off the hill, it's on the right, on a bend.'

'Are there any others that have closed?'

'Not in this area.'

'Thank you. You've been very helpful.'

'You're not going up there now, are you?' asked Hicks. 'It's pitch dark.'

'I've got a torch, which is more than that boy's got, if he's down there.'

◆ ◆ ◆

As farm tracks go, it wasn't too bad. The odd pothole here and there, easily avoided; long grass in the middle, flicking the underside of my car as we bounced along. I'd turned the internal light on, and Angela was following on Fred's hand-drawn map.

'That was the first field,' she said, the gate to the second standing open.

The farm track continued along the hedge, separated from the field by an electric fence, the mud churned up on the other side by the hooves of cattle, water standing in deep hoof prints.

'We'll need to be careful,' I said. 'Otherwise, the farmer will think we're out poaching rabbits.'

The gate was closed on the far side of the field.

'We can go on foot from here.' I reached across, took a torch out of the glovebox and shone it at the gate while Angela climbed over.

'It's in that corner.' She was pointing diagonally across the next field. 'I can see the silhouette of trees.'

'Most of these bunkers are overgrown,' I said. 'Let alone the abandoned ones.'

I was lighting the way with my torch, helping Angela avoid the thistles and cowpats. She wasn't exactly wearing ideal footwear, but then probably hadn't been expecting to find herself trudging across a farmer's field at this time of night. The grass was long and wet too.

'How are your feet?' I asked.

'Soaked through.'

A fox darted into the hedge as we neared the far side, the concrete posts of the barbed wire fence around the compound looming out of the darkness. The wire had all but gone, replaced by electric fencing to keep the cattle out. A thin strand of wire that probably packed a punch.

'Can you step over that?' I asked.

'I'll go under it,' replied Angela.

'There are no cows in the field, so it's probably off.'

A narrow path through the undergrowth led to the entrance of the bunker. I shone my torch at the ground in front of me, stuck my arm out to stop Angela in her tracks.

'Footprints,' I said. 'Someone's been here recently.'

The green paint on the concrete entrance shaft had all but flaked off, small patches of it still visible where it was sheltered from the prevailing wind. I shone my torch around, but couldn't see the vents; covered in brambles, probably.

'Step over those prints,' I said.

Angela was right behind me as I pushed through the undergrowth. Then we were standing on the concrete plinth, either side of the steel hatch.

'These padlocks are new,' she said.

I banged three times on the lid with the torch, hoping the metallic clang would echo down the shaft. Angela leaned over, her ear pressed to the steel.

She shook her head, her eyes fixed on me.

I banged again. Five, louder this time.

'Nothing,' she whispered, still listening intently.

My heart was racing. 'It'll take him a minute to find the bottom of the ladder,' I said. 'It'll be pitch black down there.'

I banged again. Kept banging, until Angela raised her hand, pressed her ear tighter to the steel plate.

Then we heard it.

Chapter Seventeen

I left my headlights on and the engine running when I screeched to a halt in the farmyard a few minutes later.

I'd left Angela with the torch, left her tapping on the steel plate covering the entrance hatch, listening to the faint knock that was coming from the underside. We'd tried shouting but couldn't seem to make ourselves heard – certainly couldn't hear any reply – so she was knocking at regular intervals just to let the person trapped inside know she was still there.

I say *the person trapped inside*; it has to be Simon Horsey, doesn't it?

It occurred to me as I picked my way across the field back to my car that it might be someone else. Another one of those 'what if?' questions.

What if it's someone else?

God help us.

The moonlight had been enough to avoid the thistles, not the cowpats, but I had more pressing things to be worrying about now.

I rang the doorbell, business card ready in the other hand.

I need to be careful. I know that. It might be Simon Horsey's kidnapper who answers the door. Unlikely, though. The padlocks are new, almost certainly placed there by whoever took the boy, and he's not going to shit on his own doorstep, is he?

I stepped back, looked up, dogs barking and lights coming on in an upstairs window. Then the hall, visible through the frosted glass in the front door.

'Who is it?'

'Police,' I replied. 'I need the keys to the bunker.'

'It's not locked.'

'In that case I need to use your phone, please. It's an emergency.'

A woman opened the door, examined my card. 'You'd better come in,' she said. She was my age, greying hair tied back, dressing gown and slippers, but then it was gone midnight.

'Who is it, Joy?' The shout came from the top of the stairs.

'Police, Frank. He needs to use the phone.' She turned to me, gestured to the hall table. 'It's there.'

I snatched the phone off the table, dialled 999.

'What is your emergency?'

'I'm at Gaunt's Farm, just west of Pawlett. There's someone locked in an abandoned nuclear bunker, ROC Puriton. I believe it to be the child missing from Watchet this morning.'

'What is your name, caller?'

'Detective Inspector Mungo Willis. Retired.'

'Stay on the line, caller, we're getting someone to you now.'

'The bunker's open,' said the farmer. He was standing on the stairs, his hands on his hips.

'There are new padlocks on it,' I replied. 'And there's someone in there, tapping on the underside of the hatch.'

'I saw it on the news, Frank. There's a child missing from over Watchet way. You know Bill Horsey? It's his grandson.'

'I'll throw some clothes on, and we'll soon have that bloody hatch off with the tractor.'

'Can I leave you with this?' I asked, the telephone handset in my outstretched hand.

Joy took it from me. 'You go,' she said.

I waited while Frank loaded a heavy chain into the bucket on the front of the tractor, then I followed him back up the lane and along the farm track.

He'd attached the chain to the hinge of the steel hatch by the time I made it back across the field, and was attaching the other end to the tow hitch on the tractor, ready just to rip the hatch off by the looks of things.

'Give me a minute,' I said. 'I'll give you a signal with the torch.'

I squeezed along the narrow path, told Angela to stand clear and then leaned over the hatch, my mouth as close to the hinge as I could get it. 'Climb down the ladder,' I shouted, as loud as I could. 'Get clear now.'

There was a single tap – perhaps he could hear us, after all – then I stood back, took the torch from Angela and waved it at the tractor.

The chain pulled tight, the huge diesel engine revving hard, the rear wheels spinning on the mud. The hinge started to buckle, the padlocks snapped, and the tractor lurched forward, dragging the steel plate away through the undergrowth.

I stepped up on to the concrete plinth, shone the torch down the shaft.

The ladder was rusted, two inches of stagnant water visible in the bottom of the bunker.

Then a face appeared, blinking up into the beam of the torch. He was pale, and I could see from the top of the shaft he'd been crying. I recognised him, all the same.

'I'll go,' said Angela, leaning forward and taking hold of the top rung of the ladder.

'You'll get wet feet,' I said.

'Hardly matters,' she replied. 'Give me the torch.' She tucked it in the top of her trousers, started climbing down towards the sound of a child sobbing in the darkness below.

◆ ◆ ◆

Frank turned the tractor around, lighting up the entrance to the bunker with his headlights. He was unhitching the chain from the back.

'Better leave the hatch there,' I said. 'They'll want to dust it for prints.'

'How did you know he was down there, if you don't mind me asking?'

'A lucky guess,' I replied.

'Bob!' Angela's voice, echoing up the entrance shaft. 'Bob. Are you there?'

I leaned over, the torch shining up into my face.

'We need to get him out of here. He's freezing.'

'Can he climb out?'

'I'll see.'

Then the little boy appeared at the bottom of the ladder, looking up at me.

'Go on, Simon,' said Angela. 'I'll be right behind you and Bob will grab hold of you from above. All right?'

A nervous nod. He started climbing, Angela on the rung directly below him, a hand on the ladder either side of him, using her body to push him upwards. 'Keep going,' she said.

I was one side of the entrance shaft, Frank the other. We leaned over, each taking hold of Simon by a wrist, and lifted him up and out. The boy's legs buckled, and he collapsed on to the plinth, sobbing again.

'We'd better get him down to the house,' said Frank. 'In front of the fire.'

I could hear sirens in the distance now, blue lights seemingly all around, coming in from the north and south.

'A roaring fire sounds good to me,' said Angela, looking down at her wet feet. She'd climbed out of the bunker under her own steam and had her arms round Simon, trying to keep him warm. 'He needs to go to hospital,' she mouthed.

'Can you get them both in the tractor?'

'Aye.'

'You go down to the house in that case. I'll wait out on the lane, send the ambulance down to the farm.'

I parked my Volvo in a passing place back out on the lane, stood in the middle of the road. Two marked patrol cars were first to arrive, so I directed them to the bunker, told them to secure the scene.

I didn't know the uniformed officers and they didn't know me, so I may have neglected to mention I was retired.

The ambulance arrived next, so I told them where to find Simon. Told them to check Angela over too.

Hypothermia tends to creep up on you.

It was going to be a while before CID arrived, so I followed the ambulance down to the farmhouse, found Angela and Simon sitting in front of the wood burning stove in the kitchen, blankets wrapped around their shoulders. Angela was holding a mug in both hands, a wisp of steam rising from the contents.

'How is he?' I asked.

'He'll be fine,' replied Joy. 'Hot, sweet tea works wonders. Would you like one?'

'Thank you.'

Frank was on the telephone in the hall, his voice carrying into the kitchen. 'Bill, it's Frank Dawson, Gaunt's Farm, over Pawlett. Look, a police officer turned up a while ago, said there was someone down in my old bunker. New padlocks on it, there were, so I had the lid off with my tractor, and bugger me if your grandson wasn't down there. Yes, he's fine. A bit cold, so we've got him in front of the fire. Hungry too; Joy's doing him something to eat.'

Frank reappeared in the doorway. 'Bill's on his way over now. Said his son's still out looking.'

It would be touch and go whether CID arrived before Simon's grandfather. Either way, the ambulance would need to wait.

I turned to one of the paramedics. 'You'll need to wait for the family to get here.'

'Fine,' she said, checking her watch, a thermometer sticking out of the corner of Simon's mouth.

'What's your involvement then?' asked Joy, smiling at me. 'Only you said on the phone earlier you were retired.'

'I was on the Cold Case Unit,' I replied. 'Looking into the murder of Paul Bromfield.'

Frank was pouring himself a whisky. 'I remember it. Don't think anyone round these parts will ever forget it. Same bloke you reckon?'

'Yes.'

'Not a cold case anymore then, is it?'

Chapter Eighteen

Another night on the sofa. Well, I say *night.* We didn't get back to my flat until gone four in the morning, so it was only a couple of hours, really.

Feels like it too.

Angela was up and gone by seven. She'll go far that girl. She rang Ray Keenan from Gaunt's Farm, got him out of bed, gave him the story over the phone. It'll make the second edition, apparently. Front page, with full credit to Angela.

She did check with me first, I'm pleased to say.

'Can I print this?'

'You were there,' I replied. 'It's your story as much as mine, isn't it?'

Frank said she could use the phone in the farmhouse and that was that.

Her first exclusive.

The reality is that the story needs to be out there anyway. We were supposed to find Simon – supposed to find him *alive* – and we did.

Whoever placed him in the bunker needs to know we did, if he doesn't already.

I didn't recognise either of the CID officers who turned up at the farmhouse. They took their time too. Simon's grandfather and mother got there first, and you can imagine it, can't you? Lots of tears and hugs.

I tried to keep out of the way, but the grandfather recognised me. I got away with a firm handshake; nearly broke my fingers.

The boy's father got there just as they were leaving for the hospital in the ambulance; more hugs and tears, then off they went to Musgrove Park, a patrol car following, blue lights flashing.

Angela didn't need to go. Her temperature was fine, and Joy had lent her a pair of dry trainers that belonged to their daughter.

I stopped in the field gateway on the way back up the lane, looked across to where the bunker was, on the edge of the small copse on the far side of the fields. The sky was lit up by arc lamps and I could just make out the tops of two vans over the hedges. Forensics already doing what they do.

'What happens now, Bob?' Angela had asked.

'Not my problem now, is it?' It had sounded churlish at the time, and it was.

I was making a cup of tea when I heard footsteps on the metal staircase outside. Then there was a knock at the door, Shirley's face appearing at the kitchen window, leaning across from the top of the stairs.

'Are you in there, Bob?'

I opened the front door, still fully clothed from last night, my trousers crumpled and covered in mud.

'You've been busy, I see.' She was holding up a copy of the *County Gazette*.

'What time is it?'

'Midday. I thought you might need this as well,' she said, placing a carton of milk on the worktop.

'Thanks. Kettle's just boiled, if you fancy a coffee.'

'Can't stop.' Then she fished two pieces of paper out of her pocket. 'You've had a couple of telephone calls. Some bloke called Ash wants you at Portishead CCU office for two o'clock sharp. He said please, so I think you ought to go.' She handed me the first piece of paper. 'And this one. He said he wanted to leave a message for Bob Willis, made me read it back to him to make sure I'd got it word perfect. '*Well done, Bob*,' she said, reading aloud. '*Shame you weren't around in '62, although you were, weren't you? Sort of. You were supposed to find him that time. So, now we begin again*.'

I snatched the piece of paper from Shirley's fingers. 'Did he leave a name?'

'Of course he bloody well didn't.'

'Did you ask?'

'Yes. I'm not a complete—'

'You'll need to give a statement, so it would be good if you could write down everything that was said, what he said to you and what you said to him.'

'I've already done it, recorded the time and everything. I was married to a police officer for the best part of twenty years, you know.' She turned for the door. 'And another thing.'

'What?'

'You've got time for a shower and a shave before you go to Portishead. There's a clean pair of trousers in the wardrobe, leave those in the laundry basket and I'll do the washing tomorrow.'

'Thank you.'

She hesitated. 'I'm proud of you, Bob,' she said, softly.

◆ ◆ ◆

The car park at the CCU office was empty apart from two cars and a couple of vans, men in brown coats loading boxes off sack trucks into the back.

I knew immediately what was happening. Paul Bromfield was a live case again, so the files were going off to the major investigation team. It made sense.

I hesitated at the bottom of the stairs. The doors were open on the first floor landing, voices murmuring, even some laughter. They'd have seen me turn into the car park so would know I was there.

The pessimist in me tells me I'm going to get a ticking off for interfering in a live investigation, using my business card when I'd been dismissed from the CCU, impersonating a police officer even.

The optimist on the other hand . . . well, actually, there isn't one. There used to be, but he's long gone these days.

Ash stood up when I appeared in the doorway. 'Bob,' he said. 'Thank you for coming.'

The ACC had been sitting with his back to the door. He stood up too, turned, his hand outstretched. 'You were right, Bob. And I was wrong. I hope you won't hold it against me.'

'No, sir.'

'You know Detective Sergeant Mary Simpson, I think,' said Ash.

'We've met.'

'Simon Horsey is doing fine, thanks to you,' said the ACC, gesturing to the chair opposite him. 'He's at home now and we've got some specially trained officers going to speak to him later this afternoon; see what he can tell us about his kidnapper.'

'Good.' I wasn't intending to appear tight-lipped, but I was still reeling from the ACC's apology, to be honest. You know what I'd been expecting. 'You'll need this, sir,' I said, handing Shirley's scribbled message to the ACC. 'He rang the post office in Blagdon this morning, spoke to my ex-wife, left that message for me.'

The ACC read it aloud, then took a deep breath. 'He's playing bloody games with us.'

'Then why the twenty-four-year gap?' asked Ash.

'We closed the case,' I said. 'There's no game left to play when your opposition walks off the pitch.'

'I suppose not.' The ACC handed the note to DS Simpson. 'You'll need to get someone over there to take a statement from her.'

'She's expecting that,' I said. 'She's written out a transcript of the call.'

'Well, you're probably wondering why you're here, Bob,' said Ash. 'We're losing the Bromfield case, obviously, and you're going with it to join the live investigation. A consultant on the same terms as before, working with DS Simpson here.' He nodded in her direction. 'No one knows the Bromfield case better than you, Bob, and the ACC has agreed.'

'I have.'

'How long have I got?' I asked.

'As long as it takes,' replied the ACC.

'Then there'll be more cold cases, Bob,' said Ash. 'There are always more cold cases.'

Chapter Nineteen

'Call me Mary, for goodness' sake.'

'I'm Bob.'

We'd sorted that out before we left the car park outside the Cold Case Unit.

'Where to?' she'd said, standing by the open door of her car.

The bunker seemed the obvious place to start.

We left our cars in the lane, went on foot. Forensics had finished by the time we got there, the track churned to mud by their vans. Several sections had been taped off, forcing the vehicles on to the field alongside it, the electric fence taken down. Little red flags were fluttering in the breeze, marking tyre tracks.

I left my car keys with a uniformed officer so they could look at my tyres for comparison purposes. I'd driven down there last night, after all.

The boot prints on the narrow path through the undergrowth had also been marked with red flags, although they would have been photographed by now; plaster casts taken of them as well.

The young detective constable Mary had been teamed up with the day before was there. It took me a moment, but I remembered his name before it became embarrassing.

'Here's a list of what they've taken,' said Mitchell, handing a clipboard to Mary.

She passed it to me without looking at it.

'The farmer said the bunker wasn't locked. He'd go down occasionally to check on it, find the odd bit of rubbish: bottles, cans, crisp packets and sweet wrappers, stuff like that. He thought some local kids had found it and been mucking about down there.' Mitchell was looking at Mary's feet. 'There's two inches of water in the bottom so you'll need wellies.'

'You can see everything from the bottom rung of the ladder,' I offered.

'That'll do,' she said. 'When will the photographs be available?'

'Later on today, they said,' replied Mitchell.

It was a short list of items taken for forensic testing. I'd expected a Bunsen burner, immediately scanned the list looking for it, but there wasn't one. There was a transistor radio – kids wouldn't have left that down there – a couple of seat cushions from an old sofa, a bucket and two large bottles of water. Left him with water, so he'd last a bit longer this time.

Nice.

The bunker had been decommissioned eighteen years ago, according to Fred Hicks, so it would be interesting to see what was left.

'The hatch was usually open,' said Mitchell. 'So, the water in the bottom is probably rain. Either that or it's getting in somewhere else. There's plenty of mould on the walls, so that's damp penetration.'

I sat on the edge of the entrance shaft, looked around the small enclosure in the last of the daylight. The vents were hidden in the dense undergrowth, the wire long gone from the fence, leaving just the concrete posts poking out of the brambles. A small area had been cleared around the concrete plinth, wildflowers trodden into the mud.

The narrow path continued into the copse on the far side of the enclosure.

'Where does that path go?' I asked.

'Just into the trees,' replied Mitchell. 'Forensics had a look, found a few deer in there, sent them bounding off across the field the other side.'

I started climbing down the ladder, holding the sides, trying to avoid the mud on the rungs. I stopped on the bottom rung, leaned back against the wall and took my torch out of my pocket.

The door of the lavatory was hanging off, the chemical toilet itself long gone, which explained the bucket left for the boy.

A nice touch that.

The ceiling tiles had come down at some point and were lying in bits on the floor, crushed underfoot, probably, the pieces visible in the water in the bottom of the bunker. The beds were still there, but the mattresses had gone: steel-framed with springs, a single bed against the side wall, bunk beds at the back wall. It was much the same layout as at Chilton Polden, although the table and shelf had gone – for firewood, almost certainly.

I shone my torch at the graffiti but couldn't make head nor tail of it. No doubt it would all have been photographed by the forensic team.

It felt freezing, but the water wasn't frozen. I stepped off the bottom rung, sending ripples across the floor of the bunker, the water oddly dark, like black tea. I braced myself, took a stuttering breath through my nose, but there was no smell. None at all.

Two empty glass bottles were lying on their sides in the water opposite the single bed. Just the sort of thing kids would leave behind, which might explain why Forensics hadn't bothered with them. What caught my eye was that the labels were still intact. They should have come off in the water, surely?

I rolled the bottles over with my foot.

Smirnoff vodka and Wood's Navy Rum.

I waded to the bottom of the ladder, shouted up the entrance shaft. 'Has the last forensics van gone?'

'They're just leaving, guv.' Mitchell's face appeared at the top.

'Get them back down here, will you?' I said. 'With a couple of evidence bags.'

There'd be some grumbling, but that was just tough.

Someone started climbing down, then Mary appeared, her feet on the bottom rung, back braced against the wall behind her, a beam of light searching for me in the darkness. 'What've you found?' she asked.

'Empty bottles,' I replied, illuminating them with my torch.

'Just kids, probably.'

'Paul Bromfield's father was in the Navy, and so was this lad's grandfather. This is a bottle of Navy Rum.'

'Oh, right.' She shuddered. 'Cold, isn't it? He wouldn't have lasted long down here.'

'It was a test,' I said.

'One that we failed, and you passed.'

I was sitting on the edge of the bed when the forensics officer climbed down the ladder. Mary had gone back up to get out of his way. 'We had a statement from the kid,' he said. 'Told us about the bucket and bottles of water but never mentioned anything about empty rum or vodka bottles.'

'He'd have had other things on his mind, I expect,' I said.

'Yeah.'

I was looking at the graffiti, shining my torch from one image to the next, all of them in the same black spray paint. A toadstool, possibly. Pretty much nothing else made any sense at all, just random letters, squiggles.

The forensics officer had emptied the water out of the bottles, bagged them up. 'Anything else?' he asked.

'Any of this graffiti mean anything to you?'

'No, sorry.'

'Me neither,' I said, following him to the bottom of the ladder.

◆ ◆ ◆

The farmhouse was quiet when we turned into the yard at Willow Grove Farm, although lights were streaming out of the cowshed, the evening's milking under way.

We'd left my car at Bridgwater police station and gone over to Watchet in Mary's pool car. There were three others in the yard, the family's Land Rover and two tractors. 'That's the interview team,' said Mary, pointing to a Sierra blocked in by a tractor.

The boy's father opened the front door as we walked up the garden path. 'Simon's in there with his mother and your interviewers,' he said, gesturing to a closed door. 'They're using the living room. Everybody else is in the kitchen.'

'How is he?' asked Mary.

'Fine. He's a strong lad, got his head screwed on.'

'It might hit him later.' She gave a reassuring smile. 'The enormity of what's happened to him.'

'That's what the doctor said, but we've been told what to look out for and the school are going to keep a close eye on him as well.'

We followed him into the kitchen, were introduced to aunts, uncles and in-laws sitting around the kitchen table.

'This is the one who found him. Mungo Willis.'

'Everyone calls me Bob,' I said. 'After the cricketer.'

It got the usual polite laugh.

'So, you think it's the same bloke who kidnapped Paul Bromfield?' asked an uncle.

'I do.'

What else could I say?

'They've been in there over an hour already.' Simon's father shrugged. 'They said it would probably be the first of several interviews.'

'They won't want to put him under any stress,' said Mary.

'Good.'

Then the door opened, footsteps running across the hall and up the stairs. We listened as they continued across the landing, ending with a bedroom door slamming.

'He's all right,' said his mother, appearing in the kitchen doorway. 'He just got a bit upset when they were asking him about the bunker. They're going to come back tomorrow morning. He's not going to school for a week or two, so that should be fine.'

'I'd like to have a word with the interview team, if I may,' I said, making my excuses and heading for the door. Mary followed.

I waited until she closed the living room door behind us.

I didn't recognise either of the officers, but then they'd come down from Bristol. Jeans and woolly pullovers, pop music on in the background, all designed to keep the young lad at ease.

Clearly it hadn't worked.

Mary made the introductions.

DS Lorna Taylor was watching her colleague packing away a tape recorder. 'He said he was cycling to school, saw a van parked on the farm track. As he approached, a man got out, knocked him off his bike, put a bag over his head and bundled him into the back. The next thing he knew he was being marched across a field and told to climb down a ladder. Then the lid was slammed shut and locked.'

'What did the man look like?' I asked.

'Blue overalls and a black baseball cap.' Lorna was reading from her notebook now. 'The drive took about half an hour.'

'Did the man say anything to him?'

'Not a word. He played the same piece of classical music over and over again in the van, but Simon didn't recognise it.'

'What did he do when the bunker was locked?'

'He fumbled about in the darkness, stumbled across the single bed and got on that, mainly to get his feet out of the water. There were cushions on it, so he sat on those. After a while he felt around under the bed with his hand, found the bucket and the bottles of water. Then, the next thing he knows, you're tapping on the hatch.'

'And the man didn't go down inside the bunker with him?'

'No.'

'He wasn't assaulted, was he?' asked Mary.

Lorna shook her head. 'He says not, and they found no evidence at the hospital.'

'Thank God for that.'

'This isn't about that,' I said.

'What is it about?' asked Lorna.

'I really don't know.'

'So, what have we learned?' asked Mary. 'That's of any use, I mean.'

'That it's a man, for a start, and he'd visited the bunker before he took Simon there. The bucket and bottles of water must've been placed down there already. The sofa cushions too, probably, given that they were dry. The other thing we've learned is that the man knew he wouldn't be seen. He took Simon there in broad daylight.'

'Another farmer, possibly? A cowhand?'

'Was it market day, something like that?' I asked.

Mary slid her notebook out of her pocket. 'I'll check.'

'You're back tomorrow?'

'We are,' replied Lorna. 'Is there anything in particular you want us to ask him?'

'I want him to identify that piece of music. Use any classical albums they've got here.' I looked around the room. 'There's a record player there. If needs be, get his music teacher up here. Keep playing him stuff until he recognises it.'

'Really? You think that's important?'

'This man is playing games, leaving us clues. He wants us to find out what this is all about, what it's always been about. And he won't stop until we do. The music is just another part of the puzzle.'

Chapter Twenty

I've never worked on a major investigation team before; never worked on a major investigation, come to think it. Apart from the A303 thing, of course, and look how that ended up.

I never thought I'd come to one of these places again either; *hoped* I wouldn't, anyway.

'There's a briefing at eight,' Mary had said.

She's a lot like Lizzie. Efficient, driven, determined; three things I was once, but I got lost somewhere along the way.

In the bottom of a glass, possibly.

Lizzie would be proud of me now, though. She always said I was wasted, stuck away in the back end of beyond. That I was capable of more.

We'll see.

Mary parked behind Bridgwater police station. 'D'you know Superintendent Sharp?' she asked, casually.

'I do.'

We go back a long way, me and Sharp; or Blunt, as some call him. Everything that came before the A303 thing is prehistory and doesn't matter. The A303 thing mattered. Still does. To me, anyway.

It turned out he was following orders. *Used*, just like the rest of us.

He's still a twat, mind.

Even though it's thanks to him that I'm on the Cold Case Unit at all.

Mary punched in the entry code, opened the door. 'Come on, Bob,' she said. 'We're late as it is.'

I get the feeling she's more of a chaperone, if I'm honest. Under orders to keep me out of trouble, probably.

I followed her up the stairs to the incident room on the first floor. Sharp was sitting at a table just inside the open door, officers at desks in front of him, more perched on tables around the walls. The Bromfield boxes were on the floor at the back, open.

'Sorry we're late, guv,' said Mary.

Sharp stood up, his hand outstretched. 'Hello, Bob,' he said. 'Everybody, this is Bob Willis. Well done, mate.' He was shaking my hand and gesturing to the tables at the side of the room at the same time. 'See if you can find somewhere to sit. Everyone's had a copy of the message Shirley took earlier.'

I found a table to lean against.

'What did young Simon Horsey have to say for himself?' asked Sharp.

I listened while Mary gave her report. Some officers were making notes, others doodling on their notepads or staring into space.

I noticed a bundle of crime scene photographs on the corner of the desk in front of me, leaned forward and picked them up, a glance at the officer sitting at the desk, returned with a nod. I'd been down in the bunker, but I hadn't seen it before the items had been removed for forensic testing.

Photographs had been taken from all angles, close-ups of the bucket, bottles of water, the sofa cushions on the single bed and the radio; all of those items gone by the time I got down there. The mention of my name dragged me back to the present.

'Bob thinks the music the kidnapper was playing in the van might be significant and has asked them to try to get Simon to identify it.'

'The music?' asked Sharp.

'It was a classical piece,' said Mary.

'Why don't you come up to the front, Bob, and fill us in on your thoughts?' Sharp looked smug. 'I've split the team into two; we're going to be revisiting all the Bromfield witnesses, starting with those who were children at the time, and the peat cutters. Then we've got another team focusing on the Horsey boy, but it would be useful to know where you are with it. You have some theories, I gather?'

An ambush if ever there was one. You're probably thinking I'm overreacting, but I know Sharp, don't forget. And he knows the old Bob.

'This is a man who wants to be caught,' I said. 'He wants us to find out what this is all about. He wanted that last time, with Paul Bromfield, blames us for Paul's death. Simon Horsey was a test and there will be another kidnapping. Soon. Make no mistake about that.'

'So, how do we find him?' asked Sharp.

'He's leaving a trail for us to follow. It's deliberate, premeditated, and it'll lead us to where he wants us to go. We'll find what he wants us to find.'

'He doesn't want us to find him, though, does he?' A voice from one of the desks in the room. I didn't see which one.

'I think he does, but on his terms. When he's ready.'

'Tell us about this trail,' said Sharp.

'Look at the Bromfield crime scene photographs and ask yourselves what that Bunsen burner was doing in the bunker. There was no gas supply, and not one of the ROC observers had seen it before.'

'Perhaps he took it down there to give Paul a means of keeping himself warm?'

A comment to be ignored, if ever there was one. 'Then there was the transistor radio,' I continued. 'What was that doing down there? There was no radio reception, apart from the ROC communications system, and it wasn't plugged in to that.'

'There was a radio in the bunker at Pawlett too,' said Sharp, flicking through a photo album.

'Look at it closely,' I said. I paused while albums were snatched off desks around the room, other officers leaning over the shoulders of colleagues. 'Compare it to the radio left with Paul Bromfield.'

Photograph albums being held side by side now.

'They look like they're tuned to the same frequency,' offered Mary.

'They do.'

I've only just noticed that, between you and me, but then I've only just seen the crime scene photos from the Pawlett bunker.

'So, that's a Bunsen burner and radios tuned to *approximately* the same frequency, assuming the dials haven't been fiddled with,' said Sharp, shaking his head. 'We can't really tell anyway. They're calibrated to the nearest fifty megahertz, or whatever it is. Not terribly compelling, if I may say so.'

'Then there are the rum and vodka bottles in the Pawlett bunker. Wood's Navy Rum, and both Paul Bromfield's father and Simon Horsey's grandfather served in the Royal Navy.'

'A coincidence, surely, left by kids having a piss-up down there.'

'The bottles were new, the labels lying in water but intact. There are no coincidences in this case. Everything has been carefully stage-managed. Every single thing.'

'We should get their service records, guv,' said Mary.

'Good thinking. Right then,' Sharp said, clapping his hands. 'What else have we got?'

'Tyre tracks, guv,' said someone perched on a table in between the windows. 'And footprints.'

'We ought to check for a match with those at the Bromfield scene, but the chances of that must be nil after all this time. What about fingerprints?'

'None. Must've been wearing gloves.'

The briefing broke up after that. Mary used the noise as cover to lean across, whisper in my ear. 'Cut you off a bit, didn't he? Probably didn't like you stealing the limelight.'

Another one who knew Sharp only too well. The thought had crossed my mind, not that this was about limelight. I'm well past worrying about that.

'Good work, Bob,' said Sharp, intercepting me as I headed for the door. 'Keep on it.'

'I will.'

He hesitated, waiting for a *sir*, probably, but he wasn't getting one.

I'm retired now, don't forget.

◆ ◆ ◆

'What time in the morning?' Mary had asked. 'I'll pick you up.'

'Nine,' I'd said, thinking it would give me plenty of time to get clear of Blagdon. I've always worked better on my own, or at least I did until Lizzie came along.

In another life, who knows what might've happened. If I hadn't been old enough to be her father. And if I hadn't been married to Shirley at the time . . .

It was a long night, sitting in my deckchair, staring at the wall, random thoughts popping in and out of my head. There was a time I'd have gone down to the lake on a night like this, sat in my car and watched the trout rising in the moonlight.

Lost its appeal somehow.

Then again, it is February.

I woke early, still sitting in my deckchair, the sunrise poking around the curtains. I can see the lake in the winter months, when the leaves have fallen off the trees. I walked over to the window, stretching my left leg; trying to, anyway.

I've got a sentence going round in my head. My own words, oddly enough. I'd fallen asleep thinking about them, woken up thinking the same.

Everything has been carefully stage-managed. Every single thing.

That means every little thing, doesn't it?

Every – apparently insignificant – little thing.

And therein lies the plan for the day.

I made myself a cup of tea, waited for Mary. I know I said I work better on my own, but I might need a serving officer for this; carries more authority, what with her warrant card. I've only got a bloody business card.

Chapter Twenty-One

'They've put a tap on the line, in case he phones again,' Shirley said, when I walked into the post office just before nine.

'He won't, don't worry.'

'How did it go yesterday at Portishead?'

'I'm working with the major investigation team out of Bridgwater,' I replied. 'And it'll get worse before it gets better.' Things usually do in my experience.

'You always say that. At least you know the killer's still out there. You won't crack the case only to find he's dead.'

It was a good point, although I felt sure Simon Horsey's parents could've done without knowing.

'Just don't be alone in here,' I said.

'I'll be fine. I've got Pam coming in later.' She took a bar of chocolate off the rack, slid it across the counter. 'Here,' she said. 'Put that in your pocket.'

'Thanks.'

'It was the shave that swung it,' she said, over the noise of the bell jangling above the door on my way out into the rain.

Mary must've seen me going into the post office and parked on the pavement outside. I'd spotted her through the window, waiting patiently.

'Where to?' she asked, when I climbed into the passenger seat.

'The nearest garden centre or plant nursery.'

'There's a nursery on the edge of Taunton. Loads of greenhouses.' She frowned. 'What are we going there for?'

'Every. Little. Thing.'

Half an hour later we were standing by the tills, waiting for the manager. A message had gone out over the tannoy. 'Will Mr Stevens please come to the front desk.'

'Shall I tell him the police are waiting for him?' asked the young lad on the checkout, with a mischievous grin.

'Better not,' replied Mary.

He looked disappointed.

'I'll be out by the plants,' I said.

'You still haven't told me what we're doing here,' protested Mary.

Nurseries are gloomy places in February. You might find a few bulbs in bloom, but everything else is dead, even the cut flowers. I know a daffodil when I see one, and there were a few of those in pots. The little white ones too, snowdrops I think they are, but I've never been much of a gardener and neither was Shirley. We had a few roses, a lawn that we gravelled over in the end, mainly because she could never get me to mow it.

I was standing by a display of crocuses, admiring the different colours, reading the little plastic tags on each, when Mary appeared with the manager in tow.

'This is Brian Stevens, Bob,' she said, trying to hide her exasperation. 'He's the manager.'

'How can I help?' he asked, nervously. A small man, smaller than me anyway, hands covered in compost.

'Who's your flower expert?' I asked. 'The best person you've got on flowers.'

'That'll be Jean. There's nothing she doesn't know about them.'

'Sounds perfect. And where's Jean?'

'Down at the polytunnels, I expect. Why?'

'Can we borrow her for a couple of hours, please? She'll need a coat and a pair of wellies.'

◆ ◆ ◆

Jean was pleased to help, particularly when I told her the job involved identifying varieties of flower. What I didn't tell her was if it came to court, we'd need an expert witness with letters after her name, but at this stage I just needed someone to tell me whether I was imagining things.

It's not unheard of, as Shirley would tell you.

We parked in the gateway on the A39, just along from the stile on the footpath that leads to the Chilton Polden ROC bunker.

There were fresh footprints on the stile and in the mud on the other side, but then the observers had been out here the day before yesterday looking for Simon Horsey.

Mary slid her boots on and followed us along the grass verge, over the stile and into the field. 'This is where they found Paul Bromfield, isn't it?' she asked.

Jean knew the name, judging by her reaction.

'We're not going down in the bunker, Jean,' I said. 'I just need you to identify some flowers by the entrance for me. All right?' I put my foot on the wire fence, so Jean and Mary could step over it.

It looked very different to the Pawlett bunker, freshly painted vents and entrance hatch, shiny new padlocks. Fresh boot prints on the concrete plinth were gradually being washed away by the rain.

'These flowers here, Jean,' I said, gesturing to the vegetation around the base of the plinth where large leaves flattened the grass underneath them, making way for bunches of little pink flowers with yellow centres. 'These are primroses, I think.'

'Yes, and no,' she said. '*Primula* is the botanical name for them. Those ones are actually *Primula Obsidian Antique Rose*. Most people call them primroses, though.'

'Are they wildflowers?' I asked.

'No. The wild ones are yellow with white centres; known as *Primula vulgaris*. Any other colour is cultivated.'

'And they'd grow here naturally?'

'Once they'd been planted here, yes. It's ideal for them. Sheltered by the hedges and this concrete block thing. Perfect.'

'What about these shoots? I'm told they're bluebells.'

She bent over and examined the leaves that were poking out of the long grass. 'Yes, they're bluebells all right. They'll flower in May, I expect. Maybe late April.'

'How could they have got here?'

'Birds drop the seed pods, but equally they could've been planted by someone. We sell the bulbs at the garden centre.'

'And these are crocuses?'

'That's right. Early crocuses to be exact. They flower a month earlier than the spring crocus, hence the name.' She straightened up, looked me in the eyes. 'Someone has put those there.'

'How can you tell?'

'They're all separate. The bluebells there, the primulas there, crocuses here. If that had happened naturally, they'd all be mixed up. Also, early crocuses aren't native to this country and rarely go to seed. Plant them and the bulbs divide and multiply, but it's rare for a new patch to appear without a helping hand.'

Mary was taking an interest now. 'So, you're saying these flowers have been planted here by someone?'

'Yes, dear,' replied Jean.

I'd heard enough and was already standing with my foot on the wire fence.

'Where are we going now?' asked Mary.

'Pawlett,' I said.

◆ ◆ ◆

The mud was worse, if anything. The rain hadn't helped and, once again, we left the car out in the lane. Mary had turned into the field gateway, quickly reversing out again, muttering, 'Sod this.'

'How far is it?' asked Jean.

'A couple of fields over,' I replied.

'I'm just a bit worried about my hip.'

'We could do it from photographs,' said Mary.

'No, no. It's important,' replied Jean, steeling herself.

We walked slowly along the edge of the track, avoiding the ruts, puddles and little red flags that had been left in the visible tyre tracks.

It was the first time I'd had a chance to take in the view, walking along the ridge towards the bunker, which was at the high point, before the ground shelved away towards the River Parrett. The end of the Polden Hills and an ideal spot for a bunker with a grandstand view across the North and West Somerset coasts, the river winding its way out to Bridgwater Bay below.

The little wharf at Combwich was visible, and the old barrage balloon hangar, the corrugated iron glinting in the sun that had come out at last, mercifully.

Not that anyone down in the bunker would see the view, of course. Their job was to stay safely underground and measure radiation levels in the event of a nuclear attack.

Mary and Jean were walking in front of me, picking their way across the field, dodging the thistles.

'Was it you who found that little boy?' Jean asked.

'That was Bob,' replied Mary. 'I can't take any credit for that.'

Jean looked over her shoulder at me. I was limping a bit this morning; that night in the deckchair had played havoc with my leg.

'Have you got hip trouble too, dear?' she asked.

'Knee,' I said. 'Got hit by a car. There are pins in it and I slept awkwardly.'

'You need a nice hot bath.'

Mary ducked under the blue tape at the entrance to the narrow path through the brambles, lifted it up for Jean. I followed.

The steel hatch had been taken away by Forensics, so the ladder was visible at the top of the shaft.

Jean leaned over, gasped. 'They left that little boy down there?'

'In the dark,' I replied.

'And Paul Bromfield was in one of these places?'

'He was.'

'Good God Almighty.'

I thought it best to keep the conversation moving, not give her too much of a chance to dwell on it.

I've dwelt on it, and I don't recommend it.

'These are the flowers I want you to look at, please, Jean,' I said.

All three of us were standing on the concrete plinth, and I shuffled along to let Jean get a better view.

'Can I get off here?' she asked.

'Just try not to tread on them,' said Mary.

Jean looked aghast, the idea of treading on flowers clearly horrifying.

Someone had trodden on the bluebells, though. Even I could see that, the shoots flattened into the long grass.

'These are the same primrose, or primula, as I said. *Obsidian Antique Rose*.' Jean bent over, lifted the leaves carefully and peered underneath. 'Yes, they've been planted here in the last two days, I'd say. You can still see the compost underneath.'

'Those are the same crocuses,' I said.

'Earlies, yes. They've wilted a bit where they've been moved,' said Jean. 'They'll soon recover. Same for the bluebells, although some oaf has trodden on them.'

'It might've been me in the dark,' I said.

'Moved?' asked Mary.

'Yes, they've been transplanted. They always take a day or two to recover. The crocuses have probably come out of a pot, the primroses certainly have, so you should see compost if I pull one—'

'No, don't do that,' I said, just in time to stop her pulling one out of the ground. 'We'll need to get someone up here to analyse the soil.'

'So, two days, you reckon, Jean?' asked Mary.

'About that. Possibly three, it'll have been frosty up here at night and that will have set them back a bit too.'

Both of them were staring at me, but I was deep in thought. There was something else, but I couldn't quite . . .

'So, there's bluebells, primroses and crocuses at both scenes, both planted there by person or persons unknown,' said Mary. She had taken out her notebook and was resting it on the edge of the entrance shaft, writing in it as she spoke.

'If he'd planted them at the time he left Paul Bromfield in the bunker at Chilton Polden they wouldn't have come up until the following spring,' I said, thinking out loud, really. 'It was August.'

'That's right, dear,' said Jean. 'At that time of year, he'd have been planting bulbs and seeds.'

'Which explains why no one saw it at the time.' Mary was nodding, slowly. 'They didn't come up until the following year.'

'This time it's already spring so he has to use mature plants,' I said. Then it came to me. It'd been staring me in the face, actually. One of those things that's obvious when you see it, but easily missed all the same. 'They're in the same configuration.'

'What d'you mean, dear?' asked Jean.

'North to south: primroses to the north, bluebells in the middle, then the crocuses to the south. The planting at both bunkers is identical.'

'That could just be a coincidence, though, couldn't it,' said Mary.

'There's no such thing as a coincidence with this man,' I said. 'Everything is significant. Every little thing.'

Chapter Twenty-Two

I lied. It's what you do in a situation like this.

All contact with the families is to be made through Superintendent Sharp. No exceptions. That's what Mary said.

We dropped Jean back to the nursery, then I got Mary to drop me home, told her I'd catch up with her back at Bridgwater. A trip to Exeter for an appointment with the good doctor – it was the best I could come up with at short notice. It was either that or a dental appointment.

Now I'm on my way to Wincanton to speak to John Bromfield.

Sharp has been to see him, filled him in on the developments so far, taken the credit for finding Simon Horsey, no doubt. But I'm not after credit. I'm after information.

The front door of the Bromfield house opened just as I turned on to the gravel drive, a golden retriever on a lead, followed by John, coat on.

'I was just taking Buster for a walk,' he said, as I climbed out of the driver's seat.

Perfect. 'Can I walk with you?'

'Er, yes,' he replied. 'You might need wellies.'

'I've got some in the back of my car.'

'We go down the lane, cross the main road, then off across the fields,' he said, watching me pull on my boots.

'Lead on,' I said, with a cheery smile. I threw my shoes into the back of my car, slammed the boot and set off after him.

'Have you got a dog?' he asked.

Small talk then, at least until we were clear of the house. I glanced over my shoulder and noticed his wife, Eleanor, watching us from an upstairs window.

'No,' I replied. 'I might get one when I retire.'

'I thought you had retired?'

'So did I.'

John was doing his best to get Buster to walk to heel. 'The little sod pulls like a train, I'm afraid. My wife tells me I'm too soft with him, but after a lifetime of discipline . . .' His voice was tinged with sadness.

That said, the dog sat patiently on the kerb, waiting to cross the main road. John unclipped Buster's lead on the far side, the dog darting under the stile and setting off across the field.

'Superintendent Sharp came to see me,' he said, once we were both over the stile and hidden from the house by the hedge. 'I gather the Horsey family have you to thank for finding their son?'

'I knew where to look from working on Paul's case.'

'What made you think the two cases were connected?'

'The timing, mainly.' Time to get to the nitty-gritty then. 'And the boy's grandfather is ex-Navy.'

'Horsey?' John was shaking his head. Stopped. 'There was a chief petty officer. Can't be the same family, surely?' He picked up a stick, threw it, but the dog ignored it.

'Yes, it can,' I replied.

'Superintendent Sharp seemed to think Simon Horsey was kidnapped *because* Paul's case was being looked at again. Mentioned you'd received a message from Paul's killer.'

'Did he tell you what the message said?'

'That Paul was supposed to have been found.' John curled his lip. 'I don't believe that. If that was true, why didn't he make an anonymous call? Leave some clues to where Paul was?'

'He did,' I said, matter of fact.

John stopped in his tracks. 'What clues?'

'Did you see the crime scene photographs at the time?' I asked.

'Yes.'

'What did you make of the Bunsen burner?'

John fixed me with a steely glare, his eyes questioning me, even behind his thick lenses.

If I had to guess, I'd say he's wondering how much I know. How much I *really* know. The answer is bugger all, but I'm not going to tell him that. Maybe I'm reading too much into his body language.

'Eric Hall said it was to give Paul some heating down there,' he said.

'There was no gas.'

'Perhaps his killer was intending to return later with a gas bottle?'

'D'you really believe that?'

John turned, walked on towards a gate in the far corner of the field. 'I have to believe that,' he mumbled.

'Or else what?' I demanded.

No reply.

We walked on in silence, reached the gate. John lifted the loop of baler twine off the post, letting it swing open. Buster darted through and began barking at something in the hedge on the far side.

'We have a witness who says that the following spring, primroses, bluebells and crocuses came up in the grass around the entrance hatch at the Chilton Polden bunker.'

'I've seen them,' said John. 'I go up there sometimes, just to sit, be near to where Paul . . .'

'They were planted by his killer. We found the same flowers around the concrete plinth at Pawlett, planted there within the last seventy-two hours.'

Silence, apart from the squelch of our boots in the mud, where cattle had been standing inside the gate.

'Same positioning too, north to south: primroses, bluebells, crocuses.'

John stopped, breathing deeply.

'Do you remember the transistor radio?' I asked.

'Yes.'

'There was no reception down there.'

'Eric was up front about that; said he had no idea what it was doing down there.'

'We found another radio in the Pawlett bunker, and it looks as if they were both tuned to the same station. Forensics are looking at it now; about 270 on the medium wave or 1250 long wave. Do either of those numbers mean anything to you?'

Because one does, to me. Now. It had just slammed into me like a fist.

'No.' He hesitated. 'Sorry.'

So, that's it. He knows more than he's letting on.

'Your ship, the River class frigate,' I said.

He turned to face me. 'What about it?'

'The picture of it on the wall in your hall, back at the house. When was that taken?'

'After the war.'

'The number on the side of the ship is K271.'

'Look, Bob. There's more at stake here than you could possibly begin to—'

'More than the life of your son?'

'Paul is gone,' he said, firmly. 'And nothing is going to bring him back now. Besides, I have a wife, two daughters, a grandchild on the way.'

I'm not letting him off the hook. Not now. 'There were two empty bottles in the Pawlett bunker. Wood's Navy Rum and Smirnoff vodka.'

I was right. He recognised the references.

They are significant, and he knows why.

'The killer's message to me finished with the words *So, now we begin again.* What do I tell the next family when their child is taken?'

'I don't know. Look, there are official channels. You need to go—'

'I'll tell them that John Bromfield knows exactly what's going on but isn't saying anything.'

His composure left him and he sank to his knees in the mud, Buster running up to him, licking his face. 'Nobody knew about the flowers. Nobody could've known, if they came up the following spring. And the radio, it was just a fucking radio, for heaven's sake. It could've been down there for any number of reasons. They checked and it wasn't tuned to a station. How the hell was I supposed to know?'

'That leaves the Bunsen burner.'

'I never made the connection,' he said. 'If I had, I'd have said something.'

'What connection?'

'I can't. It's classified, the highest level. And I've got a family.' He was clenching his fists in the puddle in front of him, thick brown mud oozing from between his fingers. 'Eleanor saw us leaving. If I speak up now, she'll think I knew all along, put the precious Navy first. She's always spat that at me over the years – putting the bloody Navy ahead of your family. That'll be us done; she'll leave me.'

I stood there for a moment, watching him wallowing in mud and self-pity.

He knows, but won't speak up, and I'd dearly love to beat it out of him. But then, on the other hand, he has lost his son, and just found out it was his fault. Or, at least, down to something he did.

Perhaps there's another way round this?

'If I go public with these details, ask anyone who knows anything to come forward, guarantee anonymity, that'll give you cover, won't it?'

He looked up at me, pleading.

'I won't tell anyone where I got the information from, and once it's all out in the public domain, it could have come from anywhere. Then you'll tell me what this is all about?'

'I will.'

◆ ◆ ◆

'I need to speak to Angela, please.'

'Who's calling?'

'Bob Willis.'

'She's a trainee crime reporter. You'll want someone in the sport sect—'

'It's a nickname. Just put me through to Angela, please.'

I'm standing at the call box in the entrance foyer of the Little Chef at Camel Hill. I've got ten minutes while they cook my All Day Breakfast. I haven't got a lot of change either, so I need to make this quick.

'Hello, Bob,' said Angela. 'How's it going?'

'Making progress. Look, I need you to print an appeal for help. Anyone with any information about the following items found at the Chilton Polden and Puriton ROC nuclear bunkers.'

Then I listed everything, feeding the last of my coins into the slot while she read the list back to me.

'And I can run this now?' she asked.

'Yes. Anyone with any information is asked to contact the Bridgwater incident room, quoting the usual reference, and ask for me.'

'I'll check with Ray, but we'll probably lead with that tomorrow.'

'Good.'

'Where are you?'

'Camel Hill.'

'Have a Jubilee Pancake for me.'

Chapter Twenty-Three

'You got a minute, Bob?'

Sharp's voice. I'd heard the door open behind me, speeded up a bit, but hadn't made it to the swing doors at the far end of the corridor.

Bollocks.

It was just after five and I'd arrived at Bridgwater police station a few minutes earlier. It had taken that long for Mary to come down to reception and sign me in.

'Not you, Mary,' said Sharp, when she turned to follow me.

'Oh, right, guv.' She looked relieved more than anything.

Sharp closed the door of the interview room behind me. 'Bob, this is Commander Jeffery from defence intelligence.'

The man remained seated, no outstretched hand; didn't even bother to look up. He was wearing a pinstripe suit, white shirt and red tie; come straight from Whitehall, probably. Made himself comfortable too, sitting back from the table with his legs crossed.

'Bob is the one who believes there to be a naval connection,' continued Sharp, trying to distance himself from what was to come, by the sound of it. 'We put in your request for the service records of John Bromfield and William Horsey, Bob, and Commander Jeffery has come down from London to deliver the files personally.'

My request?

Twat.

Jeffery lit a cigarette, ignoring the 'No Smoking' sign on the wall. 'What makes you think there's a naval connection?' he asked.

'Both John Brom—'

'A coincidence.' He looked at me coldly, gave me an acid smile.

'Probably,' I said. 'But I have to look at it.'

'There are tens of thousands of men and women out there who've served in the Navy.'

'I know.'

'Have you served?'

'I did my national service.'

Jeffery flicked his ash in the bin. 'Have you gone public with this?'

'No.'

'Then we would prefer it if you don't.'

I looked at Sharp, didn't get any support, not that I'd expected any.

'There's to be no mention of any connection with the Royal Navy and no mention of the Bunsen burner or the radios,' continued Jeffery. 'None whatsoever. Is that clear?'

'Can I ask why?'

'You can't, Bob,' replied Sharp. 'It's classified.'

'The information is not to be made public under any circumstances,' said Jeffery. 'And the same applies to the rum and vodka bottles.'

'How can we investigate—?'

'Say it,' demanded Jeffery.

'Yes.'

Mary obviously hadn't told Sharp about the flowers. I thought it best not to mention the front page of tomorrow's *County Gazette* as well.

'These are their personnel files,' said Jeffery, sliding two orange document wallets across the table towards me.

I leaned over, picked them up.

'They're redacted, so I'm not sure how much use they'll be, I'm afraid, but there we are. You've requested them, and Her Majesty's Navy is always happy to cooperate with the police.'

'Thank you.'

I glanced at Sharp again. I'm not sure what I was expecting, but all I got was a blank look and the smallest of nods in the direction of the door.

I let it slam behind me. There's no point causing a scene, and I need time to think.

◆ ◆ ◆

'What the hell is it with these fucking people?'

There's only one place you can guarantee a bit of privacy in a police station. You guessed it. I'm sitting here flicking through the personnel files, although a better way to describe the contents would be random bits of paper covered in thick black lines.

Utterly useless.

There's a two year gap in John Bromfield's records, 1951 to 1953, and nothing at all for Bill Horsey after the end of 1951 apart from his discharge papers. Even the names of the ships they served on have been redacted.

A couple of people have come and gone while I've been sitting here. Neither of them washed their hands, but that's by the by.

Then the door opened slowly.

'You in here, Bob?'

Mary's voice.

'Yes, give me a minute.' I flushed the loo, just to make it sound genuine. Washed my hands as well, given that she was still at the door.

'Here,' I said, handing her the files I'd tucked under my arm. 'The personnel files, such as they are.'

'Useless?' she asked.

'Completely.'

'How did you get on at the doctor this afternoon?'

'Fine, thanks.' I'm not a suspicious person by nature. Actually, that's bollocks. Sorry. Of course I am. What sort of police officer would I have made if I hadn't been suspicious? I've got to think she's checking up on me, though. Under orders, probably.

Then she surprised me.

'Let's get out of here,' she said. 'You can drive. I'll drop these files upstairs and meet you outside.'

I'd reversed out of my parking space and was waiting in the middle of the car park, headlights on. The electric gates were still opening when she climbed into the passenger seat a minute or so later.

'Where to?' I asked.

'How about the Edgar Lamb?' she said. 'Then we can go back to your place.'

I know what you're thinking. The thought crossed my mind too. It's the phrase *your place*; it has that certain something to it, doesn't it?

Problem is there's only ever been Shirley. No one else. Ever. And I'd rather like it to stay that way. I'm sort of hoping we might . . .

Maybe I'm getting ahead of myself.

On both counts.

'Have they been able to identify the piece of music Simon heard when he was in the van?' I asked, as I drove past the stile on the A39. I slowed, looking along the path to Paul's bunker. That's what I call it now.

It was pitch dark in the copse beyond the hedge, could see nothing.

'Not yet,' Mary replied. 'The music teacher's going in tomorrow morning.'

I drove on in silence.

'I'll get the drinks in,' she said, once we were through the door of the pub.

'Orange and lemonade for me, please.'

She looked pleasantly surprised. If it was a test, I passed.

Fred Hicks was behind the bar, and I didn't need to be a lip reader.

'You with him?' he asked, glancing in my direction.

Mary had her back to me, turned round, then must've said 'Yes'.

'How's it going?' He looked embarrassed, as if he knew he shouldn't be asking.

Then disappointment crept across his face. She must've fobbed him off with some crap.

I'm putting two and two together, making assumptions. I do that a lot. You may have noticed.

'We had a call this afternoon, put through to me,' Mary said, placing the drinks on the table, a packet of crisps between her teeth.

'Who from?'

'Eleanor Bromfield.' She ripped open the bag, offered it to me. 'Crisp?'

'No thanks.'

'She said she thought all contact was to be made through Superintendent Sharp, and yet there you were, out walking the dog with her husband. He came home in a right state, wouldn't tell her what it was about. He was covered in mud, came up with some story about Buster pulling him over.'

My turn to look embarrassed.

'I calmed her down,' continued Mary. 'Said I'd find out and call her back tomorrow.'

'Did you tell anyone else?'

'No. You told me you were going to see your doctor.'

I shrugged. 'You can end up on a disciplinary,' I said. 'I can't.'

'A nice thought, Bob.' She was taking a sip of gin and tonic, looking at me over the top of her glass.

'It wasn't an easy conversation, let me put it that way. I asked him about the flowers, the rum and vodka bottles, the Bunsen burner. He knows what it's all about but won't say. The radios too. Forensics reckon they were both tuned to about 270 medium wave and there's a picture of his ship on the wall in his house, the number K271 on the side.'

'Fucking hell. Why won't he say anything?'

'It's classified and he's got a family, hasn't he? One thing it did do, though, was confirm that his son's death was because of something he'd done. It hit him hard, even after all these years, and that's why he was in such a state. I reckon, as far as he's concerned, his son's murder was his fault.'

'It wasn't.'

'Of course it wasn't, but he doesn't see it like that.'

'How on earth did they miss this in the sixties?' she asked.

'Nobody knew about it then. The flowers came up later, there was only the one radio, and the Bunsen burner. We've got the new evidence from the Pawlett bunker as well, don't forget.'

'Yeah.' She took another drink, a swig this time. 'So, what happens now?'

'We'll have to find out another way, won't we?'

She's making all the right noises, getting me to trust her, but I don't.

And I make no apology for that.

◆ ◆ ◆

I dropped her back to her car at Bridgwater police station, made my excuses.

There's just too much at stake. After all, it's not too late for them to pull the first edition of tomorrow's newspaper, change the front page. And I can't risk that if we're to make any progress with this case.

Then there's Shirley. She believed me when I said I'd slept on the sofa when Angela stayed the night; not sure she'd be so understanding if she saw me leaving with Mary in the morning.

It's going to be another long night.

I'm sitting in my car down by the lake, engine running to keep the heaters blasting out warmth. Doors locked, just in case.

I'm going to need to keep out of Angela's way for a while after tomorrow as well. Steer clear of the Little Chef at Camel Hill, maybe sleep in my car, or a B&B somewhere. You can imagine the sound and fury that's going to rain down on her head when the story I gave her is printed. Ray Keenan's too. Naval intelligence, the Ministry of Defence. I just hope she doesn't lose her job over it.

I'll do the decent thing, if anyone asks me. I gave her the story, confirmed she could print it, so it's on me. Not her fault at all.

I'm not sure her editor will see it that way.

Still, needs must.

Like I said, there's just too much at stake.

Chapter Twenty-Four

I went home in the end, managed to get a couple of hours' sleep.

Shirley woke me just before nine, banging on the door of the flat, thrusting a copy of the *County Gazette* into my hand before I had a chance to focus.

'You've been busy, I see,' she said, smiling. 'Front page news.'

'Thanks.' I snatched the paper, set off down the metal staircase.

'Have you slept in those clothes?'

I heard her drop the latch and shut the front door of the flat behind me.

'And you could do with a shave!'

There was a tap on the line at the post office, so I needed a phone box. I needed to get clear of Blagdon too, before Mary was knocking on my door. She'd be coming along the A38, so I decided to go over the Mendips, find a phone box at Cheddar.

It was just after nine-thirty when I stopped at the phone box at the bottom of the gorge, dialled the number.

'Hello?' Eleanor's voice.

'Could I speak to John Bromfield, please?'

'He's gone for his newspaper. Who is calling?'

'Bob Willis.'

'Oh.' I often get that reaction when I tell people it's me. 'Well, he's taken the car, and I've got no idea what time he'll be back.'

Then she added, 'He should've been back by now. He's taken Buster so he might've gone for a walk.'

I said I'd try again later, rang off.

I know where he's gone.

And so do you.

◆ ◆ ◆

A bright, clear morning. A car parked in the field gateway just along from the stile.

John Bromfield's car.

I left mine behind it, with the offside wheels on the grass verge, hazard lights flashing.

There were footprints in the dew on the stiles, pawprints in the mud underneath. The first flush of green was beginning to show on the trees in the copse, early buds on willow, possibly.

I followed the tracks in the wet grass, along the hedge towards the gate in the far corner of the field, looked along the track to the compound.

John Bromfield was sitting on the entrance hatch, staring out across the Somerset Levels, Buster sniffing along the edge of the undergrowth.

John was wearing one of those waxed jackets, a rolled-up newspaper sticking out of the pocket. He turned, saw me coming, then went back to staring at the view.

His brown leather brogues were saturated, the water creeping up the legs of his trousers. A plume of smoke was rising, and I could smell a cigar as I approached.

'It feels a bit like the bridge of a ship, sitting here,' he said. He shuffled along a bit, gestured to the concrete next to him. 'Sit.'

'Your wife said you'd gone out for your paper.'

'Spur of the moment thing, really, coming up here.'

We sat in silence for what seemed like an age but was probably only a minute or so. Then he threw the end of his cigar into the wet grass.

'You kept your part of the bargain,' he said. 'So, now I suppose I'd better keep mine.'

'Nobody will know it was you who told me.'

He nodded, slowly.

'We got your personnel file from the navy, but it was heavily redacted; even the name of your ship.'

'HMS *Plym*,' he said, the memory clearly a fond one. 'A frigate. Two years without a scratch on convoy duty in the Atlantic. We sank U772, but it was credited to another ship. She did a troop convoy to South Africa too; anti-submarine escort, and we damaged another on that trip. She was a fine ship. She was *my* ship.'

'What happened to her?' I asked.

He took a deep breath. 'She was used as the detonation platform during Operation Hurricane in October 1952. I sailed her out there with a skeleton crew.' He hesitated. 'Had to watch.'

I decided to wait, let him talk at his own pace, when he was ready.

'The Montebello Islands off the west coast of Australia. We gave the individual islands names, they're still on the naval charts,' he said, turning to me. 'Primrose, Bluebell, Crocus. There was even a Vodka Bay and a Rum Cove.'

He lit another cigar.

'The ship was moored in Bunsen Channel for the test, got vaporised by Britain's first atomic bomb.' He took a long draw on the cigar, looked me in the eye. 'So, now you know,' he said, before exhaling through his nose. 'It occurred to me last night Paul's killer left us the biggest clue of all, only we never saw it.'

'A nuclear bunker.'

'Exactly. It never crossed my mind his kidnapping was anything to do with Operation Hurricane. Not even after they showed me the Bunsen burner, but it was my fault all along.'

'It was many things, but your fault is not one of them.'

'Thank you for saying that.'

'How many were on the skeleton crew?'

'We took eighty from a full complement of a hundred and forty.'

'How many on the operation as a whole?'

'Fifteen hundred or so. Then there were the Aussies.'

He's got more to tell me. All I have to do is wait.

'I've never understood why they had to give something like that such a lovely name. The bomb was codenamed Blue Danube, would you believe it? One of the loveliest pieces of music ever written and they name a nuclear bomb after it. Buster, come!' He stood up. 'Days we waited, for the right weather, then the meteorologists fucked it up. When the mushroom cloud reached ten thousand feet a westerly wind took it right over the mainland. I watched it, and there wasn't a fucking thing we could do about it. So, there you have it. I did all that, and Paul paid the price.'

'That explains your personnel file,' I said.

'This is classified to a level you can't begin to imagine, Bob. Be very, very careful.'

'Thank you.'

'Some of the lads went ashore, suited and booted, to look for bits of the ship. They found a few fragments, but they were highly radioactive. To all intents and purposes, she completely disappeared.'

A bit like his son, Paul, all those years ago.

'I will find who killed your son,' I said.

'I hope you do,' he replied. Then he clipped on his dog's lead and trudged off along the footpath, back to his car.

Chapter Twenty-Five

'Ah, there you are,' said Mary, when I walked into the reception area at Bridgwater police station an hour later. 'I was just telling Bert to keep an eye out for you.'

It took me an hour mainly because I spent half the time sitting on the entrance hatch to Paul's bunker, letting what his father had just told me sink in.

'Sharp's on the warpath after that newspaper headline,' continued Mary. 'And there's a briefing going on.'

'Lead on,' I said.

'We found out what the piece of music in the van was.' She opened the door at the bottom of the stairs. 'Simon's music teacher got him to identify it.'

'"The Blue Danube",' I said, matter of fact.

'That's right.' She frowned. 'How could you possibly know that?'

Once through the doors of the incident room, Mary sat down behind a desk, putting a bit of distance between her and me by the looks of things.

'What the bloody hell have you done, Bob?' demanded Sharp. He was standing at the front of the room, all of the desks occupied, the tables too. 'I've had the ACC on the phone, bending my ear about the front page of the *Gazette*. He's had the MoD on the phone to him and they've had the Cabinet Office on the phone to them. You are in deep, deep shit, mate. Commander Jeffery made it quite clear—'

'With the greatest of respect,' I said. 'Fuck Commander Jeffery. He's not trying to find Paul Bromfield's killer before another child goes missing.'

There was an overhead projector at the front of the room, an image from the Pawlett bunker lit up on the wall behind Sharp. One of the pieces of graffiti, from the wall above the single bed.

Time to get it all out in the open, I think.

'We were going to ask Frank Dawson if he could identify any new pieces of graffiti in the bunker,' I said.

Sharp spun round, looked at the image behind him. 'Yes, he said he hadn't been down there for a while, but he hadn't seen this one before. We think it's a toadstool.'

'It's not a toadstool,' I replied. 'It's a mushroom cloud.'

◆ ◆ ◆

I took over the briefing after that, Sharp sensible enough to sit down, shut up and listen.

By the time I was finished fifteen minutes later, everybody knew everything.

There were a lot of shaking heads, a bit of murmuring as I sat down next to Mary.

'Fucking hell, Bob.' She looked at me, her eyes wide. 'Well done, mate.'

'Right, well, that's a major breakthrough if ever I've seen one. Changes everything,' said Sharp. 'Where has this information come from, Bob?'

'It came in response to the newspaper article, on condition of anonymity,' I replied.

'Yes, but you can tell us.'

'I assured the person I would tell no one.'

Sharp decided to let it go. For now, probably. 'What d'you suggest we do?' he asked, clearly unsure which way to jump.

'I'd start with the skeleton crew on HMS *Plym*. They sailed for Australia with the bomb on board, so they must've known what was going on; even those who flew home before it was detonated would've known. There were eighty of them, from a full crew of one hundred and forty.'

'I don't fancy our chances getting that list out of Commander Jeffery.'

'Then you've got the other naval vessels down there at the time,' I continued. 'Basically, everyone who took part in Operation Hurricane, the Australians who were there, and then civilians on the mainland. Their relatives too.'

'That could run to thousands of people.'

'John Bromfield was the captain of HMS *Plym* and it was his son who was taken, so it sounds closer to home to me. Someone in the skeleton crew, possibly. Someone who knew him, and his family. It's as good a place to start as any.'

'Bob's right.' Sharp puffed out his cheeks. 'We'll start with the ship's crew, work out from there. It's going to be a very interesting conversation with naval intelligence.'

'I'd get the ACC to earn his money, guv,' said Mary.

'Good idea.'

I lost count of the handshakes and pats on the back I got as the briefing broke up; from officers I'd never even spoken to before.

Then Sharp appeared, blocking my exit. 'I'm going to ring the ACC. Don't go anywhere, Bob. I may need you.'

◆ ◆ ◆

Turned out Sharp did need me in the end, but not for what I'd expected.

The call came in before he'd had a chance to ring the ACC; reports of a gunshot at an address in Wincanton.

The Bromfields' house on Bayford Hill.

John had gone home, sat his wife down in the kitchen, and told her everything. Then he'd locked himself in his office, and you can guess the rest.

For the second time in eight months, I found myself standing over the body of an ex-serviceman who'd killed himself with his sidearm, this time a Webley service revolver.

At least I didn't have to witness it this time.

He was sitting in his leather office chair, pitched forward, blood seeping into a large naval chart that had been opened out and covered the whole of the desk. I could make out the names of some of the islands, but Crocus was hidden by the pool of blood.

It had congealed before it reached Bluebell to the north.

It makes me wonder whether they keep their service weapons as souvenirs when they retire. I didn't even get to keep my truncheon.

I'm also wondering whether this is somehow my fault, but it can't be.

Can it?

What happened, happened. I didn't make it happen. All I did was uncover it, bring it out into the light. John would've found out sooner or later.

The bullet passed clean through his skull, taking brain tissue and bone fragments with it, and there was a corresponding hole in the front window where it continued on its way. That side of his office had been taped off, pending the arrival of the pathologist.

The gun was on the floor, next to his chair, where you'd expect to find it, I suppose. Dropped when . . .

Best not to dwell on these things, I find. Other people get paid to do that. I can't help but feel sad, though. He was a good man, who did his duty.

None of this is his fault. He just happened to be the captain of a ship the Navy decided it didn't need anymore. In the wrong place at the wrong time.

I'm guessing someone else was in the wrong place at the wrong time and took it out on John Bromfield by snatching his son.

Killing his son.

What was it the good doctor said?

. . . someone who's been confronted with that in their past.

Well, now we know what *that* is.

The Blue Danube.

'How's his wife doing?' I asked, when Mary appeared beside me.

'One minute she's remarkably composed, then she breaks down. Sharp's with her.'

There was a familiar scratching at the inside of the door opposite.

I wonder who's going to take Buster for his walks now.

Raised voices were coming from the kitchen, footsteps in the hall.

'Keep that door closed!' Sharp, shouting.

Then Eleanor appeared in the doorway.

'What's he doing here?' she demanded, glaring at me. Her face was almost crimson, sobbing, tears streaming down her cheeks. 'It's thanks to him I've lost my husband!' she screamed, hurling the rolled-up copy of the *County Gazette* at me. It glanced off my shoulder, landed in the pool of her husband's blood on the desk. 'It's not enough my son is dead, now John. I want that man out of my house!'

I'm not sure what I'd been expecting, to be honest, but it wasn't that. It hit me like a car, and I should know what that feels like – do know what that feels like. This felt worse.

'I saw you yesterday, out with Buster. John came home covered in mud. What was that all about?' She dropped to her knees.

Sharp was behind her, trying to help her up, move her back in the direction of the kitchen. 'John shot himself because of that article.'

So, there you have it. She thinks it was the article, when actually the article was just cover for John to tell me about Operation Hurricane.

And I can't tell her that – can't tell anyone that – without breaking my promise to him.

So be it.

'It wasn't your fault, Bob.' Mary tried a reassuring smile. 'When she's had a chance to think about it, she'll realise.'

'Doesn't make it any easier.'

'Get him out of this house!' The shout came from the corridor as Sharp led Eleanor back to the kitchen.

'I'd better go,' I said.

'I'll hang on here. Sharp can give me a lift and I'll catch up with you back at Bridgwater.'

Chapter Twenty-Six

Their daughter Rachel had arrived just as I was leaving, driven down from Stroud, probably. It must've been her because she was heavily pregnant. Right age too.

In any other situation, I'd have taken the opportunity to ask her about the day Paul was taken. After all, she'd been sitting opposite her brother in the railway carriage, with her back to the direction of travel. That meant she'd have had a view along the platform to where Jenny Pugh had seen the figure in the smoke.

Rachel was on my list to interview, but now was hardly the time.

Instead, her arrival just served as a reminder that John hadn't waited to meet his first grandchild. Sadness heaped upon sadness.

I'd recovered my composure by the time I got back to Bridgwater. I hadn't lost it altogether, but I was glad there was no one else in my car for the drive back to the station.

I can tell you that; I know you won't tell anyone else.

People deal with grief in a multitude of ways. I've learned that over the years. And Eleanor dealt with it by lashing out at me. The article on the front page of the *Gazette* mentioned my name, so it must've been my fault John was dead. He clearly hadn't told her that we'd met again at Paul's bunker this morning. Otherwise, she'd have been blaming me for forcing him to breach the Official Secrets Act on top of everything else; saying that pushed him over the edge.

It may have done, but I didn't force him. I persuaded him. There's a difference.

It must've been lunchtime when I walked into the incident room on the first floor. Only one desk was occupied. Mitchell, the young detective constable Mary had been working with the day Simon Horsey had been taken.

'We're getting bugger all from the MoD,' he said, shaking his head. 'I've spoken to three different people, each one higher up the food chain, and I'm just getting blanked every time. They're denying all knowledge of Operation Hurricane.'

'Leave it to the ACC,' I said.

'He's on his way down here, apparently. Sharp is on his way back too.'

'Where's Mrs Bromfield?'

'Gone to Stroud to stay with her daughter.'

I sat down at a vacant desk at the back of the room, was still sitting there when the ACC and Sharp walked in. Most of the desks were occupied around me by then and, to be honest, I hadn't noticed. Mary was weaving her way between the desks towards me.

'They've been in an interview room downstairs for ten minutes, Bob,' she whispered. 'It's not looking good, mate. First thing the ACC did when they came out is ask where you were.'

'Could we have a word, please, Bob?' asked Sharp, gesturing to the door.

'Good luck,' said Mary.

The ACC sat down behind the table in an interview room, leaned back in his chair and folded his arms, waiting while Sharp closed the door behind me.

'Who gave you the authority to leak that information to the *County Gazette*?' he asked.

'No one,' I replied.

'But it was you?'

'Yes.'

'And why did you do it?'

'I needed help understanding the significance of the items listed. They'd been left at the crime scenes deliberately. Paul's killer was leading us somewhere and we needed to know where. Now we do.'

'I'm told Mrs Bromfield believes that article was the cause of her husband's suicide.' He's looking at me over the top of his glasses now.

'She's mistaken,' I replied. 'Her husband took his own life because he blamed himself, and his part in Operation Hurricane, for Paul's death. That much was clear from the map open on his desk.'

'Was it John Bromfield who told you about Operation Hurricane?'

'No.' No hesitation, careful not to blink.

'Who was it then?'

'I'm not at liberty to say. The information was given on condition of anonymity.'

'If you don't tell us, Bob, then I'm afraid you're off the case.'

'Then I'm off the case,' I said, turning for the door.

'Not so fast, Bob.' Sharp stepped to one side, blocking the door.

'Mrs Bromfield has made a complaint,' said the ACC. 'Superintendent Sharp here seems to think she'll calm down, when she's had a chance to think about it.' He was looking me up and down. 'You've done well. Blown this case wide open, but at what cost?'

'If her husband hadn't found out the truth from that article, he'd have found out some other way, sooner or later,' I said.

The ACC nodded. 'We have another problem,' he said. 'The MoD are furious about it as well. I've had to get the Home Secretary to intervene. They'll release the information we need, but due to the obvious sensitivity, only to a strictly controlled group of serving police officers who can be trusted not to leak it to the press. And that doesn't include you.'

'Bob's work is done here,' said Sharp. 'It'll be old-fashioned police work from now on, tracking down and interviewing witnesses. Now we know what it's about.'

'I think the answer is to send you back to the Cold Case Unit, Willis.' The ACC stood up. 'I'll let Clive Ash know.'

◆ ◆ ◆

I took a moment, considered my options.

I'd been thinking it might be fun to buy a vice and start tying my own flies. After all, the lake opens for trout fishing in a few weeks. Then there was back to the Cold Case Unit. That was what they wanted me to do, but I'm not very good at doing what people want me to do, particularly when I don't think it's the right thing.

Shirley will vouch for that.

It probably explains why I retired a detective inspector.

'Out on the tractor, cutting hedges,' they'd said, and I eventually found Bill Horsey in a field. I'd seen the lights and the top of the cab over the newly cut hedge.

The engine was running as I approached, the little flap on top of the exhaust pipe bouncing up and down, but even that couldn't drown out the birdsong.

It had turned into one of those barmy spring afternoons you sometimes get in late winter, when Mother Nature lulls you into a false sense of security, lets you believe the worst is behind you.

It rarely is, in my experience.

Late, though, so it's getting cold quickly as the sun goes down.

There was no sign of Bill when I waded through the mud in the field gateway. If he'd nipped into the bushes for a pee, he'd have been back at the tractor by the time I got across the field. Then I spotted a plume of smoke rising from the hedge trimmer at the back, remembered he was a pipe smoker.

I walked around the front of the tractor, and there he was, leaning against the side of the hedge trimmer.

'John Bromfield is dead,' I said.

He looked at me blankly. I was blinking furiously, my eyes adjusting to the light after I'd walked through the headlights.

'Captain John Bromfield, Royal Navy retired. Father of Paul Bromfield, who died in the Chilton Polden bunker in 1962.'

'I know who he is. How did he die?'

'He took his own life.' I left it at that. He might not have a service revolver, but farmers have shotguns. 'We got your personnel file, but pretty much everything is redacted after 1951. Even the name of your ship. I'm guessing you were on HMS *Plym*?'

'We're not supposed to talk about her.'

'We know about Operation Hurricane and the Blue Danube.'

'That was the music the man was playing in the van. I was there this morning when Simon's teacher put it on the record player. Poor little bugger nearly passed out.' Bill tapped his pipe out on the back tyre of the tractor, embers falling into the wet grass. 'So that's what this is all about, is it?'

'We found bluebells, primroses and crocuses planted at the bunker, all islands at the test site. There was a Rum Cove and a Vodka Bay. A Bunsen burner was left in the Chilton Polden bunker.'

'We anchored for the last time in Bunsen Channel.'

'And the graffiti on the wall in the Pawlett bunker, above the bed where we found Simon, we believe, is a mushroom cloud.'

I waited, watching him filling his pipe with fresh tobacco, pressing it down with his thumb. Then he lit it, clouds of smoke rising into the darkening sky.

'I was Chief Bosun's Mate,' he said, eventually. 'Last one off the ship. We piped the captain off, and that was that. I retired then, came home to run the farm. My father was knocking on, slowing down, you know how it is.'

'Tell me about the bomb.'

'It was a bloody great big thing, in the forward hold. A sphere. The plutonium was added later, when we docked at Fremantle, which was a good job because it was a wild ride down there, crossing the Indian Ocean. We could only make ten knots, and the storms were the worst I'd seen in my eight years in the service.' Lighting his pipe again. 'The Suez Canal was out because of all the trouble, so we had to go the long way round.'

'How many were on board?'

'We left Sheerness with a crew of eighty.' He shrugged. 'Didn't need the guns or the depth charge crews, so that was less than full complement. Once we anchored in the Montebello Islands the crew gradually shrank until there were only thirty of us left, come the end. I watched the test from the deck of the *Campania*, twenty miles away. There were loads of us, out on deck with goggles on. There was a blinding flash, then the blast a minute or so later. A huge ball of flame, the mushroom cloud. It was a sight to behold, I can tell you. And my home for eight years ceased to exist. After that, I came home on the *Campania*, and that was that. My naval career was over.'

'Were any of you ever exposed to radiation?'

'No. We spent days training on the way down and it was all tightly controlled. We all wore film badges that measured the radiation dose. Then there were dosimeters for anyone going into the contaminated area. It was a small thing that looked like a pen. You clipped it on your chest and there was a scale. If the radiation went above a certain level, off you went for decontamination.'

'Did any of the *Plym*'s crew go into the contaminated area?'

'A few. Most of the lads flew home once they left the ship. There was only a handful of us who stayed on for the main event.'

'Is there an HMS *Plym* Association?' I asked.

'There was; disbanded now. We met for a while, to remember those we lost, have a piss-up, but it was mainly lads who'd served on the Atlantic convoys.'

'Did you lose many?'

'We were lucky. There was a fire, and we lost two in that, but none to enemy action.' He looked at his watch. 'I ought to get back, said I'd help with the milking tonight.'

'How many were in the association?'

'A couple of hundred, maybe. To begin with. We had regional branches. There was one for the South West, then it became one national organisation, then it just sort of fizzled out.'

'And when was that?'

'Oh, I don't know, late seventies, possibly. I'd stopped going by then. People move on, don't they?' He tapped his pipe out again, was standing with one foot on the bottom step up to the cab, his hand on the rail. 'I got a letter. The committee had voted to wind up the organisation and the money held in the bank account was donated to the Royal Naval Benevolent Trust.'

'Was John Bromfield in the association?'

'He was the patron. All past captains of the ship were honorary members.'

'Did they go to meetings?'

'Bromfield did, until he lost his boy. Maybe once more after that. None of the other captains ever came, from memory.'

'Was there ever any anger or bitterness about what happened to the *Plym*?'

'There was disappointment, but no anger that I remember. It was one of those things. Surplus to requirements, she was.' He was sitting in the driver's seat of the tractor now, looking down at me.

‘If she hadn’t been blown to bits by the bomb, she’d have been sold off, probably for scrap. She was being decommissioned anyway. We’d known it was coming.’

‘Who ran the regional branch?’ I asked, raising my voice over the revving of the engine. He needed to be on his way, was being polite.

‘Evan Williams. He became a schoolteacher over at Burnham. Retired now, I think.’

‘Thank you,’ I said, shutting the driver’s door of the tractor, giving him a cheery wave.

◆ ◆ ◆

I followed the tractor’s lights across the field, walking in the tracks. It was pitch dark by the time I got back to my car in the lane.

I was kicking myself, because I’d forgotten to ask Bill not to mention our conversation to officers from the major investigation team when they turned up to ask him exactly the same questions, as they surely would.

I’m going to need to rethink my strategy. Sharp will get the lists from the MoD and go through them one by one. Every single person who took part in Operation Hurricane will be spoken to, if needs be, let alone every sailor on board the *Plym* for her final voyage.

What the hell can I realistically achieve on my own?

Bugger all, is the answer to that, which leaves going back to the CCU or learning to tie my own flies.

Chapter Twenty-Seven

I must've been miles away when I turned into the small car park behind the post office in Blagdon. I saw the red bonnet; just never made the connection.

Not in time, anyway.

Next thing I knew, Angela had wrenched open the driver's door of my car. 'You fucking bastard, Bob!'

She was waiting for me to get out, so she could give me a good slap, probably. Wouldn't have been the first time.

'You knew I'd get in deep shit for printing that stuff you gave me. You used me.' Her left hand was on the door pillar, her right fist clenched, ready to swing it at me.

Wearing jeans and a pullover, didn't look as though she'd come from work.

'Have you been sacked?' I asked.

'No.'

'Well, I have.'

'Good.' She took a step back, allowing me out of the car. Obviously, a trap.

'It's what we do. You'll get used to it,' I said. 'It's all part of the game. Police officers use journalists and journalists use police officers.'

I decided to give her a minute to calm down, stayed sitting in my car.

'I got called into the editor's office; asked me what the bloody hell I thought I was doing.'

'What did Ray say about it?'

'He said it was all my fault.'

I shook my head. 'Conveniently forgot you're a trainee and covered his own arse. Twat.'

'The editor said he'd had head office in London on to him, demanding he sack someone over it. The government were threatening all sorts.'

'Let them. Journalists are supposed to annoy the government.'

'That's what Ray said.'

She was calming down, so I thought I'd risk it – got out of the car.

'Have you eaten?' I asked.

'Yes. I've been waiting for you in the Little Chef all afternoon.'

'Pub then?'

'So, you've lost your job,' she said, as we walked up the road to the Seymour Arms.

'I've been booted off the major investigation team.'

'Did you find out what it was all about?'

We found a quiet corner of the pub; a glass of white wine for her, sparkling water for me.

It took ten minutes.

HMS *Plym*. Operation Hurricane. Everything. From the top.

I owed her that.

'Even I know I can't print that,' she said, puffing out her cheeks.

'It'll all come out eventually when they catch him, and he has his day in court. I'm beginning to think that's what this is all about.'

'What are you going to do?'

'I had thought I'd try to find him on my own, but how? I'm not going to have access to the lists of service personnel and the major investigation team will be speaking to them anyway.'

'Well, at least we know what it was all about now. Why Paul Bromfield died down in that bunker. They'd never have got that far without you.'

'Maybe not.' She's softening, but Angela won't forget. She owes me a good slap.

'I'm assuming you got a response to the article then?' she asked.

Actually, I didn't, but I won't tell her that. And, besides, it was never about that anyway. It was about giving John Bromfield the cover to tell me himself – to breach the Official Secrets Act.

'Is this why the boy's father killed himself?' asked Angela. 'The one from 1962.'

'He blamed himself.'

'Ray's dealing with that. Local man took his own life, that's it though. Nothing else until the inquest.'

I nodded.

'So, what happens now?'

'I don't know what else I can do,' I replied. 'I've been frozen out.'

'There must be something.'

'I've got a name for the bloke who used to run the local branch of the HMS *Plym* Association.'

'Right, I'll be over at nine in that case.'

'You'll be at work.'

'I might ring in sick for a few days. It'll serve them bloody well right anyway.'

◆ ◆ ◆

Ten o'clock at the Little Chef at Farrington Gurney, we said. Only I never got there.

The knock was earlier than usual. Louder than Shirley's knock too. She knows I'm a light sleeper.

Lighter than usual at the moment.

I threw on a pair of trousers and a shirt, trudged along the corridor doing up the buttons. There was a figure standing behind the frosted glass. Short, dark hair. Tall. Looked like Mary Simpson.

I opened the door, began tucking my shirt in.

'Morning, Bob,' she said, her voice flat.

'I'm off the case. I was binned yesterday; sent back to the CCU.'

'Then you went to see Bill Horsey, but it's not about that,' she said. 'There's a body in the peat fields opposite Ashcott station. Sharp wants you there. Now.'

'Who is it, do we know?'

'There's no ID yet.'

'What time is it?'

'Just gone nine.'

'I'll take my own car,' I said.

It's a rule of mine. Take your own car and you can leave when you want. It applies to nights out too, dinner parties.

I'd left my jacket hanging over the back of my deckchair last night; tie on the floor next to it. My coat was on the back seat of my car.

'I just need a word with Shirley in the post office, then I'll follow you.'

She looked as if she was about to protest but thought better of it.

I poked my head around the door of the shop. Shirley was standing behind the counter, a coffee in one hand, turning the page of a newspaper with the other.

'I was supposed to meet Angela at ten, but I've got to—'

'I'll make your excuses for you if she turns up here,' said Shirley. She looked up. 'Anything exciting?'

'I got the boot yesterday, now they want me there immediately.'

Shirley gave me a knowing smile, then a wave.

Mary was turning around at the top of the lane that leads down to the lake. I tapped on the driver's window.

'Quicker the other way,' I said. 'Over the Mendips.'

'I don't know that way.'

'Follow me in that case.'

Mary kept up with me, not that I'm much of a driver to be honest. I've never been pursuit trained or anything like that. And I'm in a Volvo estate too.

A Saturday morning in late February, so there wasn't much traffic about. A few rock climbers in Cheddar Gorge as I took the bends a little too fast, perhaps, the cliffs towering over me on both sides of the road. It's impossible to drive that road without your tyres squealing. Then we were off across the Levels. Single track lanes, rhynes either side full of water.

I pulled into a field gateway when we left Meare, waved Mary past me. There'd be a road closure ahead, and we'd need her warrant card to get past it. Then we were being directed into the car park of the Railway Inn.

The grass verges were lined with cars and vans, a patrol car parked across the road on the far side of the old railway line, blocking it from the south.

I left Mary to speak to the uniformed officer directing the traffic, took in the view. It would've looked much like this in 1962, when Paul Bromfield had been taken. The lanes lined with marked cars and police vans. I seem to remember when we arrived by coach it parked in the pub car park, and we went the rest of the way on foot.

'It's south of the railway line,' said Mary, bringing me back to the present. 'Three fields over.'

'Do we know who it is yet?'

'No. One of the peat cutters thinks they've seen him around, though.'

I looked over my shoulder at Andrew Bucknall's caravan, all but hidden in the undergrowth in what was the old railway siding. I could just about make out the roof, stained green by the algae.

'The body's still in the water,' continued Mary. 'Face down.'

I followed her across the bridge over the South Drain and along the track that ran along the edge of the peat fields. It occurred to me that what we were actually walking on was the old railway line, the rails and sleepers long gone, the gravel still there in places.

There was a thin layer of ice on the puddles, but that would soon go when the sun was a bit higher in the sky. The deeper water hadn't frozen overnight. It's strange stuff, the water that accumulates in the peat cuttings; has the look of strong black coffee about it. I remember it from the sixties, when we were out searching for Paul. It has that stagnant stink to it; stayed in my nostrils for weeks afterwards, that did.

I could see several officers standing in a group on the far side of the next field. They had their hands in their pockets and were looking down. Some were stamping their feet, trying to ward off the cold. Sharp was there, in the middle of the group.

I'm guessing he wants to pick my brains, see if I think there's any connection to the Bromfield case.

The peat had been cut from parallel trenches, all of them full of water, giving the appearance of lattice work, green islands of grass in coffee-coloured water. The next field over had been dug in circular pits, narrow green paths winding in between each. The hedgerows were still there, trees at random intervals.

I remember seeing it being dug. My father took us on the steam train for days out at the beach as kids; that would've been just before the war. There's the old peat works siding half a mile or so further along the track, and you could see the peat cutters, hard at it in the fields.

The water will be deep. I remember that as well.

No peat has been cut from here for years, though, the fields and their new ponds gradually reclaimed by Mother Nature.

'Ah, there you are, Bob,' said Sharp. 'How did you get on with Bill Horsey?'

Bollocks.

Actually, I spent much of the night thinking about my meeting with Bill. Thinking about what I'd learned. Now is not the time, though.

'Fine,' I said. If Sharp was expecting an apology, he was going to be disappointed.

'Well, let's not worry about that now.' The group had gathered at the corner of the field, an area of long grass trodden flat beneath their feet. He stepped to one side, allowing me to see the water behind him. A narrow strip, perhaps ten or twelve feet across, the remains of reeds in the margins. 'D'you recognise him?' he asked.

The body was lying face down at the edge of the cutting; would've sunk to the bottom had it not been for the mat of dead reeds.

'We just need to know if you think it's connected to this other business,' said Sharp.

I recognised the boots, and the filthy coat. The matted hair too, sticking out from underneath the bobble hat. It was blond but hardly looked it in that water.

'It's Andrew Bucknall,' I said. 'He lives in a caravan in the old siding on the other side of the road. I spoke to him only the other day. He confessed to the abduction and murder of Paul Bromfield, spent six weeks in custody in early '63, before they realised it wasn't him; couldn't have been him.'

'For fuck's sake,' hissed Sharp.

Cause of death wasn't going to be difficult either. I could see the cut to the left side of Andrew's neck; I'm guessing now, but it probably went all the way around to the other side.

An officer appeared, trudging along the track in a pair of thigh waders.

'Get in there and roll him over,' said Sharp.

'I wouldn't do that, if I were you,' I offered. 'That water's eight feet deep, the banks are steep, cut in steps.'

'We'll have to get a rope on him then, pull him out.'

'Pathologist is on his way, guv. Shall we wait for him?' I heard the voice behind Sharp, didn't see who had been brave enough to question him.

'All right, Bob.' Sharp ignored the comment, turned back to me. 'I want you and Mary to focus on this murder. We've got our hands full with the naval personnel, speaking to them one by one. We've found two who went on to join the Observer Corps, but keep that to yourself.'

'What about the ACC?' I asked. 'He gave me my marching orders yesterday.'

'You let me worry about the ACC, mate.'

Mate?

Chapter Twenty-Eight

Sharp and his team disappeared, leaving us to wait for the pathologist. A dive team arrived soon after and they helped get a rope on the body, lift him out of the water and on to a tarpaulin.

I was right. It was Andrew, his throat cut almost from ear to ear.

Chances were the knife had been thrown in, so the search began; two divers side by side feeling their way along the bottom in the murky water.

The pathologist didn't take long, though.

Sometime last night between ten and midnight.

The killer was right-handed, the cut sweeping from left to right across the throat.

Then his body was carried out on a stretcher to a waiting mortuary van.

I've seen bodies that have been in water before, the skin pale, bloated, but this was something different altogether.

Mary had spent the time organising house to house enquiries all along Station Road. She went to see Andrew's father too, the old stationmaster still living in the station house; took a couple of uniformed officers with her. I've done my fair share of breaking news like that over the years and was grateful to be spared it this time.

A search of Andrew's caravan was under way too, forensic officers carrying bits and pieces out to plastic crates on the ground, bagging them up, labelling them. I picked up the clipboard, glanced down the list.

Nothing.

Nothing of any consequence anyway; not that I can see.

If it is the same killer, there'll be something, though, surely? He left clues at both bunkers; even played a waltz to Simon in the van as he drove him out to the Pawlett bunker.

There must be something.

Buggered if I can see it.

I'd memorised the names of the islands when I was leaning over John Bromfield's desk; those islands that hadn't been covered in his blood as it seeped across the naval chart. I'm looking for things like claret, and cocoa. There was a Flag Island too, but I can't see a flag anywhere in Andrew's belongings.

That's assuming the killing of Andrew Bucknall was planned, of course. That it is part of the strategy.

And there is one.

A strategy.

Make no mistake about that. This killer wants Operation Hurricane out in the open, wants everyone to know what happened. And that brings me back to my meeting with Bill Horsey yesterday – chief petty officer, Royal Navy, last off HMS *Plym* before she was blown to smithereens. What I learned from him tells me that Sharp is wasting his time interviewing the naval personnel who took part in the operation.

I simply don't believe any of them have an axe to grind, a grievance. They were doing their jobs, their duty as they saw it. They knew the ship was being decommissioned anyway; all but a few weren't exposed to dangerous radiation levels.

John Bromfield was even the patron of their association. So why kidnap and murder his son?

No, this is someone else.

Someone with a different agenda.

But d'you think Sharp will listen to me?

◆ ◆ ◆

'How was he?' I asked, when Mary appeared next to me. I was standing in the old siding, watching the forensic team trying to cut back the undergrowth around Andrew's caravan. A flatbed lorry was waiting to take it away once they'd been able to clear it.

I'd still not found anything to connect his murder to the kidnappings. No bluebells, primroses or crocuses. None out in the peat fields and none here. Maybe they don't like acidic soil. Gardening has always been a mystery to me, I'm afraid.

There was a vodka bottle; one of those half-bottles, half empty too, so my guess is it was Andrew's.

Never half full; always half empty, but how could it ever be anything else, doing this for a living?

And, yes, I know people do take their own lives by cutting their throats, but this was murder. Pure and simple. I've seen a couple of suicides in my time, and the cut never goes right across the throat, ear to ear. It's usually one side of the neck, depending on whether they're left or right handed, then the sight of blood stops them. They'll have severed the carotid artery or the jugular vein; the artery and they're dead in less than a minute, the vein and it takes half an hour.

Three suicides, thinking about it. I can remember the names, and the inquests, even now. Some things stay with you.

The other thing is, if it was suicide, Andrew would probably have done it in his caravan. No, my guess is he was lured out into the peat fields, throat cut and pushed into the water.

'How d'you think he was,' said Mary, her voice flat. 'His wife's dead and his only son has just been killed.'

It was a fair point.

She was struggling to keep her composure. Not been an easy one, then.

Some are, some aren't.

'Who found the body?' I asked.

'Some woman out walking her dog. Lives in the village.'

'Let's go and have a word with her.'

The formalities didn't take long. Mary made the introductions, asked the usual questions. Betty Langdon her name was, her dachshund, Polly, sitting on her lap. It had been their usual route, along the old railway line, and there he was, face down in the reed bed.

Betty ran home and dialled 999.

Hardly enlightening.

'I thought it looked like Andrew,' said Betty. 'Poor lad.'

There'd been no formal identification yet – the old stationmaster still had that treat in store.

Mary looked at me blankly, wondering where to take the interview. Back in time, was the answer to that – was where the answer to all of this sorry mess would be found.

'How long have you lived in Ashcott?' I asked.

'All my life,' replied Betty. 'I was born here, married my childhood sweetheart. He worked over at ROF, the Royal Ordnance Factory.' She glanced up at a photograph on the mantelpiece, gave a sad smile. 'He was lovely.'

Past tense, so a widow.

'You'll remember the disappearance of Paul Bromfield in that case?'

'Vividly.' She stood up, took another photograph off the mantelpiece. 'My son, Graham, was home from university, had a holiday job cutting peat. You must remember it, surely?' She was looking at me, rather than Mary.

'I was in uniform back then, out in the fields looking for him.'

'There was another boy found in a bunker only a few days ago, wasn't there? Alive this time, thank God.'

'Presumably you knew Andrew quite well?' I asked. 'He lived in his caravan on the old railway line, and you walk your dog down there—'

'Every day,' she interrupted me, finished my sentence for me. 'Yes, I knew Andrew. As well as anyone, mind you. Nobody knows him very well. He keeps . . . kept himself to himself. A bit . . . odd . . . if you know what I mean.'

'Did you ever feel threatened by him, worried by him?'

'Not really. I know some of the mothers were worried about him, told their children to stay away from him. Particularly after he confessed to kidnapping the little boy, obviously. Some people seem to believe there's no smoke without fire. But you got used to him hanging around the station. I mean, that was hardly surprising when his father was the stationmaster.'

'Were you surprised when he confessed to the kidnap and murder of Paul Bromfield?'

'We all were.' Her response was immediate, no hesitation. 'I mean, there was no way he'd have done that, no way he was capable of that. I told the police at the time.' She looked at me, frowned. 'What was all that on the front page of the *Gazette*? The flowers and the alcohol bottles?'

'We can't really talk about that, I'm afraid, Mrs Langdon,' said Mary.

'Is Andrew's death connected to the kidnappings?'

It was a natural reaction. She'd found a body and wanted to know what it was all about.

Don't we all?

'Did he drink?' I asked.

'There was the odd empty bottle in the grass sometimes, the little bottles, you know. I assumed it was him. I don't think he could afford anything else. But I never saw him the worse for wear, if that's what you mean. If he drank, he was private about it.'

'And did you speak to him?'

'Not really. I'd say hello if our paths crossed, but that was it.'

'You said Andrew was hanging around the station.'

'Yes, he was always there. I think he was a trainspotter, always had a notebook in his hand, writing down the numbers. Filthy, smelly old things, the steam engines, but they were lovely, all the same. Andrew was fascinated by them. I spoke to his father about it once, just remarked that Andrew was always there, you know, watching the trains. He said it was his boy's only interest. Sad, when you think about it. When they closed the line, they took the father's job and the son's only real interest in life.'

◆ ◆ ◆

Mary waited until the front door of Mrs Langdon's bungalow closed behind us. 'Where to now?' she asked.

'We need to go and see if Andrew's father kept his old notebooks.'

'His trainspotting books?' She folded her arms. 'Really?'

'Yes, really.'

The old man reeked of whisky when we knocked on his door a few minutes later. There was a glass in his hand, an open bottle on the table in the front window.

'They said the identification would be tomorrow.'

'It will be, Mr Bucknall,' replied Mary. 'We just had a few questions for you and were hoping you might still have Andrew's trainspotting books.'

'They're in the loft, but I can't go up there now, not at my age. I haven't been up there for years.'

I looked at Mary, exaggerated my limp up the tiled steps into the hall.

'Looks like it's me then,' she said.

'It's at the top of the stairs, there's a hatch and a ladder pulls down. The box is on the left, labelled, so you'll see what it is. It's heavy, mind.'

I followed Mary up the stairs, waited while she pulled down the ladder, climbed it, before disappearing into the loft.

'Is there a light?'

'No, sorry,' replied the old man, from the bottom of the stairs.

Then I heard a box being dragged along the loft boards, until it appeared at the top, Mary peering over it. 'There's a handle, so I can lower it down to you, Bob, but you'll need to be on the ladder, just the first few rungs.'

The old man had been right. It was heavy. My knee wasn't too bad, but a sharp pain tore through my left elbow when I took hold of the box.

I left it at the top of the stairs, went into the living room just in time to see the old man filling his glass again, right to the top.

Then Mary came in, carrying the box. She placed it on the table in front of the old man.

'We're looking for the twenty-eighth of August 1962,' I said.

The old man slammed the bottle down. 'I've told you before, it wasn't Andrew.'

'I know it wasn't Andrew, but he would've been there, standing on the end of the platform, taking down the train numbers. Then he got on the train and went to the beach. We know that from the witnesses who gave him an alibi when he was arrested. I believe that what he saw that day got him killed last night.'

The old man took a swig of whisky, then opened the top of the box.

'We've got a new witness,' I said. 'She was a child at the time, and she thinks she saw someone standing on the end of the platform when the train pulled out of the station, exactly where Andrew would've been standing to get the numbers, but he was on the train by then, so it must've been someone else and my guess is Andrew saw him.'

'He used to stand at the eastern end, at the top of the ramp. Said it gave him more time to write down the numbers because the trains had slowed almost to a stop.'

'What did you do when a train pulled out of the station?' I asked.

'Went back in my office, usually.'

'The guard hopped back on the train when he'd waved his flag, which means this person would've been alone on the platform as the smoke cleared. Only that day he wasn't alone, was he? He was there with Paul Bromfield.'

The old man was flicking through the pages of the notebook. 'There it is,' he said. 'Twenty-eighth August 1962. She was an 0-6-0, number 2204. An ex-Great Western Railway locomotive. Underneath he's written the six coach numbers, probably couldn't see the number on the engine at the back.'

'What's the 0-6-0 bit?' asked Mary.

'It's the classification. It was done by the wheels and where they were. None at the front, six in the middle, two on each axle, then none at the back. The *Flying Scotsman* is a 4-6-2; much bigger.'

I knew that. Don't ask. I may have had a train set when I was a child.

'I'm sure I've got a photograph of 2204 somewhere.' The old man stood up, walked over to a cabinet, and took out an album. 'There,' he said, placing it on the back of the sofa in front of me. 'That's the engine.'

A classic steam engine. The image was black and white, of course, the number in white paint on the front, where you'd see Thomas the Tank Engine's face. Two chimneys, one for the smoke and one a steam valve. The locomotive had been backed into a siding, the tender resting against the buffers.

'That looks like Templecombe in the background,' offered the old man.

'What did Andrew say to you about that day?' I asked.

'Nothing.'

'Did he tell you he was going to confess to Paul Bromfield's murder?'

'No.'

'I'm guessing you went to see him when he was in custody?'

'He just kept saying he was sorry. I asked him what for and he didn't say.'

'How about when he was released?'

'He said nothing about it at all.'

'When he kept saying he was sorry, what did you *think* he was sorry for?'

'I knew he hadn't done it, so I assumed it was for wasting everyone's time and putting me and his mother through it, God rest her.'

'Could it have been something else?'

'Like what?'

'That he knew where Paul Bromfield was all along, perhaps, but didn't say anything.'

No reaction. The old man had retreated into memories. If I had to guess, he was back sitting in the cell with Andrew, his son apologising over and over again.

He tipped his head, sighed at me – you can sigh *at* someone. Shirley used to do it all the time.

Now he was starting to wonder whether he'd got it wrong all these years.

Time to go in for the kill. 'That he knew who'd taken Paul, but didn't say anything,' I said.

It took a while, but we got there in the end.

'Could've been, I suppose,' he mumbled. 'I never thought . . .'

I picked up the book. 'Can we keep this?'

'Er, yes. No use to me. Not now.'

'Is this the last one?'

'No, he filled a few more. The line stayed open for freight, peat mainly, and he was out with his pen every day.'

'We'll take them all, in that case,' I said.

Mary made a half-hearted attempt to stifle a sigh. 'I'll carry them then, shall I?'

We were back in the Railway Inn car park, the box resting on the boot of her car, before Mary spoke again. 'What I don't get, right, is why Andrew was never spoken to as part of the original investigation. Not before he was arrested.'

'There's a note somewhere. He was spoken to, informally, and his notebook checked, but they didn't think he had the mental capacity to give a formal statement. I'm translating the exact words used, but you get the picture.'

'Didn't stop them arresting him, taking his confession seriously.'

'Read his police interviews,' I said. 'Just like his father. No one ever asked him what he was sorry for. Not once.'

Chapter Twenty-Nine

'We need to get round to Avalon Peat,' Mary had said. 'It's on the road between Shapwick and Westhay.'

I was following, driving slowly enough to take in the changing landscape, looking out of the driver's side window, east across live peat workings now. Ashcott had been abandoned years ago, much like the railway line, but here it was very different.

Drainage ditches weaving in between earthworks and digger tracks, deep trenches and vast mounds of raw, exposed black earth.

I leaned forward and closed the air vents, shutting out the sickly sweet smell of damp peat, slowing as we crossed the South Drain.

I can imagine the battlefields of the First World War looked much like this, the ground churned to hell by artillery shells instead of diggers. I'd seen the pictures of the bare mud and shell holes filled with murky water.

The only difference here was the hedgerows were still intact, and the trees hadn't been shot to pieces.

Mary turned into a large industrial compound. Several diggers, more trailers and other machines had been parked behind high fencing, razor wire on the top of it, padlocks and heavy chains on the gate. Several pallets had been loaded with white bags and wrapped in plastic, awaiting collection, a forklift truck standing by to load them on to a lorry.

A man was standing with two uniformed officers in front of a Portakabin, the conversation animated.

I waited for Mary. At least she had a warrant card to hide behind.

One of the uniformed officers recognised her and walked over. 'The manager's here, Mary,' she said. 'He was fishing in a match on the canal; isn't a happy camper.'

Mary looked at me, pleading almost, I thought.

'Don't look at me,' I said. 'I'm just a consultant.'

'His name's Wally Fletcher,' said the officer. 'Been the manager here for years, apparently.'

I recognised the name from the statements on the Bromfield file. He'd been working in the fields that day in 1962, saw nothing, but then no one had.

'Good morning, sir,' said Mary, warrant card at the ready. She introduced herself and me, ignored the huffing and puffing.

'What the bloody hell's so important on a Saturday morning?' He folded his arms. 'The burglar alarms haven't gone off. I was fishing in a competition over at North Newton and my son had to come and get me.'

'A dead body, Mr Fletcher,' replied Mary, her voice flat. 'In the old peat workings opposite Ashcott station.'

Took the wind out of his sails, did that.

'They never said.'

'Can we go inside?' she asked.

'Yes, of course.'

'You two can go.' Mary was speaking over the jangling of keys as Fletcher unlocked the front door of the office. 'Get over to Ashcott and join the house to house team.'

Fletcher was maybe ten years older than me. That put him right on retirement age, or thereabouts. Grey hair was poking out from under his bobble hat. He kicked off his boots inside the door.

'Do we need to—?'

'It's just my fishing boots, don't worry.'

'How long have you worked for Avalon Peat?' I asked. Mary was still outside, talking to the uniformed officers.

'All my life. I started in 1936, aged fifteen. It wasn't Avalon Peat back then. Petfu it was, then it was bought by Fisons. Now we're Avalon. Something like that. I lost track of all the changes over the years.'

'What happened during the war?' I asked, more out of idle curiosity than anything else.

'Reserved occupation. Peat was fuel in those days.'

I nodded. 'How long have you got left before you retire?'

'I go at the end of March.'

'Mr Fletcher,' said Mary, appearing in the doorway. 'We're investigating the murder of Andrew Bucknall.'

'Andrew?'

'You know him?'

Fletcher sat down behind a desk. 'Everyone knows Andrew. He worked for us for a while, but it didn't last.'

'Third field over from the old level crossing,' I said. 'He was found by a dog walker following the old railway line this morning.'

'We haven't worked those fields since the fifties.' Fletcher looked up. 'Was he in the water?'

'Face down in the reeds.'

'Some of those trenches were dug in steps, so you get reeds around the margins. Up to ten feet deep, some of them.'

'When was the last time you saw Andrew?'

'A while ago. Last summer, maybe. I don't tend to get over that way these days. We're working the fields around here now.'

'What about in 1962?' I asked.

'We were cutting peat by hand back then, the fields east of here mainly.' He hesitated. 'You're talking about the little boy that went missing, ended up in the nuclear bunker?'

'Paul Bromfield.'

'I remember that, yes.'

'Andrew confessed to his murder.'

'Wasn't him, though, was it? He was harmless. Everyone knew it wasn't him, except you lot.'

'How often did you see him?'

'Most days. He'd just be hanging around the railway. Sometimes you'd see him in the sidings, walking along the canal, or even out in the peat fields. He never did any harm. That was back in the days when there were loads of us, cutting the peat by hand. We'd cut the turves, about the size of a breeze block, then he'd help us stack them for drying. That's when we gave him a job, but all he wanted to do was work on our narrow-gauge railway, and when we said he couldn't he just didn't turn up one day and that was that. Lost interest. That was back in the good old days when peat was used as fuel. Now it's used as fertiliser, so we just dig it out with machines and bag it up.'

'Can you remember where you were the day Paul was taken?'

It might seem like an odd question, but to local people at least, it's one of those events you just remember, no matter how hard you might try to forget it. A bit like the moon landing. Everyone can tell you where they were that day.

'I'd been out in a field over Westhay with Ken Birch. He's dead now. We saw all the activity on the railway line, but didn't know what it was. Heard about it when I got to the pub. Then it was weeks of your lot out every day looking for him.' He looked Mary up and down. 'You'll have been too young to remember it.'

'I was at school, but I remember enough, the horror of it.'

'We did our bit,' said Fletcher. 'Checked all the peat workings, stuff like that. Poor little bugger.'

'So, there's no one working over at Ashcott now?' asked Mary.

'No. We shut down all workings south of the drain when the railway closed.'

I left Mary asking the usual questions: did you see anything, know of any reason why someone might wish to harm Andrew, etc. etc. She'd need formal permission for a search of the fields too.

I was starting to like being a consultant, spared all the mundane tasks that come with being a police officer. And there are mundane tasks. Lots of them.

The post mortem would be another. Mary could go on her own to that.

Poring over Andrew's trainspotting notebooks too. Pages and pages of numbers, apparently random to most of us, but each corresponded to a locomotive or carriage that had passed through Ashcott station that summer of 1962.

Fletcher was showing Mary out of the office.

'How many staff on the payroll now?' I asked, when they stepped out into the winter sunshine.

'Forty,' replied Fletcher. 'Including the part-timers and lorry drivers.'

'Any of them ex-Navy?'

◆ ◆ ◆

I made my excuses after that. Having my own car on hand helped.

'The post mortem's at five,' Mary said.

'I'll leave you to it, if that's all right. I saw enough in the peat field.'

She couldn't really argue with that. Didn't bother trying. There'd been some bruising around Andrew's mouth, but no doubt the pathologist would confirm in due course. And there'd be photos in the appendices to his report.

'What time tomorrow?'

'I'll see you at Bridgwater at ten,' I replied.

That gave me a whole evening to myself. To think.

It's a dangerous business when a police officer thinks too much. An investigation is about finding the evidence and going where it takes you. Thinking leads to assumptions and half-baked theories, the risk being that you then try to find the evidence to support them. I've seen it happen before. Time and time again, actually. Some former colleagues even going to great lengths to *find* the evidence, if you know what I mean.

They made the same mistake in 1962; believed Andrew's confession and then wasted six weeks trying to find the evidence to back it up.

I got back to the flat just as Shirley was closing up the post office; didn't feel able to turn down her offer of supper. There was enough fish pie left for two, apparently, if I fancied it.

Actually, I didn't want to turn it down.

I don't remember when it was, but somewhere along the way I lost sight of the fact that life goes on, even for a police officer. I don't even remember which case it was now; we'd got a guilty verdict, then came the inevitable piss-up to celebrate, and I got home late to find I'd lost Shirley.

She'd left a note with the solicitor's letter, though, which was a nice touch.

Not a mistake I intend to make again.

And that's assuming this really is the second chance I'm hoping it is.

It's late now and I'm sitting in my deckchair, staring at the pictures on the wall.

It was a nice evening, we talked a lot, but you'll forgive me if I leave it at that. When there's anything to report I'll let you know. All right?

I've been thinking a lot about Operation Hurricane. Sharp and his team are focusing on that side of it, working their way through the naval personnel, but I can't get rid of the feeling that one of them with an axe to grind is unlikely to take it out on one of their own, unless it was some petty grievance, some incident on board HMS *Plym*. I can't see that either, because if that was the case, why kidnap Simon Horsey?

Why the trail of evidence pointing to the Blue Danube?

So, we come back to the bomb itself.

And something John Bromfield said to me when we were sitting on the Chilton Polden bunker.

Chapter Thirty

Mary was coming out of the post office when I walked around the corner just before nine-thirty the following morning.

Shirley opened for newspapers for a couple of hours on a Sunday, usually put some croissants in the oven too. One of them was sticking out of Mary's mouth.

'Morning,' she said, spraying crumbs everywhere.

'I thought we said the police station at ten?'

'There's a croissant left if you fancy it.'

'I had some cornflakes.'

'You did well to miss the PM.' Mary shuddered. 'This is the first thing I've had to eat since.'

I waited.

'There was some petechial haemorrhaging, so a hand had been across Andrew's mouth for some time, restricting his breathing. Bruising to match. And what looked like boot prints where he'd been kicked. Throat cut from left to right, so a right-handed killer. Unusually sharp blade too, a razor possibly. Definitely murder and the time stands: between eight and ten.' She curled her lip. 'I arrived at just the wrong time.'

'I can imagine.'

'There were some boot prints at the scene and they're being compared to the ones we got at the Pawlett bunker. Apart from that, there wasn't a lot going on at the station, so I thought I'd come and get you, save a bit of time.'

'I just need a word with Shirley,' I said, opening the front door of the shop.

Shirley was standing behind the counter, shuffling piles of Sunday papers. She looked up as I entered. 'She's nice. Speaks very highly of you.'

'She's just here to keep an eye on me, I think. Keep me out of trouble.'

She looked relieved. I think.

'It's nice to see my old Bob back again. The man I married.'

'No messages for me?'

'Were you expecting any?'

'From Angela. She was supposed to meet me yesterday,' I said. 'The Little Chef at Farrington Gurney at ten, but I had to go early. I thought she might come here.' I grimaced. 'It was the body in the peat field.'

'She didn't come in the shop, if she did.'

'See you later then.'

'I'm doing a roast chicken. Christine's coming over with Rufus. Usual time.'

'Will there be—?'

Shirley rolled her eyes. 'Yes, there'll be bread sauce.'

'Wouldn't miss it for the world.'

Mary had finished her croissant, was standing on the pavement, brushing the crumbs off her pullover. 'Where to?' she asked.

'Did you get an address for Evan Williams over at Burnham?'

'I thought we were supposed to be investigating the murder of Andrew Bucknall?'

'We are.'

'I have got an address, in that case.'

'He used to run the HMS *Plym* veterans' association, until it disbanded. Then I'd like to go and see Eric Hall's bagman again, Jack Welshman.'

'*Bagman*.' Mary shook her head. 'There's a term you don't hear much these days. I suppose I'm your bagman?'

'I thought you were my chaperone?'

'Nothing anyone said about you is true, Bob. You do know that.'

'It was, once. People change. Rarely for the better, but it does happen.'

She was fishing her car keys out of her pocket. 'We'll take my car. No point in taking two everywhere.'

Bollocks.

◆ ◆ ◆

It was one of those Victorian villas, with high ceilings and picture rails. An airtight front porch, judging by the sound the internal door made when it was opened, but you'd probably need that when the wind was sandblasting the front of the house.

Even the brickwork was beginning to show signs of it. The front hedge was starting to lean with the prevailing wind.

There was a scaffolding tower at the side of the house, a rope around the chimney. Must've had a few tiles off.

The front gate had been newly painted, all the same.

The man was still in his dressing gown. Balding, with wire-framed glasses and a greying moustache.

'Who is it?' he asked, without opening the front door.

I let Mary deal with the formalities, her warrant card coming in handy again.

'That's the living room,' he said, gesturing to a door. 'I'll just go and throw some clothes on.'

A large bay window overlooked the front garden, the lawn appearing more like a sand dune, but then we were only a hundred yards or so from the beach.

I took the opportunity to look at the photographs on display, some on the wall, others either side of a carriage clock on the mantelpiece.

There was a photograph of a much younger Evan Williams in naval uniform, mounted in a silver frame on top of a chest of drawers behind an armchair. Black and white, taken during the war, probably. An officer, clearly, but naval insignia was a mystery to me.

'Is that the *Plym*?' asked Mary. She was staring at a photograph on the wall, above a glass-fronted display cabinet.

'K271,' I said.

'That is her, then.'

'Sorry about that,' said Williams, closing the living room door behind him. 'Now, how can I help?'

'We wanted to ask you about HMS *Plym*,' I said.

'I was the First Lieutenant, second in command. I joined the ship when she was commissioned, left after the war,' he said, lowering himself into the armchair. 'Became a maths teacher after that.'

'Do you remember John Bromfield?'

'Yes, he went on to captain the ship in the fifties. Had the dubious honour of sailing her to her doom. That was how he put it, anyway. I saw him once or twice at reunion do's in London and he came to a couple of committee meetings.'

'I'm sorry to tell you that he died a few days ago. Took his own life.'

'I'm not surprised to hear that. Very sorry but not surprised. After what happened to his son.'

'We understand the association just fizzled out?'

'People get old, die. Memories fade. It becomes less important over time. Sad, but that's the way it is. We were lucky that we didn't have fallen comrades to remember. And lots of the lads had served on other ships and were members of their associations as well.'

'Are you still in touch with any of them?'

'Not really. I'm still a member of the Atlantic Convoy Association, a lot of the individual groups got rolled into that.'

'Where were you in 1962?' I asked.

'Here. I was deputy head at St Dunstan's. The school was in Grove Road then.' He took a deep breath. 'I know what you're going to ask; what I remember about the disappearance of John Bromfield's son.'

'Paul.'

'Tragic. I do remember it, yes. We took boarders back in those days and we had parents on the phone night and day wanting reassurance their boys were all right.'

I glanced around the room, looking for a copy of the *County Gazette*; couldn't see one. 'Would it surprise you to learn that Paul Bromfield's disappearance seems to have been connected to Operation Hurricane, the nuclear test when the *Plym* was destroyed? Clues left at the scene, and the scene of a second kidnapping only a few days ago.'

'A second kidnapping? I must've missed that.'

'A nine-year-old boy was found alive and well down a different nuclear bunker, just west of Pawlett. The boy was Bill Horsey's grandson.'

'Chief?'

'Chief Petty Officer Bill Horsey, that's right.'

'We brought a sub to the surface and were exchanging fire, our forward gun turret took a direct hit. He went in, got everybody out, then went back in and carried on firing the damn thing.

They surrendered pretty sharpish after that. He should've got a gallantry medal.'

'He never said.'

'Bill wouldn't.' Williams leaned forward, turned the gas tap and pressed the pilot light, holding it down until the fire next to his chair lit with that familiar whoosh. 'If you're speaking to him again, do pass on my best wishes.'

'Was there ever any ill feeling towards John Bromfield after Operation Hurricane? After the ship was destroyed. Any remarks made, threats, anything like that among association members?'

'Certainly not. It wasn't his fault. He was just doing his job. And he was a good captain, as I understand it. Like I say, I didn't serve under him – I'd retired by the time he took over the ship – but those who did had nothing but praise for him.'

I picked up a photograph from an oak trunk at the back of the room; several older men in dinner jackets, raising glasses towards the camera. I recognised Evan Williams, sitting in the middle.

'That was our farewell dinner,' he said. 'At the Army and Navy Club in London.'

'Was John Bromfield there?'

'No. We only saw him at one committee meeting after his son was . . .' He clenched his fist, slammed it down on the arm of his chair. 'I've got a lever arch file somewhere with the meeting minutes and other stuff in it. You're welcome to take it if you think it might be useful.'

'Thank you,' said Mary.

'Did veterans of the operation ever talk about it?' I asked.

'Only in general terms. Some of it had been reported at the time anyway, that there'd been a test and it'd been successful, that Britain was now a nuclear power. We knew the bomb had been on the *Plym*, obviously, and that she'd just disappeared.'

I know what I'm doing. I'm asking Williams to confirm what I think, looking for someone or something to corroborate my theory about what's happened. The *Plym* left Sheerness with eighty on board, and there were over fifteen hundred on the other ships, including scientists.

It's going to take Sharp and his team weeks to wade through all the naval personnel one by one; weeks we haven't got, if that message Shirley took is to be believed.

So, now we begin again.

'John Bromfield believed that his son's death was his fault,' I said. 'That he was killed because of what he'd done.'

'He hadn't done anything, except his duty. Everyone in the Navy would've understood that.'

◆ ◆ ◆

'Talk about leading a witness,' said Mary, when we stepped out into the road. 'You practically put the words in his mouth.'

'Sharp's wasting his time,' I said. 'There's no way any naval personnel would've done that to John Bromfield's son. He was part of Operation Hurricane just the same as they were, and they were all following orders. Just cogs in a much bigger wheel. We need to look elsewhere.'

'Any ideas?' She looked at me, quizzically.

'I have, as it happens,' I replied. 'Let's go and see Welshman first, though. See what he makes of this new information.'

'They'll have had other suspects, apart from Andrew Bucknall,' said Mary. 'Even if they never made another arrest.'

'Let's hope so.'

Chapter Thirty-One

We never got to Welshman's flat in Langport. Mary rang in and it turns out Sharp's made an arrest, but I'm not holding my breath. He's still barking up the wrong tree, so my guess is it will be the wrong person for the wrong reasons. I may be mistaken though; it happens often enough.

Let's hope so.

'He's in with his solicitor,' Sharp said, when we arrived at Bridgwater police station half an hour later.

The incident room was full, even though it was a Sunday afternoon, the team apparently bigger now it had become a murder investigation.

You and I knew it was a murder investigation already, of course, but poor little Paul Bromfield seems to have been forgotten in all the excitement of Andrew Bucknall's killing. *Excitement* is probably the wrong word, but you know what I mean.

The first seventy-two hours and all that, the majority of the team redirected to the live murder case. Yes, Sharp really said that.

Live murder case.

Words fail me.

I'm sitting at the back of the incident room watching all the chatter, the back slapping, thumbs up, grins. They'll be off to the pub to celebrate next, and that's before the interview has even taken place.

I remember Jack Welshman's workshop and I'm starting to feel like that one little screw that's left behind when he's put the clock back together. Best forgotten about, stick it in a dish on the windowsill and move on.

As far as they're all concerned, I made my contribution when I unravelled what this was all about and now I'm surplus to requirements, getting in the way, keeping Mary from doing real police work instead of babysitting me.

We'll see.

His name is Steven Porter, and he lives in Meare, which is about a mile or so north of Ashcott station. He was part of Operation Mosaic, which was basically more British atomic bomb tests in 1956; a cook on board HMS *Concord*, stationed fifty miles west of the Montebello Islands for weather reporting purposes, so well out of the danger zone. All very interesting, possibly, but what's got Sharp hot under the collar is the fact that Porter is now an active member of the local branch of the Campaign for Nuclear Disarmament. And he works in the kitchen at the Railway Inn, just yards from Ashcott station; has done since he left the Navy in 1961.

Circumstantial, you might think. And you'd be right.

You might also be wondering why any of that would necessarily persuade him to kidnap and murder the son of the captain of HMS *Plym*. I know I am.

He was interviewed during the original investigation, and I've read his statement. Saw nothing; heard nothing. Never made it on to Eric Hall's radar either.

He was on my list and I'd have spoken to him sooner or later.

No, there must be something else.

The interview is taking place downstairs. It'll be tape recorded, and there's a video feed to the room next door. I'm on my way down there, to get a spot in front of the monitor before the scrum starts.

'Where are you off to, Bob?' asked Sharp.

'Just nipping to the loo.'

◆ ◆ ◆

It was a tight squeeze, but I got a seat at the front.

There were two screens, side by side. One camera looked down at where the police officers would be sitting, the other looking down at Porter and his solicitor on the other side of the table.

They were sitting in silence. Waiting.

They'd have had their conference in a side room, where there are no cameras. Or bugs. Not these days anyway. Not with the new Police and Criminal Evidence Act.

Porter was a large man, carried it well, although there was a bit of a beer belly and his shirt was too tight. Bald, greying at the sides, a pair of glasses on the table in front of him.

I didn't know the solicitor, but he was local, from Bridgwater; even bothered to change into his suit on a Sunday afternoon.

I was still watching the screen when the door opened and Sharp walked in to the interview room with Mary. They sat down opposite Porter and his solicitor.

I'd wondered where she'd got to, but her presence made perfect sense now. To me, at least.

Porter must have had a history of sex offences, post 1962, because there was no mention of them on the Bromfield file. Child sex offences, if he was a suspect in the Bromfield case and the disappearance of Simon Horsey, although neither boy had been interfered with.

It's an old tactic, interviews with sex offenders undertaken by female officers; puts the suspect on the back foot immediately.

I'm still not convinced. Paul Bromfield was taken because of who his father was and what he'd done. I'd go as far as to speculate it was opportunistic, the kidnapper just happened to be on the same train, saw father and son together and took his chance.

The murmuring in the room died down when Sharp spoke. He introduced himself and Mary, invited Porter and his solicitor to state their full names for the tape and then reminded Porter of his rights. God bless PACE.

I'm surprised Sharp is doing the interview himself, to be honest, although that's more about taking the credit for cracking the case, I expect.

There was muttering behind me from someone standing at the back of the room. 'What the fuck's he doing here?' Aimed at me almost certainly, but I didn't recognise the voice; probably irritated I'd got a seat and he hadn't.

It's standing room only, as you might imagine.

'Where were you on the twenty-eighth of August 1962, Steven?' asked Sharp.

'How the hell am I supposed to remember that?'

'It was the day Paul Bromfield was snatched from Ashcott station. In my experience, everyone living locally remembers where they were on that day.'

Nice one, even for Sharp.

'I'd have been in the pub, wouldn't I,' replied Porter.

'At that time in the morning?'

'We used to serve a bit of food back then and I'd have been getting ready for lunch, buttering bread for sandwiches, stuff like that. It was August, the holidays.'

'How long would that have taken you?'

'Most of the morning.'

'Did you walk down to the station for a last look at the steam train before the line closed?'

'No. I'm not interested in trains. Never have been.'

The solicitor was scribbling furiously in his notebook.

'Only, we have a statement from a new witness who says that she saw a man on the platform as the train left.'

The solicitor looked up. 'This is the witness who was nine years old at the time?'

'That's right,' replied Sharp.

'Hardly a reliable witness, and my understanding is that she doesn't give a description of this mysterious figure she *says* she saw in the swirling smoke.'

'Nevertheless,' Sharp retorted. 'She saw someone and I'm asking your client if that person was him.'

'It wasn't,' said Porter, emphatically.

There's a surprise.

'Were you aware of the Royal Observer Corps bunker at Chilton Polden?'

'Yes. Everyone round here was.'

'Were you a member of the ROC?'

No, he wasn't. Even I know that one. If he had been he'd have been much higher up my list.

'No. I applied to join, but they wouldn't have me.'

'And why was that?'

'They said my membership of CND was inconsistent with it. They were very nice about it, they just said thanks, but no thanks.' Porter shrugged. 'It was no big deal.'

'When was that?'

'After I left the Navy, so early '62, maybe.'

News to me. It shows he was aware of the ROC and the bunker; had a chip on his shoulder too. Possibly.

'Did the ROC ever meet in your pub?' asked Sharp.

'They met at the Edgar Lamb. Still do, as far as I know.'

'What can you tell me about Operation Mosaic?'

'Not a huge amount. I was a cook on a ship miles away. There were five ships with meteorologists on board and we were stationed all around the restricted zone, reporting on the weather. That was it, really. The worst part was it kept me away from home for eighteen months.'

'Did you see the tests?'

'We were allowed up on deck to watch them. There were two.'

'And I'm guessing the experience shaped your attitude to nuclear weapons?'

'If you're asking whether that's why I became an active member of CND then the answer is yes. I'm one of the few people who's seen one of these explosions up close. Make no mistake about it, those two tests that I saw were small ones. The mushroom cloud still reached twenty thousand feet.'

'And you're still subject to the Official Secrets Act,' said Sharp.

'Sod the bloody Official Secrets Act. They can prosecute me, then it'll all come out in court, won't it, with a public gallery full of reporters.'

'Have you heard of HMS *Plym*?'

'Of course I have. Everyone in the Navy knew what happened to her.'

'Did you ever serve on the *Plym*?'

Sharp must know the answer to that question, surely? He'd have Porter's service record.

'I joined the Navy in 1954, after she was blown up.'

Maybe not, then.

Porter folded his arms. 'Join the Navy, see the world, blow it up.'

Sharp looked at Mary, nodded.

'D'you have an interest in children, Steven?' she asked.

'That was all a mistake,' he replied, his face reddening.

'You pleaded guilty.'

'That's what my solicitor said I should do. I'd be convicted if I went not guilty, so plead guilty and get a lighter sentence, that's what he said.'

'You were committed to Taunton Crown Court for sentence and received six months' imprisonment, suspended for two years.'

'It was just possession of images.'

'Of children,' said Mary.

'Did you take pictures of Paul Bromfield?' asked Sharp, abruptly.

'I never took Paul Bromfield, never saw Paul Bromfield.'

'My client has made his position clear in relation to the abduction of Paul Bromfield,' said the solicitor. 'You are also aware that he has an alibi for the material time in August 1962.'

Sharp was going through the motions now, putting to him what he had to put to him; the allegations. I leaned across the officer sitting next to me, asked for a piece of paper. Then I scribbled a note, looked over my shoulder, handing it to the officer blocking the door.

'Give that to Sharp, will you?'

He started reading the note.

'Now,' I said.

I turned back to the screen, in time to watch Mary shuffling the papers on the table in front of her, while Sharp put to Porter the material details of the abduction of Simon Horsey. Surprise, surprise, Porter denied that too.

Then the door opened, the officer leaning in and handing my note to Sharp. He looked at it, then passed it to Mary.

'Have you ever been to Australia?' she asked.

'No.'

'What about during Operation Mosaic?'

'We never went ashore the whole time we were down there, never went in sight of the mainland.' Even Porter was frowning now.

'Do you have any Australian friends?'

'No.'

'Family?'

'No.'

Sharp glanced up at the camera, rolled his eyes at me. Then he turned back to Porter. 'Did you know Andrew Bucknall?'

'Everybody knew Andrew. He came in the pub sometimes, when it was quiet.'

'Were you friends with him?'

'Not friends, no.'

'Why did you kill him?'

'I didn't.'

I'd seen enough, stood up and left the room, squeezing past the officers standing against the back wall. Of course Porter would know the peat fields, they were on his doorstep and he had a dog. And of course he was going to deny slitting Andrew's throat.

Wouldn't you?

Chapter Thirty-Two

'There you are,' said Mary, sitting down next to me at the back of the incident room a few minutes later.

I'd crept in, past the open bottles of cheap fizzy plonk on the table at the front, and had been sitting at the back of the room, watching the scene unfold. Porter's denials hadn't dampened spirits. Neither had the fact that there didn't seem to be any direct evidence to connect him to anything at all. Not Simon Horsey's kidnapping or the murders of Paul Bromfield and Andrew Bucknall.

They had twenty-four hours from the time of Porter's arrest to find something, otherwise they'd have to release him.

And they wouldn't find anything. Because it wasn't him.

'What did you think of his interview?' asked Mary. 'I'm guessing you saw it.'

'It wasn't him,' I replied, matter of fact.

'He fits the—'

'So do any number of people involved in the nuclear bomb tests, in that case.'

'Yes, but—'

Sharp appeared at the front of the room, clapped his hands, silencing any further protest from Mary. 'We nicked him at eleven-forty-seven, so we've got until the same time tomorrow to find something or we're going to have to release him. What have they found at his house?'

'Nothing yet, guv,' said a voice at the front.

'Tell them I'll be on my way over there when we've finished here. And they'd better have found something by then.'

'Yes, guv.'

I do hope Porter hasn't got any primroses or bluebells in his garden. Sounds like that would be enough for Sharp in the mood he's in.

'And what was all that crap about Australia, Bob?'

I was wondering when he'd get round to that; hadn't expected him to do it front of everyone, though. Sitting at the back of a crowded room is all well and good, until everyone turns around and stares at you. Then there's no escape.

Time to stick my neck out. 'It's not him,' I said.

After all, what have I got to lose?

'And why does the great Bob Willis think it's not Steven Porter?' Sharp folded his arms. If he tried to hide his exasperation, he failed dismally. He was probably regretting getting me that job on the Cold Case Unit now as well.

I stood up. There was nowhere to hide anyway.

'He was a serviceman,' I said. 'They were doing their duty. All of the veterans I've spoken to have said the same thing. And that'll apply equally to the British and Australian service personnel who took part. They were doing their jobs and knew that John Bromfield was just doing his.'

'Porter's a member of CND.'

'And there was me thinking CND were pacifists.'

'All right. If our killer isn't ex-Navy, who the bloody hell is he?'

'Eight a.m. on the third of October 1952, the Blue Danube was detonated in the forward hold of HMS *Plym*. Weeks, they'd waited for the right weather. They needed an easterly wind to take the fallout away from mainland Australia, out over the Pacific, out of harm's way. And all went according to plan, initially at least. The mushroom cloud reached three thousand feet in three seconds. But when it got to ten thousand feet the wind changed direction and they watched in horror as a strong westerly wind at the higher altitude blew the cloud right over north-western Australia.'

'You are joking.'

'Radioactive fallout was deposited over an area sixty miles wide and two hundred miles long; most of it uninhabited, but not all of it.'

'They kept that quiet, didn't they?' A voice at the front of the room.

'Where did you get this information, Bob?' demanded Sharp.

'It was given in response to the article in the *County Gazette*. And that guaranteed anonymity. We've had this conversation before.'

Sharp gritted his teeth. 'So, you're saying our killer's going to be Australian.'

'Or have some connection to that part of Australia, at least,' I replied. 'Maybe married an Australian, had to watch them die of cancer. I spoke to a consultant psychologist who said the manner of Paul Bromfield's death will be significant, that he died slowly; wasted away, effectively.'

'In a nuclear bunker.' That same voice again.

'So, what d'you suggest we do with Steven Porter?' asked Sharp.

'Look for any connection to that part of Australia,' I said. I was making my way to the door, albeit slowly. 'And if you don't find one, let him go.'

'Brilliant.'

'After that, get on to the Home Office for a list of all visas granted to anyone from that part of Australia; Somerset House in London for UK death certificates of Australian citizens issued between 1952 and 1962. Marriage certificates too.'

'But surely the local population were kept in the dark about what happened?' Sharp was scowling at me. 'They wouldn't have known about the test.'

'They did. They even knew which ships were involved,' I said. 'The arrival of the *Plym* in Fremantle was plastered all over the front page of the *West Australian* newspaper. They even had journalists camped on a hill watching for the explosion. The buggers broke the news before the government put out a press release announcing that Britain was now a nuclear power.'

'And where d'you think you're going?'

'I've got roast chicken waiting for me.'

I'd almost reached the door at the top of the stairs when I heard footsteps running along the corridor behind me.

'Where are you *really* going, Bob?' asked Mary, her hand on the door, stopping me opening it.

'I thought I'd get out while the going's good,' I said.

'Sharp's barking orders left, right and centre in there.' Mary shook her head. 'It doesn't help it's a Sunday. What time tomorrow?'

'I'll meet you here at nine. Just remember that message the killer left when he rang the post office,' I said. '*And so we begin again*. Remind Sharp.'

◆ ◆ ◆

It was dark by the time I got back to my flat, but there was a light on in the post office.

Shirley would've closed at lunchtime, surely?

I left my car in the car park at the back, walked around the corner to the front and looked in the window, between the handwritten postcards offering this and that for sale that had been Sellotaped to the inside of the glass. Shirley was leaning on the counter, her head in her hands.

I tried the door, but it was locked, so knocked loudly.

She saw me, ran over and opened the door.

'Thank God you're here, Bob,' she said. She looked up and down the road, then closed the door behind me, locked it. 'I had Angela's father in here earlier, looking for you. Well, actually, he was looking for her. She hasn't been home since she left for work the day before yesterday. She went into her office on Friday evening for a couple of hours, but they haven't seen her since either. She was due in yesterday and today, apparently.'

'She said she was going to ring in sick, so I'm not surprised she hasn't been into work. Has he reported her missing?'

'Not yet. I told him to, but he said she's done it before. They thought she'd met someone because she'd stayed out a couple of nights last week. I didn't have the heart to tell him she was staying with you, not after what happened to Lizzie.' Shirley picked up the answerphone, placed it on the counter. 'Then I nip down here to get some peas and there's this,' she said, pressing play.

'*Seems to me the best way to get a story in the news these days is to kidnap a journalist*,' said the message. '*What d'you think, Bob?*'

The voice was male, muffled, a hint of a Brummie accent, possibly, but that was easily put on.

'It's the same voice as last time,' said Shirley. 'Definitely.'

He's got Angela.

Fuck.

My fault too. That article on the front page of the *Gazette*. Her scoop. It was bad enough that it got her in trouble with her editor, but this?

Fuck.

There's a cold sweat in the small of my back and I'm suddenly fighting the urge to vomit. It's Lizzie all over again. The sting operation that got her killed had been my idea, not that I've admitted that before. Not even to myself. I've always been careful to say *we* had this idea, when actually it was me. And now Angela's been taken because I put her in the firing line with that article.

I used her.

Used her to print an article that gave John Bromfield the cover to tell me what I needed to know.

I'm glad there are no mirrors in the post office because I really don't want to look at myself right now.

You arsehole, Bob.

'Ring the number they gave you,' I said.

'I've done it,' replied Shirley. 'You found that little boy, Bob. You'd better go and find Angela.'

I nodded, turned for the door.

Chapter Thirty-Three

I was in hospital for Lizzie's funeral. A shattered left knee and elbow, but it still felt like the easy way out. Easier than facing her parents.

Shirley always said that I'd take the easy way out of any situation. I like to think that was *the old Bob*, but I'm about to find out.

I'm sitting in my car outside Angela's house, summoning up the courage to face her parents. It took me far too long to visit them after Lizzie's death, and then to find they didn't blame me for it, that was too much.

Two nights Angela's been gone; that's if she was taken when she left my flat the night before last. My guess – let me rephrase that – my *hope* is that she's somewhere similar to where Paul Bromfield and Simon Horsey were found. If that's the case then she's got time. I've got time.

On the other hand, there's Andrew Bucknall now, isn't there?

Throat cut.

It's a nice house on the hill, steps up to the front door. Angela's father must've spotted my car and opened the front door before I reached the top step. Looking out of the bay window, probably, waiting for his daughter to come home.

And come home she will, if I've got anything to do with it.

'You've not seen her, I suppose, Bob?' he asked.

'Not since the night before last,' I replied.

'We've tried her friends.' He shrugged. 'We even thought she might've met someone, because she stayed out a couple of times this week.'

'She was staying at my place,' I said. 'We've been working on something together. I slept on the sofa.' I thought I'd better clarify that, just in case of any misunderstanding.

'Oh, right.'

I'd followed him into the front room, where his wife was sitting. The television was on in the background, the sound muted. She stood up.

'She was staying with Bob both nights,' he said, when his wife looked at him, pleading.

I should tell you their names, really. Keith and Lynn. Good people. Too good.

'We thought . . .' Lynn's voice tailed off.

'Was it this you were working on?' asked Keith, picking up a copy of the *Gazette* from the coffee table, the newspaper folded to reveal Angela's front page article in all its glory. 'She said it was to do with the Paul Bromfield case and finding that little boy, Simon Horsey.'

'It is.' I cleared my throat. 'Have you reported her missing yet?' I asked.

'Not yet,' replied Keith. 'We're not really sure she is missing.'

I asked them both to sit down, waited until they were, then told them about the message on the answerphone at the post office. I told them where we'd got to with the Bromfield case too, said it was thanks to Angela's article, left out the murder of Andrew Bucknall, though; that was probably too much information.

Better to keep it to what they need to know.

Lynn ran upstairs, sobbing.

'Can I use your phone?' I asked.

'In the hall,' replied Keith. He looked shell-shocked, staring at the photos on the mantelpiece. I'd recognised the one of Lizzie, taken at the party to celebrate her promotion to sergeant. Angela was much younger in her picture, still in school uniform.

I rang Bridgwater, spoke to Sharp, who was still there. No point in poncing about with a routine missing person report.

There's nothing routine about Angela's disappearance.

Keith had followed his wife up the stairs, and they stayed there for the duration of my call, only appearing on the landing when I put the phone down.

'What happens now?' asked Keith.

'A full search. An alert will go out for her car, the Observer Corps will be paged to check the bunkers, and I've reminded them about the decommissioned ones this time. Officers are on the way here to get as much information from you as they can, friends, family, stuff like that.'

'We can't lose another daughter,' said Lynn. She'd tried to come down the stairs but slumped back on to the top step.

'They'll be checking everywhere, Lynn,' I said. 'Water tanks, old air raid shelters. No stone will be—'

I nearly said it; stopped myself just in time.

'Can I see her room?' I asked.

'Yes, of course,' replied Keith.

I managed to squeeze past Lynn, still sitting at the top of the stairs, and followed Keith into Angela's bedroom, one of those floral tiles stuck on the outside of the door announcing it was Angela's room, a sign underneath it saying *Keep Out*.

I'm not sure what I'm looking for, really. She'll have been doing her own research on the case, of course she will, and there might be something useful lying around. You never know.

A single bed against the wall, a wardrobe, chest of drawers. I didn't feel inclined to rummage through her clothes, not with her father watching.

'Can you check the drawers, Keith?' I asked.

Just clothes, as it turned out.

I looked in all the usual places. Under the bed, mattress, on top of the wardrobe. There was a notebook on the top of her dressing table, but nothing in it that made any sense to me, not at first glance.

'Can I keep this?' I asked, showing it to Keith.

'Of course.'

There was a knock at the front door. 'Police, Mrs Harper,' said a voice when Lynn opened it. I stepped out on to the landing in time to see three officers file in – two in uniform, followed by Mary.

That was a relief, for two reasons. Firstly, it meant that Sharp was taking Angela's disappearance seriously. Secondly, and more importantly, it would keep Mary out of my hair.

Shackled to Mary I have to play by the rules, but I'm not a serving officer, am I?

And there are no rules. Not for me.

Keith took me to one side on the landing, out of view from below. 'I know you'll blame yourself for this, Bob,' he said. 'But don't. It's not your fault. She's a crime reporter and loves it. She'd have been reporting on this story with or without you, and if that's what has put her at risk, then she'd have taken that risk all the same. I know she would.'

I gestured to Mary on my way out of the house and she followed me out into the darkness.

'Sharp's doing everything he can,' she said. 'He's got the ACC to call the RAF, put the Observer Corps lot on alert. We've got uniformed officers checking all the abandoned bunkers, local farms. We're looking for her car. We've got patrol cars following all her routes home from your place. Plus, we're doing everything else you suggested to try to find who is doing this. If we can find him, we find Angela.'

'I know.'

◆ ◆ ◆

Police stations leak like sieves. A few quid here, a few quid there, and the local hack will get a tip off something's going on.

Another message from the killer, another kidnapping.

There was a throng of journalists hanging around outside the car park when I arrived at Bridgwater. Well, I say *throng*; three, but that's enough in my experience.

I spotted Ray Keenan from the *Gazette*, leaning against the wall, lighting a cigarette, the pockets of his waxed jacket bulging as usual. He had the look of a man who'd rather be somewhere else, so he can't have known it was Angela.

'We're setting up a press conference for ten in the morning,' said Sharp, when I walked into the incident room. 'D'you think the parents will do it?'

'Yes,' I said.

He waved at someone sitting at a desk with a phone to their ear, then turned back to me. 'This isn't your fault, Bob.'

It is. And the fact that people feel the need to keep telling me it isn't just confirms it.

It was the same with Lizzie.

If I hadn't picked this case in the first place . . .

If I hadn't got Angela involved . . .

If I hadn't fed her that story . . .

If she hadn't managed to get it on the front page . . .

Sailors have a name for people like me. A Jonah.

It took me ten minutes to make sure that everything that could be done, was being done. The coastguard were out, checking the fort on the end of Brean Down; even cave rescue up on the Mendips had been called out. Everywhere underground was being checked.

Patrol cars were out, looking for Angela's car. Farmers were being asked to check water tanks, slurry pits.

I made myself a coffee, left it on the windowsill. It took me a moment, but I got there in the end; found something useful I could do.

I marched across the car park, grabbed Ray Keenan by the corduroy collar of his waxed jacket, pulled him out of earshot of the other journalists loitering with intent.

'What's going on, Bob?' he asked, dropping a cigarette in the gutter.

'What d'you know?'

'I got an anonymous tip,' he said. 'There's been a girl taken.'

'It's Angela.'

'You're joking.' Eyes wide now.

'Because of that fucking article I fed her. And you let her take the blame for it, you prick. You and I are going to have a talk about that later.'

'It wasn't my fault.'

'I want to see her desk, what she was working on.'

'Now?'

'You drive.'

◆ ◆ ◆

I can't help thinking Angela deserves better than this. Than us. Here we are, two of the men in her young life: a seedy, yes *seedy*, journalist and the broken-down old copper responsible for the death of her sister. Bitter with it. At least, I was. Not so much now, perhaps.

Both of us wondering whether what's happening to her is *our fault*.

And it is.

It's Ray's fault she took the flak for that article. Angela's a trainee, and he's her boss. Enough said.

And you know about my part in that article.

She's a bright kid, though. She'll have been working on something else, and I'd like to know what. After all, there's nothing else I can usefully do.

Keenan parked on the double yellow lines outside his office in St James Street, Taunton.

'I won't get a ticket at this time on a Sunday,' he mumbled, climbing out of the driver's seat.

There were lights on inside the office, journalists at work getting ready for the Monday morning edition.

'Did she ring in sick?' I was following Keenan around the back.

'No. I've not heard from her since Friday night. Her father rang a couple times to ask if I'd seen her, but I haven't. I just thought she'd be sulking, to be honest, wasn't expecting to see her until Monday.'

She's got a temper, has Angela. I found that out a few months ago when she caught up with me at Wincanton racecourse.

'Then she turned up here on Friday evening,' continued Keenan. 'Spent a few hours looking at the microfiche, printed off some stuff and left about one-thirty from what I can gather.'

'What stuff?'

'Old news articles from Australia, I think. She was still here when I left about midnight.' He was turning a key, the sign on the side door making it clear it was the staff entrance. 'I just thought she'd be back when she'd calmed down a bit,' he said, rolling his eyes.

Up the stairs, through a pair of doors at the top.

'That's her desk,' said Keenan. 'And this is mine.'

Open plan, either side of the partition. Keenan's desk was a mess, piles of paper, copies of old newspapers, a bin on the floor with more paper around it than in it.

Angela's bedroom had been tidy, and her desk was much the same, even though she'd left in a hurry by all accounts. There was a paper cup on its side, a trickle of coffee that had dried on the desk. An electric typewriter, still switched on.

'Did she take anything with her when she left?' I asked.

Keenan was craning his neck, watching me over the partition. 'Nope, she just took her coat off the back of her chair and walked out.'

'So, let me make sure I understand this correctly,' I said, fixing him with a cold stare. 'She's a trainee and you'd have approved that article before it went in. Then, for it to get on the front page, your editor-in-chief will have approved it as well.'

'He did.'

'And you let her take the fall for it?'

Keenan reddened and looked away.

'You bunch of wankers.'

Sounds like journalists have the same hierarchy as the police – take the credit and pass the buck.

I sat down on Angela's swivel chair, looked at the drawers either side of the desk, started opening each in turn.

Stationery, packet soups, the usual stuff you'd find in any office worker's desk. One drawer contained old notepads, full of her scribblings. I flicked through them one by one, but mostly it was coffee morning details, fetes, old notebooks from before she became a trainee crime reporter.

It looked like she'd spent her first couple of months down at Taunton Crown Court. There were a couple of inquests in there too.

Then came the drawer of personal stuff – if you know what I mean – but what caught my eye was the yellow cardboard underneath it, hidden from view, but not quite. It looked like a paper drawer liner at first glance, but I knew it wasn't, so I took hold of the edge and slid it out, managing to leave the rest of the contents untouched.

It felt creepy enough searching her bedroom.

A yellow file, marked *Australian articles.* I recognised her handwriting from the birthday card she'd sent me.

'What's that?' asked Keenan, standing up to get a better view over the partition.

'Never you mind,' I replied.

'That's the property of the *County Gazette*,' he protested, half-heartedly, I thought.

'It's evidence.'

Chapter Thirty-Four

Keenan dropped me back to my car, must've been gone eleven, and the police station was alive with activity. Patrol cars coming and going; dog vans too.

A few more journalists had congregated at the entrance to the car park, and I watched as Keenan checked to see whether he'd missed anything.

He hadn't, judging by the shaking heads.

I was at the bottom of the stairs when I heard the commotion at the top, the incident room door flying open and hitting the wall.

Sharp was halfway down the stairs before he noticed me standing at the bottom.

'They've found her car, Bob,' he said, when he reached the bottom. 'It's behind the Kentucky Fried Chicken on East Reach in Taunton. I'm on my way over there now.'

I followed the blue lights out of Bridgwater, lost them on the M5 before I got to Taunton, finally getting to the restaurant just as they were about to load Angela's car on to a flatbed lorry.

'There's no sign of her,' said Sharp, blocking my path to the car. 'No blood or anything like that.'

'I want to see for myself.'

Sharp turned, waved at the lorry driver, who had been about to start winching it up the ramp.

I stepped over the tow line that had been attached to the front of the little red Allegro, reached out to open the driver's door, but a scenes of crime officer wearing gloves opened it for me. The passenger compartment was lit by arc lamps that had been placed either side of the car.

'It's clean,' he said. 'I've searched it and there's nothing. It wasn't locked, so we think she came out of the restaurant, put her key in the lock and then—'

'I spoke to the manager,' interrupted Sharp. 'She came in the night before last, picked up a takeaway and then left just before they closed at two in the morning. It was quiet, and apart from staff clearing up, she was the last one in the car park.'

'There's no sign of a struggle,' continued the scenes of crime officer. 'I've checked all the usual places, but we'll take it to bits back at the lab tomorrow.'

'And we're extending the search to this area,' said Sharp. 'I've already rung the RAF and they're putting the Observer Corps on alert. We're extending it to Hampshire and Wiltshire as well.'

I turned for my car.

'Where will you be, Bob?' asked Sharp. 'In case I need you.'

◆ ◆ ◆

I got home just before two o'clock in the morning, made myself a cup of tea and sat down in my deckchair in the dark.

Angela is somewhere out there, curled up on a bed, cold. Deep underground, probably. But where?

She knows who's got her, knows why. She's not daft. I hope she doesn't do anything stupid all the same, doesn't try to wind him up, whoever he is.

She'll wait. Assuming she's got no food or water, just like Paul Bromfield, she's got a few days. And she knows I'll be looking for her; knows I'll have everyone else out looking for her.

There's a desk lamp on the floor next to my chair, so I flicked that on, reached down and picked up the folder of HMS *Plym* Association meeting minutes that Evan Williams had given me. For no other reason than I can't sleep, and my tea is sitting on the file I took from Angela's desk drawer.

Not terribly enlightening.

I found the two meetings John Bromfield had been to – March 1962 and then again in March 1964 – his name taking pride of place at the top of the list of attendees. The minutes were the usual crap, but under *Any Other Business* in March 1964 were the arrangements for their farewell dinner; the last before the association was wound up.

There was a *Date of Next Meeting*, oddly enough. Presumably that's when they made the decision to donate the remaining funds to a naval charity.

I could feel my eyes closing as I turned the page.

◆ ◆ ◆

You won't be surprised to learn that I didn't get a lot of sleep. It wasn't just because I was in the deckchair either. I kept waking up, wondering where Angela was. How she must be feeling; whether she was cold, hungry, thirsty. She's strong, of course she is, but we're into day three now.

She's got three to five without water. At best.

That was Paul Bromfield's fate, and I have to work on the basis the same fate awaits Angela. Unless we can find her.

I said *we* then, but it feels like it's down to me. And I'm not exactly Sherlock Holmes, am I? I think we've established that.

I missed the rush hour, and was sitting in my car on Southernhay in Exeter bright and early on Monday morning, waiting for the good doctor to arrive at her office. I know she likes to get to work at some ungodly hour. If I knew where she lived, I'd have knocked on her door in the middle of the night, so it's probably best I don't.

Strictly a professional relationship, you understand.

It was just gone seven when I saw her, walking along the lane from the cathedral, so she really is an early riser.

I caught up with her before she opened the front door of her office.

'You're up early, Bob,' she said, turning at the sound of my footsteps behind her.

'*Up* implies I've been to bed.'

'Like that, is it?'

It took me ten minutes or so to bring her up to speed with the investigation. I talked while she made the coffee, the sunrise hitting the top of the cathedral by the time I'd finished.

'And you say you've ruled out anyone in the Navy?' she asked, handing me a mug of strong, black coffee. 'No milk until the receptionist arrives, I'm afraid.'

'I have, but I'm not sure anyone else has.'

'Whoever he is, he's well organised, intelligent. Highly motivated. Could very well be military personnel.'

'Thanks.'

'How d'you feel about John Bromfield's suicide?' she asked, sitting down behind her desk.

I'm in the leather armchair again and it's starting to sound like another therapy session. 'He killed himself when he found out why his son was taken. He blamed himself.'

'And d'you blame yourself?'

'No.'

'You chose the case.'

'The Cold Case Unit would've got to it sooner or later, with or without me.'

'What about Angela?'

'Of course I blame myself for Angela. That's why I have to find her; why I'm here, asking for your help.'

She's mulling it over, I think. Most people would tell me at this point that Angela is a crime reporter and knew the risks. Even her father said that, but the good doctor is smarter than that. She also knows I'm not interested in hearing it.

'There's a lot I don't know,' she said, taking a slow, deliberate sip of coffee.

'Me too.'

'I don't think she's going to be underground. It's not about that anymore. The bunkers were nuclear, that was their relevance, and he knows you found Simon in the Pawlett bunker; he's not going to do that again. He's smarter than that.'

'So, we're wasting our time?'

'You are.' She shrugged. 'But then you have to check.'

I waited. She'd turned on her chair and was staring out of the window, seemingly watching office workers walking across Cathedral Green. Looking for her receptionist, hopefully, arriving with some milk.

'Angela's kidnapping isn't another test, Bob. This is the real thing. Simon Horsey was just a test. He knew full well the boy would be found. It was just a case of who by and how quickly. That was when he knew he'd found someone who'd help him.'

'Help him? Who?'

'You.' She spun round to face me. 'He's highly motivated. He wants the world to know what happened to someone very close to him, someone hurt by Operation Hurricane, who died in much the same way as Paul Bromfield. His wife, child, maybe even both; wasting away slowly. I knew about the bomb tests, they were announced officially at the time, but I had no idea the mushroom cloud blew over the Australian mainland. He wants that out in the open and he's banking on you helping him with that.'

'By catching him.'

'Exactly. It's a high-profile case now, if it wasn't before, and he's going to have his day in court; tell the whole world his story. Make the British government pay.'

'He doesn't need to kidnap Angela for that.'

'Kidnap a journalist and no D-Notice in the world is going to stop that story being printed.'

'So, where is she?'

'I don't have a crystal ball, Bob. What I would say is that, wherever she is, it's likely to have some relevance to the bomb test, some aspect of Operation Hurricane, but she certainly won't be in a nuclear bunker, and I doubt she's even underground.'

◆ ◆ ◆

The receptionist arrived with the milk just as I was leaving, my coffee still sitting on the corner of the good doctor's desk. Stone cold.

I drove north on the M5, my head spinning. It always did when I finished a therapy session with the good doctor, but this time it was for a different reason.

If Caroline is right, and Angela isn't underground, where the bloody hell is she?

I arrived in Bridgwater just after nine. The press conference was fixed for ten and I had been hoping to be safely out of the way for that. Not because I was expected to appear in front of the cameras, more because I didn't want to have to face Angela's parents again.

I know, I know.

The car park was full of journalists and TV vans, microphones being thrust in front of any officer who had the misfortune to be arriving for their shift. I spotted Ray Keenan – before he spotted me, mercifully – and was able to make it to the door without him seeing me.

Cables had been laid on the floor, running from the vans into the press suite, the staff entrance propped open with a fire extinguisher. There were cameras being set up on tripods, microphones on the table at the front of the room.

Keith and Lynn would be somewhere in the building, being briefed by Sharp. No doubt the ACC was here too. A ten o'clock press conference would make the lunchtime TV news and the regular radio bulletins almost immediately. It might even go out live on local radio.

Proof that it was a high-profile case, just like the good doctor had said.

I felt a hand on my elbow, turned.

'DS Simpson was looking for you, sir,' said the desk sergeant. 'I'm to ring her as soon as you arrive.'

'Thank you.'

I was halfway up the back stairs when Mary appeared at the top. 'Thank God, at last,' she said. 'There's someone here to see you, Bob. Won't speak to anyone else. You alone.'

'Who is it?'

'Rachel Bromfield.'

Chapter Thirty-Five

'I've got her up here,' said Mary. 'Out of the way of the press.' She turned on the stairs, went back up.

I followed. 'How long has she been here?'

'About an hour. Where the bloody hell have you been?'

'To see a psychologist.'

'Are you all right?'

'Not about me. About the case.'

Both, actually, as it turned out, but that's the good doctor for you.

'I gave her a coffee and she said she'd wait.' Mary stopped next to a closed door. 'I put her in here.'

'Does anyone else know she's here?' I asked, softly.

'No. She was adamant. You, and no one else.'

Mary opened the door slowly, glanced at the figure sitting hunched in the corner of the room, then backed out, closing the door behind me.

Rachel had short, dark hair, a stud earring glinted in the light, but apart from that there was no makeup, no jewellery. Her face was pale, her eyes red, but she was still instantly recognisable from the photograph I'd seen at the Bromfield house. A brown wool coat, done up, she was leaning forward, arms folded, hiding her pregnancy.

A full mug of coffee was sitting on the windowsill next to her.

She looked up, opened her mouth to speak, but the words caught in her throat.

'I'm Bob Willis,' I said, with a reassuring smile. 'You wanted to speak to me.' I slid a chair out from under the meeting table, sat down in front of her. 'Take your time,' I said. 'There's no rush.'

Actually, there is, but she's clearly got other things on her mind.

'This has got to stop,' she said, hesitantly. 'My father is dead. That poor man in the peat field too. And now he's taken someone else.'

She looked like she'd been up all night. Believe me, I know the signs. 'Who has?'

'I don't know his name.'

'But you've seen him?' I asked, my voice hushed. She looked at me, her eyes full of tears. Whatever it is, she's been bottling it up for years. Since 1962, if I had to guess. 'On the steam train, perhaps?'

She took a deep breath. 'I was six. Paul was nine. He used to pull my hair, stick pins in me. He killed my rabbit. I know it was him.'

She's got a speech worked out and I'm just going to sit here and listen, let her tell me in her own time.

'He was horrible. All the time.' Sobbing now. 'He'd kick me, hit me, trip me up in the garden. He used to scribble on the pictures I painted for my parents, break my toys. I know this sounds petty, and you're probably thinking it was just standard older brother stuff, but I was six and I hated him. You have to understand that. I hated him.'

'I do understand.'

Breathing deeply now, through her nose. I can't begin to imagine the stress of this, hope it's not harming her unborn child. I've seen witnesses tormenting themselves like this before, and it's almost always borne out of guilt.

I have a feeling I know what's coming.

'My father had bought us ice creams on Glastonbury station and Paul knocked mine out of my hand when he wasn't looking. Then he laughed at me. It was like that all the time. My father couldn't understand why I didn't want to take my bucket and spade to the beach, but there was no point; Paul would've just kicked my sandcastles over. He ruined everything.' She was rocking backwards and forwards on her chair. 'I was six years old, and I hated him,' she said. 'Then I saw a man take him. And I said nothing.'

Sobbing again.

I looked around the room, noticed a packet of tissues on the side, placed them on the table next to her.

'What does that make me?' she asked.

'A child,' I replied.

'I said nothing for twenty-four years. I'm thirty, and you're the first person I've told.'

'Thank you.'

'I was glad he was gone; didn't really understand what it meant at the time, though. I remember my parents were frantic, but the longer it went on, I just couldn't say anything.' She was dabbing her eyes with the remains of a sodden tissue. 'Then they found him, down in that bunker. I remember my mother trying to explain it to me, that Paul was gone and would never be coming back. I was glad. Can you believe that?'

'I can understand it,' I said.

'They went out of their way to make up for it after that; never let me and my little sister out of their sight. Life was good without Paul. Better. Apart from at night, when we'd gone to bed. They'd row. We'd hear the shouting. My father blamed himself, said he should've been watching Paul, seen what happened to him. But I saw. And I never said anything.' She buried her head in her hands. 'I saw.'

'What did you see, Rachel?'

'I saw a man get off the train. Paul was on the platform, and he led him away. He had an arm around Paul's shoulders, two or three paces and they disappeared into the steam from the train.'

'The man got off the train, which means he was on the train?'

She nodded.

'Where did he get on?'

'I don't know.'

'Did you see him on the train?' I'm firing questions at her now, praying she doesn't clam up. I have to know what she saw. All of it.

'Yes. He was standing at the end of the corridor, watching Paul running up and down.'

'What was he wearing?'

'I don't really remember that detail. I'm sorry. I think dark trousers, possibly. He had a coat with a hood on, I do remember that.'

'Did you see them again?'

'No. I remember thinking it'll be nice to have a day at the beach with Daddy, on our own. Without Paul. That's actually what I thought. Then I remember my father shouting, running up and down the corridors, looking in all the compartments. The train stopped in the middle of nowhere and everybody was looking for Paul. I told myself over the years that even if I'd said something it probably wouldn't have made a difference.'

'Did you see his face?'

'Yes. When he was standing in the train corridor. He had his back to me, but he turned to watch Paul.'

'Was he young, old?'

'I don't know now. Everyone seems old to a six-year-old.'

'Would you recognise him again?'

Silence.

I waited. Why would that question be trickier than the others, unless . . . ?

'That's just it,' she said, eventually. 'I did see him again. It must've been about a year later. I don't remember when or where it was, but I went to a meeting with my father. There were lots of men there, and they all called him "sir". I sat in the corner, playing with my dolly.'

'And this man was there?' Doing my best to hide my disbelief, disappointment even – after all, I'd told Sharp the killer wasn't ex-Navy.

'Yes, but that's all I remember. Just that he was there, at that meeting.'

Chapter Thirty-Six

Rachel stood up, abruptly. 'I need to go,' she said. 'I'm staying with my mother in Wincanton, took a taxi over here, didn't say where I was going. She'll be worried.'

I glanced at the clock on the wall. Just before ten. The press conference would be getting going soon, the station swarming with journalists.

'I'll take you home,' I said. 'First job is to get you out of here without being seen.'

'My mother doesn't know about any of this. You're the only one I've told. You won't tell her, will you?'

'I can't guarantee she won't find out, Rachel,' I said.

She puffed out her cheeks. 'I suppose I knew it was coming. One day.'

'Let me go and see if the coast is clear. There's a press conference starting in a minute and once that's got going, we can leave.'

'The parents of the missing girl?'

Mary was hanging around on the landing, keeping watch along the corridor when I opened the meeting room door.

'Well?' she asked, her eyes wide.

'I need to get her out of here without being seen.'

'I'd take the lift, go out the front in that case,' she said. 'The journos are all in the press suite, so you'll be fine. What did she say?'

'Later. I'm just going to drop her home.'

Rachel had gathered herself by the time I got back. I'd moved my car around to the front of the station, left the engine running. Nobody's going to pinch an old Volvo, not from outside a police station.

I was watching her in the mirror as we went down in the lift. A bit of rouge to give her cheeks some colour, a touch of lipstick. She was doing well in the car too, until we went through Ashcott. That's my fault, really. I should've gone via Langport. I'd forgotten the village was on the main road, the station a mile or so to the north.

'Why were you at this meeting with your father?' I asked, mainly to break the silence.

'My mother had taken Kim somewhere. It was just me and my father for a few days, and he said he had to go to a meeting. He never left us with anyone else, not after what happened to Paul.'

'Can you remember anything else about it?'

'They were all sitting around a big table and there was a model of a ship in the middle of it. My father told me it was *his* ship.'

We drove on in silence, me wondering how I was going to explain this to Sharp, Rachel staring out of the passenger window.

'Drop me here and I'll walk the rest of the way,' she said, before I turned into Bayford Hill. 'I don't want my mother to see you.'

'How long are you staying with her?'

'A few weeks. Until after my father's funeral anyway.' She climbed out of the passenger seat, then leaned back in. 'Find that girl, please, Mr Willis,' she said. 'I'm not sure I can live with another death on my conscience.'

'It wasn't your fault, Rachel. You were a child of six. And even if you'd spoken up, we might not have found him anyway.'

'You were there?'

'Out in the fields, walking the police line.'

'I'm sorry.'

I watched her walk along the pavement, turn the corner, and she was gone.

It's easy to see how she found herself in this position. The longer it went on, the more difficult it would have become for her to have said anything.

Until it became impossible.

There but for the grace of God.

What would be interesting to know is whether her father asked her if she'd seen anything and she'd lied, said she hadn't. I didn't ask her that, though. Thought it was a question too far at this stage. And what difference would it make?

She hadn't said anything, and that was that. Hadn't said anything even when she saw the same man again a year later.

But she's paying for it now.

◆ ◆ ◆

I'm getting close.

But memories fade, recollections become distorted. It happens to all of us in time, more so for a child, possibly. I have vague memories of things that happened when I was six or seven years old. I'm sure you do too. Visions, images.

I can remember a sports day at school when I won the under 8s' high jump. I know. Don't laugh. I can picture myself at the playing fields. My father was there. My teacher too, but could I pick her out at an identity parade now?

All these years later.

I'm not so sure.

The key piece of information I got from Rachel is that she saw the man again a year or so later. At a meeting of the HMS *Plym* Association, assuming that was the model ship in the middle of the table. So, now I'm sitting in my deckchair, flicking through the lever arch file of meeting agendas, minutes and accounts that Evan Williams gave me yesterday.

Williams was the XO, or executive officer. Even I know that's naval speak for second in command. It looks like he took the minutes, listing himself at the top of *Attendees*.

March 1964. Eighteen months after Paul's disappearance, but I think we can forgive Rachel that. I'd found them yesterday, flicked through them without understanding their significance. Time for a closer look.

> *HMS Plym Association.*
> *Committee Meeting.*
> *27th March 1964. 8pm.*
> *In attendance:*
> *Captain John Bromfield (CO)*
> *Lieutenant Commander Evan Williams (XO)*
> *Chairman's Opening Remarks: CO apologised for bringing his daughter to the meeting, but hoped those present would understand.*

There were no apologies for absence, no one listed as absent, so it was a full house.

Eleven names.

All of them on my list, although I can see immediately two are dead now.

One leaps out at me. Bill Horsey. He never mentioned being on the committee, but then again I never asked.

All of them ex-Navy of course, and I'd told Sharp there was no way ex-service personnel were behind this. Those I'd spoken to had been at pains to impress on me that they were doing their duty, would've borne no malice towards John Bromfield.

Now I'm wondering why they were so keen to make that point. I'm sure you are too.

I closed the folder, took a deep breath.

Time to face the music.

◆ ◆ ◆

I listened to the radio in the car, caught the local news, twice as it happened.

Police are continuing to search for . . .

An appeal for information by Sharp, followed by a quote from a tearful Keith Harper. 'We just want her back. Angela, wherever you are . . .'

You get the picture.

Twice was enough. I switched off the radio, drove the rest of the way in silence.

The car park was quiet by the time I reached Bridgwater, the press already moving on to the next story.

'Ah, there you are, Bob,' said Sharp. He was standing at the front of the incident room, staring at the whiteboard. Most of the desks behind him were empty. 'We're just waiting for the certificates from Somerset House. The Home Office have given us a list of visas granted post 1952, but there are hundreds of them, I'm afraid.'

My face must've given it away.

'What's going on?' he asked.

Mary was sitting at a desk, dialling a number on the phone. She replaced the handset, staring at me.

'I had a visit from Rachel Bromfield,' I said.

'When?' demanded Sharp.

'This morning.'

'Why wasn't I told?'

'You were busy with the press conference, guv,' said Mary. 'And she said she'd only speak to Bob.'

'Let's hear it then.'

Two officers at the back of the room left their desks, moved forward to sit on the windowsill behind Mary.

'She saw the man who took her brother,' I said.

'She *saw* him?'

'She was a six-year-old child,' I said, flatly. 'Paul made her life a misery, but that's incidental now. She saw this man standing at the end of the corridor, which means he was on the train and got off at Ashcott, with Paul.'

'Is there a description?' Sharp was shifting from one foot to the other.

'Nothing workable,' I replied. 'What she did say is that she saw the man again about a year later. At a meeting somewhere. Her father had taken her, and there was a model of a ship in the middle of the table.' Sharp opened his mouth to speak, but I silenced him with a wave of my hand. I'd got the lever arch file under my arm, placed it on the table at the front, opened it to the page I'd marked. 'I was given this file by Evan Williams, who used to run the HMS *Plym* Association, and these are the minutes of that meeting. March 1964, and the attendees are listed.'

'How many are there?' asked Mary.

Sharp seemed to be taking a moment to let it sink in.

'Eleven; two of them are dead, three if you include John Bromfield. Bill Horsey's name is on the list.'

'You fucking idiot, Bob.' Sharp waved the visa list at me; I could see the Home Office logo at the top of the first page. 'I've got officers running about all over the country interviewing Aussies, because you told me it'd never be a serviceman, and now you've got a witness who says she saw the man who took Paul Bromfield at a meeting of the HMS *Plym* Association.'

'Which means he's ex-Navy. I know.'

Sharp let out a long, slow sigh. 'Let's get everybody back,' he said, turning to Mary. 'This is what happens when you let him out of your sight.'

'Yes, guv.'

He looked at me, shook his head. 'He's one of eight people.'

'Ten,' I said. 'You'll need to check the dead ones too.'

'Yes, true.' Sharp's voice was loaded with sarcasm. 'One of them might very well have kidnapped Simon Horsey and murdered Andrew Bucknall. Good thinking, Bob.'

'Guv, I don't suppose there's a chance John Bromfield left his own son in the bunker?' One of the officers sitting on the windowsill had summoned up the courage to speak. 'He could've done Simon Horsey too, killed Andrew Bucknall, then himself.'

'Bollocks.'

'It doesn't fit with the witnesses on the train,' I replied. 'They all saw John Bromfield frantically searching for his son. It doesn't fit with what Rachel Bromfield told me, either.'

'We can rule that out,' said Sharp, impatiently.

I won't pretend it hadn't occurred to me. Probably to you too. Could he, would he have done that to his only son? If so, he must've had an accomplice, someone to take Paul off the train.

I can't see it myself. I spent most of the drive from Wincanton to Blagdon stewing on it, and I'm with Sharp on this one. It's bollocks.

And there's Angela too, don't forget.

'The best thing you can do now, Bob, is fuck off, if you don't mind,' said Sharp, turning his back on me. 'Leave the professionals to it.'

Mary looked at me, tipped her head, mouthed 'Sorry'.

I picked up the visa list that Sharp had thrown on the floor in disgust. 'Is this the only copy?'

'I made several,' replied Mary.

I folded it in half, stuffed it in my coat pocket and headed for the stairs.

Chapter Thirty-Seven

I caught the tail end of the lunchtime news on the television in the pub. A man's got to eat, and there was no Little Chef for miles around.

It was the local bulletin that comes after the national news. 'A huge search is under way across four counties for missing journalist Angela Harper . . .'

After that came pictures of helicopters, lines of officers trudging across fields, searching in undergrowth, divers in rivers. It was all horrifyingly familiar, apart from the helicopters. There'd been none of those in 1962. Not that I'd seen anyway.

Not that they'd have found Paul Bromfield either. Even one of those new-fangled thermal imaging cameras wouldn't have found him down in that bunker. Might find Angela, though, if the good doctor's right and she's not underground.

I feel bloody useless, but what the hell can I do on my own?

She knows I'll be doing everything I can. I hope she knows that anyway.

First and foremost, I hope she's still alive.

The good doctor would tell me that guilt and self-pity are different emotions; that it's perfectly possible to feel both at the same time. And I do.

I'd prefer to be worrying about blame, to be honest; about whether Angela blames me for this whole fucking mess. Why?

Because she has to be alive to do that.

A revolting toasted sandwich, but at least it's food. Angela's probably starving.

I took my notebook out of my pocket, looked at the list of names I'd scribbled down before I'd handed the meeting minutes over to Sharp. Eleven names, three of them dead.

That leaves eight. Seven if you exclude Evan Williams; didn't seem like the type to me, although he had been most anxious to point out they were doing their duty.

Eight, then.

Including Bill Horsey. Would he really have used his own grandson as a pawn in this game? It might explain the bottles of water. Paul Bromfield had none, tried drinking from the chemical toilet.

None of the eight had joined the Observer Corps when they left the Navy.

I wonder if any of them married an Australian?

I was still poring over the list of visas when the landlord called 'time', ended up sitting in my car in the car park.

I do my best thinking when I'm doing something else. Not sure why. I should get a dog really, then I could take it for a walk. Although, I've spent far too long trying not to think about anything too much, as you know.

I picked up that file of newspaper articles from the Australian press that I'd found in Angela's desk drawer. I'd stuffed it down the side of the passenger seat, thought I might find time to have a look at it at some point.

◆ ◆ ◆

'What the fuck are you doing here, Bob?'

The incident room was busier, the message to return to the station getting through slowly.

I ignored Sharp, looked for Mary.

'Have the birth, death and marriage certificates arrived from Somerset House yet?' I asked quietly. I was leaning over her desk, conscious that Sharp was eavesdropping.

He'll know when I know.

'We've got the first batch, marriage only, they arrived by courier about half an hour ago,' she said.

'Can I see them?'

'Sharp's got them.'

I waited.

'You want me to get them?'

'Thank you.'

Sharp's mood hadn't improved over lunch. Mary leaned across the table hesitantly, reached out for the files of papers.

'What d'you want?' demanded Sharp.

'Bob wants to see these,' she replied.

He glared at me, running his tongue over his teeth. He blinked first.

'All right,' he said. 'Just keep an eye on him.'

'What are you looking for?' I'd sat down at Mary's desk and she placed the file of papers in front of me.

'Confirmation,' I said. I started flicking through the marriage certificates.

If I'm right there'll be a death certificate as well, but we haven't got those yet. A marriage certificate will do for starters. Like I said, I'm looking for confirmation. I know who and I know why, but I need more. I need proof.

Sharp appeared at Mary's elbow. She was standing next to me, watching me flicking through the certificates one by one.

'What's he—?'

'Just give him a minute, guv,' interrupted Mary. 'I think he's got something.'

The whole room had gone quiet and I was suddenly conscious that everyone was watching me, still flicking through the marriage certificates one by one.

Carefully.

Methodically.

And then I found it, the certificate I'd been looking for.

I stopped. Read it again. And again. Looked up at Sharp and smiled.

◆ ◆ ◆

'Well?' He clapped his hands. 'Everybody! Let's all listen to what Bob's got to say.'

Where to start?

Angela's newspaper articles, I think.

I stood up. Sharp was expecting me to make a fool of myself. But it's not about me. It's about her now.

Listen to this. I told you she's a bright kid.

'Let's talk about Angela,' I said. 'She's a journalist. A good one. I told her about HMS *Plym* and Operation Hurricane after that article appeared on the front page of the *Gazette* and I found this file of newspaper articles in the drawer of her desk at her office. She'd been doing her own research; pieces from the Australian press coverage of the bomb test and the aftermath.' I opened the file, took out the first article. 'The *Perth Daily News*, dated third of October 1952, that's the same day as the test. *The West Australian* on the fourth carried a six-page spread with photographs of the mushroom cloud.' I held it up, so everyone could see the picture on the front page. 'Then we come to articles about the aftermath. There are even some covering the Royal Commission last year. One of the key findings was that the rate of cancers would not have occurred were it not for the fallout from the tests. But there's one set of stories you need to know about.'

Sharp leaned back against the desk, folded his arms. 'Go on,' he said.

'82 Wing of the Royal Australian Air Force was tasked with air sampling. It was their job to fly up and down the north coast, testing for radioactive particles in the air. They flew Lincolns and had buckets on their wing tips to catch samples. Trouble is, when the wind took the debris east towards the mainland, they found themselves flying through thick clouds of nuclear fallout. The planes got covered in it. Air intakes clogged, engines, filters. A few days later they returned to their base in Queensland, so now they're thousands of miles away from the contaminated area.'

'Is this going somewhere, Bob?'

'Decontamination of the aircraft took weeks, four of them had to be dumped in an isolated part of the airbase, cordoned off, because they couldn't get the radiation down to acceptable levels. Toxic runoff from the cleaning went into a holding tank underground. Trouble is, every time it rained the tank overflowed, taking the radioactive water into a nearby stream where it flowed into a pond.' I hesitated. 'Where local children used to go swimming.'

Now Sharp can see where this is going.

Twat.

'There are articles detailing compensation claims right up to the present day. All of them have failed. The Australian judges put their cancers down to UV radiation from the sun. They said there's no direct link with the bomb test, apparently; they were thousands of miles away from the contaminated area.'

'Names, Bob?' asked Sharp.

'I'm getting to that,' I snapped. 'The Burnside family of Amberley lost a daughter. It's a suburb of Ipswich, Queensland, yards from the airbase and yards from the pond. A brain tumour aged ten. Their other daughter married an Englishman, came to live in the UK. Laura Emily Burnside is listed as having been granted a marriage visa in January 1958. And here is her marriage certificate.' I held it aloft. 'Marriage Solemnized at the Parish Church in the Parish of Burtle in the county of Somerset. If I had to guess, I'd say there'll be a death certificate in her name as well.'

'We'll get them later today, they said,' offered Mary.

'You have done well, Bob,' said Sharp.

'I haven't. Angela has.'

'Is there anything else?'

'There is. Where are the minutes of that meeting of the HMS *Plym* Association?'

'I circulated copies,' said Mary. 'Everyone's seen it.'

'Rachel Bromfield said she saw the man who took her brother at that meeting.'

'That's right,' said Sharp. 'We're going to be speaking to them all today.'

'Don't bother.'

'It must be one of them.'

'Has anyone got a copy of the minutes of that meeting in front of them?' I asked.

'I have,' said Mary. She picked up a piece of paper from the corner of the desk. 'It's here.'

'Read the last line under *Any Other Business*.'

'Er. Here it is. *XO would like to extend his thanks to the staff at the Station Hotel for their hospitality*.'

I waited for the murmuring to subside. 'Laura Emily Burnside married Frederick William Hicks on the eighth of May 1958. *Age, twenty-six; Condition, bachelor; Rank or Profession, Publican. Residence at the time of Marriage, The Station Hotel, Station Road, Burtle.* The Station Hotel was renamed the Edgar Lamb in 1965 and he's the landlord. Rachel Bromfield was right. He was at that meeting, serving the bloody drinks.'

Chapter Thirty-Eight

All hell broke loose after that. Cheering, clapping. I lost count of the pats on the back.

We're no nearer finding Angela, though, are we, and I need to make sure Sharp doesn't go charging in there in his size tens and arrest Hicks. Yes, he can be that stupid, before you ask.

'All right, calm down everybody,' Sharp said.

'What are you thinking, guv?' asked Mary.

'We place him under surveillance. Twenty-four hours, and hope he leads us to Angela.'

That's a relief.

'What can you tell me about him, Bob?'

'He's Chief Observer now, was in the ROC back in 1962, but he had a key to the bunker and the padlocks had been picked, so they must've ruled him out for that reason. He never featured on the radar, as far as I could see.'

'Is there a statement from him on the original file?'

'Yes.'

'Leave it with me, guv,' said Mary.

'It'll be interesting to see what Jack Welshman has got to say about him. Go and see him, Bob.' Sharp looked at his watch. 'The pub opens at six. You two. Go home, change into something casual, go and sit in that pub while we put a surveillance team in place. And make sure you've got some change for the bloody phone.'

I'd seen the two officers hanging around the incident room, but didn't know their names.

'Is there anything else we should be doing?' asked Sharp. He was looking at me, oddly enough.

'We need to know if they had children, and what happened to them. Birth and death certificates when they get here. A phone tap, obviously.'

'You've met this bloke?'

'I went in the pub right at the start of the cold case investigation. It was him who lent me the key to go down in the bunker.'

He may lack imagination, but he doesn't lack industry, I'll give Sharp that. And he authorised the overtime without breaking sweat.

Round the clock surveillance, starting immediately. It had started before I'd even left the station with Mary to speak to Eric Hall's bagman, Jack Welshman.

Two teams in the pub, another outside. Multiple cars and the helicopter on standby to follow him.

I have a bad feeling about it, all the same. Yes, we have to try it, give him time to go and see Angela, but what are the chances of that? *So we begin again*, his message said. If you take that to mean it's a rerun of Paul Bromfield, then he just left the poor little boy to die. And there's no way I'm letting him do that to Angela.

I've got a plan. I won't tell you what it is yet because you won't like it, won't like me for it, probably. That said, one thing I'm not going to do is let Angela die.

'What time is it?' I asked.

'Just before six,' replied Mary.

'We'll wait.' I switched off the engine, unbuckled my seatbelt and wound down the driver's window.

'What for?'

'You'll see.'

A Westminster chime started first, then another.

'I see what you mean,' muttered Mary. We waited in the foyer of the converted warehouse on the edge of Langport for the chiming to stop. 'His neighbours must bloody love that. Those sodding cuckoos as well.'

'He repairs clocks for a living,' I said, knocking on the door of his ground floor flat.

'Who is it?'

'Bob Willis.'

Welshman left the front door standing open and disappeared back inside his flat.

'I've been following the case on the news,' he said, the voice coming from the living room when Mary closed the door behind us. 'What was all that stuff about bluebells and crocuses?' He was sitting in an armchair when we walked in, gestured to the sofa.

I told him the whole story, spared him nothing.

He reached over to the sideboard and picked up a bottle of whisky. 'Anyone?' he asked.

'No, thank you.' In unison.

'I thought not.' He was filling the tumbler on the coffee table in front of him. 'I remember Hicks,' he said. 'I took his witness statement.'

I knew that, had decided not to remind him, if he hadn't remembered.

'Seemed like a nice bloke.' Welshman shrugged. 'He'd lost a child, young. Brain tumour, I think, but it didn't raise any red flags because we never made the connection with the bomb test. Maybe we should've done. We knew John Bromfield was ex-Navy, looked at that as a possible reason for a grievance against him.'

'The contamination of the Australian mainland was hushed up,' I said.

'I bet it bloody well was.' Welshman took a swig of whisky. 'Hicks was Observer Corps, from memory, had a key to the bunker and still picked the padlocks to make it look like . . . Crafty sod.'

'We're watching him closely, hoping he'll lead us to Angela Harper,' said Mary.

'He won't.' His eyes glazed over. 'His wife was ill as well, I think. I remember taking his statement at the pub, one afternoon when it was closed so we were the only ones in there. He asked me if I wanted a pint, but I was on duty. He said he had to pop upstairs halfway through, check on his wife. She wasn't well.'

'We're awaiting birth and death certificates now,' offered Mary.

'I asked him about the Bunsen burner and he must've lied to my face. He was good at it; never gave me any cause for concern.' Welshman took another swig. 'I never knew about the flowers. I was at the bunker that autumn and winter, went back for the first anniversary, but that was autumn again. We did a TV appeal, hoping to jog memories, you know how it is. Never went there in the spring, so never saw them. They were at Chilton Polden and Pawlett?'

'Newly planted at Pawlett, according to someone who knows about these things,' I replied.

'We had no way of knowing about the radio frequency either.' Welshman was looking back, looking for explanations. 'I put a piece of tape on the dial at the time, in case it was significant, but we thought Paul might have fiddled with it in the dark anyway. What else was there?'

'Nothing at Chilton Polden, apart from the fact it was a *nuclear* bunker.'

'I don't think there's any criticism of the original investigation, Jack,' said Mary. 'None of this information was available to the original investigation.'

'Maybe not, but you have to wonder, don't you? Whether we should have realised.'

'What did John Bromfield say about the Bunsen burner?' I asked.

'Eric asked him about it, but he never mentioned anything about his ship or the Montebello Islands. I'd have remembered that if he had. I showed him a photograph of the radio, asked him if he recognised it and he didn't.'

'Did Hicks say anything else about his wife?'

'I got the impression she didn't have long, I'm sure I did. Not from anything he said, it was just the look on his face when he said she wasn't well.' The curtains were open and Welshman was staring out of the window, into the darkness outside. 'I wonder what Eric would make of all this. This case finished the poor bugger off, as you know.'

◆ ◆ ◆

I learned a couple of things from Welshman. Firstly, about the child. We'd have found out sooner or later from the birth and death certificates, but it makes the desire for revenge all the more understandable. Unforgivable, but understandable. Not only that, but he's taking it out on the wrong people.

John Bromfield didn't decide to use the Montebello Islands for the test; wasn't the one who decided to go ahead despite a dodgy weather forecast. He wasn't the one who hushed up the radioactive fallout drifting towards mainland Australia. None of what befell Hicks and his family was John Bromfield's fault. But there he was, sitting in a room at the Edgar Lamb, right in front of Hicks just weeks after his child had died, his wife dying upstairs.

The captain of the ship, attending his first committee meeting of the South West branch of the HMS *Plym* Association in March 1962.

I'm guessing it was pure chance Hicks found himself on the train that morning in August 1962 as well, watching Bromfield taking his children to the beach for a family day out.

Like I said, understandable, and yet unforgivable at the same time.

Then there's Angela. What the bloody hell has she done to deserve this?

Andrew Bucknall probably knew too much. Too much for his own good anyway. He said he used to go up to the bunker, so maybe he saw Hicks up there one day, planting the flowers? Perhaps even on the platform with Paul that fateful day.

The second thing I learned was that Hicks was never on the radar of the original investigation; never a suspect. That explains why the case went unsolved, went cold, but it's what happens when police officers rely on gut feeling.

Instinct.

The harsh reality is that most of us don't have it.

I've still got Mary in tow, which is a pain, but she didn't protest when I suggested paying the Edgar Lamb a visit. Not going in, you understand. Just sitting outside in the car.

I don't know what else to do, to be honest. I'm out of ideas. And the plan is just to wait, hope he leads us to Angela. I do feel closer to her somehow, sitting here, listening to the patter of the rain on the windscreen, occasionally flicking on the wipers, for something to do more than anything else.

Mary got out, walked over to an unmarked car on the far side of the pub car park. A quick word with the occupants through the open driver's window, then she ran back, jumped in the passenger seat.

'He's in there, behind the bar,' she said. 'That's his car over there, the red Montego.'

You could just about make out the colour in the lights from the pub.

'How many have we got inside?'

'We started with six, but then dropped it to two,' replied Mary. 'It's a Monday night and the pub's practically empty. Six looked odd. There's Hicks and a girl behind the bar, someone else in the kitchen.'

We're relying on Hicks leading us to Angela when there's no evidence he went back to visit Paul Bromfield. He left him down in the bunker and that was that.

We'll be into day four tomorrow, and the vision of Angela trying to drink from a chemical toilet keeps flashing across my mind.

Like I said, I've got a plan if this gets us nowhere, but I'll need to shake off Mary for that.

There was someone approaching the passenger side of my car. I recognised him from the incident room.

'Sharp's been on the radio,' he said, when Mary wound down the window. 'Wants you back at Bridgwater.'

Bollocks.

Chapter Thirty-Nine

I can't say I'd planned this, but I'm out of the car now, marching towards the front door of the pub. I can hear footsteps behind me, Mary in hot pursuit.

'You can't go in there, Bob!'

I remember years ago, when I first joined CID, I was bagman to a grizzled old DCI. He said lots of things, most of them crap, but one stayed with me over the years.

Sometimes, you have to go in with both feet, make things happen.

He was right about that. Sometimes you do.

And this is one of them. Angela's running out of time, and that's all there is to it.

'Bob!' Mary steps in front of me, her outstretched hand in the middle of my chest. 'You'll blow the whole thing,' she said.

'How long d'you think Angela's got left?'

She takes a deep breath. 'Not long.'

'I'm not going to *do* anything. I just want him to know that I know. See what he does. He'll do something, I guarantee it.'

She's mulling it over, then moves aside. 'Sharp will go ballistic.'

'At me, not you.' I stop at the front door, my hand resting on the handle, turn to face her. 'You tried to stop me.'

The pub is all but empty. A couple of locals are sitting on stools at the far end of the bar. Another couple of lads in the corner, arguing over what they're putting on the jukebox next. I can hear voices from the games room, the clack of pool balls, the sound of coins tumbling from a fruit machine.

Two police officers are sitting in the front window, doing their best to look like a couple, even holding hands across the table. They try to look casual when they see me. Fail.

Hicks is standing behind the bar, watching a young girl loading the dishwasher under the counter.

He sees me coming, doesn't react. I'm watching for it.

'How are you getting on with that case?'

He remembers me, but then of course he does. He's taken the trouble to find out where I live, left me messages. And he's lent me the keys to the bunker.

'Fine.' I'm looking idly at the beer pumps lined up along the bar. 'Nearly done.'

'Really?'

I nod.

'You'll have finished with the keys to the bunker, in that case?'

'Not quite yet, if that's all right.'

His turn to nod. 'Drink?'

'Orange juice and lemonade. A half will do.'

'On the wagon, is it?'

'Something like that.'

He flicks the lid off the small bottle, empties the orange juice into a glass. 'I saw on the news a girl's been kidnapped.'

'He seems to think that'll guarantee him news coverage when he's arrested, but he's pissing in the wind. Obviously hasn't heard of a D-Notice.'

'What's that when it's at home, then?' He's holding my glass under the lemonade tap.

'Blocks press coverage of a story, usually in the national interest.' I've got a handful of coins, and am sorting through them in my palm, remaining casual. Trying to, anyway. I'd like to reach over the bar and tear him a new—

I look up. His face has reddened, and my lemonade is overflowing.

'My drink?'

'Sorry.' He places the glass on a bar towel.

'How much?'

'On the house.'

'Very kind of you.'

'You found that boy who'd been kidnapped. That was good.'

Feels like we're jousting now. He wants to know how much I know.

'I got the shout from the ROC about checking the bunkers again. Someone else had to do it. You've got my keys.'

'Sorry about that.'

'What did you think of it, down in the bunker?'

'You'd have to be a special sort of bastard to leave a nine-year-old boy down there to die.' I take a swig of my drink, watching him over the top of my glass. 'There really is no excuse for that. No matter what's happened.'

'No.' He's got a cloth now, wiping the top of the bar.

We're both trying to act casual, but I know it's him.

And he knows that I know it's him.

'You're close to making an arrest, by the sounds of things.'

I drain my drink, leave the empty glass on the bar and turn for the door. 'Very close.'

◆ ◆ ◆

'What the fuck was all that about, Bob?' demanded Sharp, when we walked into the incident room twenty minutes later. 'And what the bloody hell were you doing letting him go in there?'

'She tried to stop me,' I said. 'It's not Mary's fault.'

Sharp sat back down. The incident room was quiet, but then it was late, and most of the team were out on surveillance duties or catching up on sleep. 'What did he say?'

'Nothing,' I replied. 'And I said nothing. But he knows I know, and that's enough for now. We'll see what he does about it.'

It's a gamble. I know that. Sharp knows that.

You know that.

But what other choice do I have? The clock is ticking.

'We got the certificates from Somerset House,' he said, opening a file on the desk in front of him, sliding out several pieces of paper: green, red and black. 'Marriage certificate, dated eighth of May 1958. You've seen that. Then there's a birth certificate for a son, Robin Thomas Hicks, dated thirty-first of March 1961. There are two death certificates.' Sharp sighed. 'The boy died on the third of March 1962, so that's three weeks before the first HMS *Plym* meeting John Bromfield went to at the Station Hotel, then the wife died in August 1964.'

'What's the cause of death?' asked Mary.

'Both of them were diagnosed with glioblastoma. That's a brain tumour to you and me.'

'The boy didn't even see his first birthday,' she said.

Sharp cleared his throat. 'There's someone else living in the owner's accommodation above the pub. Jude was in there with Mac and reported an old man suddenly appeared at the bottom of the stairs and had to be ushered back up. It's happened twice so far this evening. She reckons he's well over eighty, and seemed out of it, so dementia, possibly. We did a bit of digging and it looks like it's the father-in-law. There's a visa in his name; the Home Office faxed it over an hour or so ago.'

'I wonder if he was over here in 1962, as well,' muttered Mary.

'We're waiting to hear from the Home Office on that, but if it was a short stay there'd be no visa.'

'Might explain a lot, might that,' continued Mary. 'He'd have lost a daughter and a grandson at that point. And if he left poor little Paul in the bunker and buggered off back to Australia. What d'you think, Bob?'

'If that's right, then who slit Andrew Bucknall's throat? Who kidnapped Simon Horsey? Someone with dementia couldn't have done that.'

I know I've talked about instinct, but I've looked into Fred Hicks's eyes, and I could see the guilt.

'There's what Rachel Bromfield said too, don't forget,' said Mary. 'She saw the man who took Paul at that meeting she went to with her father. March '64, wasn't it?'

'Better check the visas for 1962 and 1964 in that case,' I replied. 'He might've come over from Australia again if his daughter was dying and that would've put him in the pub when Rachel was there. I'd get the old man's medical records as well, to be on the safe side.'

'Where are you going now, Bob?' asked Sharp.

'Home, to get some sleep,' I replied.

Lying has become a lot easier these days. I've never done a lot of it, never had to, not even to Shirley. Besides, it was only a small one.

Now I'm parked on the track that follows the old railway line, the other side of the South Drain from the Edgar Lamb. A discreet distance away, out of sight, but I can see the pub, see the lights on upstairs.

It's gone half-ten, so it'll be closing time in a minute. That's when he'll move, and if he doesn't, I've got my sleeping bag in the back of the car.

I'm not going anywhere.

Chapter Forty

I could hear tapping on glass.

I opened my eyes, saw Mary standing in the darkness. I wound down the driver's window.

'He's on the move, Bob,' she said.

'What time is it?'

'Just gone two. We've got a car behind him. We'll go in mine. I've got a radio.'

I resisted the temptation to ask how she knew I was there. Must be getting predictable in my old age.

Now we're racing north on the M5. I'm sitting in the passenger seat of her car, listening to the radio.

'Northbound M5, exiting junction 22.'

'Car Three, pick up the tail at the roundabout.'

We're a couple of miles back, just crossing the Huntspill River. We're not part of the surveillance team and would just get in the way. Mary is sensible enough to know that, even if I don't.

'Where's he going, Bob?' she asked.

I assumed it was a rhetorical question, kept quiet.

Another car took over the tail as Hicks approached Burnham-on-Sea, the radio crackling into life once more.

'He's going south on the Esplanade.'

'It's a dead end; pulling in and following on foot.'

'That's the yacht club down there,' said Mary. 'Maybe Angela's on a boat?'

'If it's a dead end, he'll have to come back this way,' I said, when she parked on the seafront. 'Park down there, otherwise he'll go right past us.'

I didn't see the road name in the darkness. All the streetlights had gone off, although it was a clear sky with a full moon. Cold too.

Mary turned behind a block of flats and parked on the nearside, just back from the junction; engine and lights off. Then we both slid down in our seats until we were peering over the dashboard, listening for anything on the radio.

Something was ticking. Either her wristwatch or the clock; a painful reminder that time was running out for Angela. The radio stayed silent for what seemed like an age.

I've never been very good at waiting. Shirley will vouch for that. I've been on surveillance operations before, of course I have, but this is different. We're into the fourth day of Angela's abduction. She's alive too. I know she is. And here I am, sitting in a car in the dark, twiddling my thumbs.

Then we heard heavy breathing over the radio. 'He went to the yacht club, but he's on the move again. Do I continue the tail?'

'Yes.' Sharp's voice. 'DS Simpson will investigate the yacht club.'

'Sorry, I've been running,' said the voice, still gasping. 'He just stood on the end of the jetty, Mary. Looking across the river at something. Ten minutes, maybe, then he got back in his car and left. Northbound on the Esplanade now.'

We ducked down further, watched Hicks drive past without so much as a glance in our direction. Then, a couple of seconds later, another car.

'Let's go and have a look,' said Mary. She sat up, turned the key. 'Let's hope your little chat with him did the trick and he's led us to Angela.'

Between you and me, I'm not holding my breath.

Mary parked her car at the end of the turning circle, leaving her headlights on full beam to illuminate the footpath to the jetty. The clubhouse was in darkness behind us, a security light on in the yard where yachts were standing on trailers, craned out of the river for the winter.

There were one or two on moorings at the bottom of the jetty, we could see the masts, hear the rigging rattling in the gentle breeze.

We followed the footpath, walked out along the jetty until we came to a gate.

Mary tried the handle. Padlocked, and it was staying that way no matter how hard she rattled it. 'He must have a key.'

'What's that over there?' I asked. The voice on the radio said Hicks had been looking across the river at something, but it was difficult to see in the moonlight.

A yacht, possibly. On the mud, the tide out.

There appeared to be an inlet on the far side of the river, opposite the jetty, the mud glistening, with one yacht-shaped darker patch.

'Is that a yacht over there?'

Mary was squinting into the darkness. 'Could be.'

'Let's get the club's keyholder out here,' I said. 'We'll need the coastguard too.'

'Maybe she's over there, he came to kill her and got the tide wrong?'

'He wouldn't make a mistake like that. He led us here for a reason.'

Mary sighed. 'He knows we're following him?'

'I'd bet my house on it.'

She doesn't need to know I haven't got one.

Mary left me on the jetty, went back to her car to use the radio.

The gate was high, with spikes on the end of fence posts that extended higher still and out to both sides, over the mud. Barbed wire too. There was no way round it, or over it, not that I'm athletic enough to have attempted it anyway. Not these days.

There's a strange smell to estuary mud, but the tide was coming in. Even I could see that. Some of the moored yachts were afloat now, the masts swaying from side to side, which meant that the yacht on the far side of the river would be afloat, surely?

'Sharp's on his way,' Mary said, appearing at my elbow a couple of minutes later. 'He's called out the coastguard and the fire brigade just in case.'

We weren't waiting long before a torch appeared on the footpath.

'That might be the keyholder. I told them to tell him we'd be on the jetty,' said Mary.

It turned out he lived in the block of flats a couple of hundred yards back along the Esplanade; got there before anyone else.

'Can I help?' he asked. He looked as if he'd pulled a pair of trousers on over his pyjamas, but then he probably had. Coat done up to the neck too, bobble hat.

Mary reached for her warrant card. 'I'm Detect—'

'Is that a yacht over there?' I interrupted – no time for the niceties. I was pointing across the river, at the inlet on the far bank.

'Yes. We've got a couple of moorings that side, but they're not usually in use during the winter. There's one yacht over there at the moment.'

'How do we get there?'

'There's a rib.'

'Can you take us over?'

'When?'

'Now.'

He looked down at the water, shining his torch at a gauge on the side of jetty. 'Tide's coming in, so it should be fine, yes.'

‘How long does that give us?’ asked Mary.

‘Five hours. It’s a ten-metre tide this morning, so it’ll still be coming in for two hours or more.’ He was unlocking the gate, his torch tucked under his arm.

‘What can you tell me about the yacht that’s over there?’ I asked.

‘Not a lot. It only arrived a few days ago, oddly enough. I don’t know the chap’s name. He’s not long bought it.’ The gate swung open with a clang. ‘Didn’t want to put his name on the waiting list for a permanent mooring this side, which I thought was a bit strange, but it takes all sorts, doesn’t it? Said he was quite happy over there, moored in the Channel.’

Chapter Forty-One

'The Channel?'

'That's what we call it. Takes six during the summer months, so it's useful overflow.'

I look at Mary, raise my eyebrows.

'Are you thinking what I'm thinking?'

I nod, slowly.

Some other aspect of Operation Hurricane, the good doctor had said. And now we've got a boat moored in an inlet known as 'the Channel'.

Painfully close to the HMS *Plym* moored in Bunsen Channel, don't you think?

Truth is I don't know what to think, but we have to check it.

'We ought to get some lifejackets from the clubhouse.'

'We haven't got time for that,' I said.

'There might be a couple in the bottom of the rib.'

The jetty extends a short distance across the sand, secured to pillars driven deep into the beach, then turns to run parallel to the river. At the far end, on the seaward side, is a small rubber dinghy with an engine on the back.

I've never been very good with boats. I've got a bit better lately, fishing on Blagdon Lake, but that's about the extent of it.

'That's the rib?' I asked.

'That's it.' The man climbs in and lifts the lid on a storage container under the seats. 'There are two lifejackets. You take them, if you're going to be transferring to the yacht over there. I'll be fine in the rib.'

'Are you sure?' asked Mary.

'It's fine.' He sits us down in the boat and helps us on with our lifejackets. Then he starts the engine, unties the mooring line and turns out across the current. It catches the front of the rib and we rock from side to side on the small waves that are rolling up the River Brue, but we're quickly under control, accelerating across the river towards the inlet.

'Here, you take this,' said the man, handing Mary his torch.

She shines it in the direction of the yacht, now lifted off the mud by the rising tide.

'It's a small one; sixteen-footer. Fine for recreational sailing in the estuary, but that's about it.' The boat slows as we approach the moored yacht. 'What exactly is it you're looking for?'

'Angela Harper,' replied Mary.

'Not that missing journalist?'

Engine off, the rib bumps the side of the yacht. The man reaches up and loops the mooring line around a stanchion, pulls it tight.

'When you're ready,' he said.

I can hear sirens in the distance now, as Mary climbs aboard the yacht, shines the torch at the door, bangs on it.

'Angela?'

'Angela!'

She listens attentively, then she turns and helps me over the railings. 'It's not looking good,' she said. 'Can't hear anything.' She tries the door handle. 'Locked.'

The curtains are drawn in the side window, so I lean over, can't see anything through the skylight.

'Pass me the torch, will you?'

It's seen better days, this yacht. The varnish is peeling off the deck timbers, some of them rotten, and I can see tears in the sail, even though it's rolled tightly around the boom. I shine the torch at the mast, two pennants at the top shredded by the wind.

I don't know about you, but I'm starting to get a bad feeling about this. I keep thinking about the *Plym* and what happened to her when she was moored in Bunsen Channel.

If Angela isn't on this yacht, then what's this all about?

The yacht is rocking gently from side to side as I lean over again, shine the torch through the Perspex.

There's a table, but no one sitting at it. No sign of Angela. What I can see, though, is gas canisters. Several of them on the bench seat. And Jerry cans. The cabin is full of them.

There's a strong smell of petrol too.

I shine the torch at an angle, tip my head, trying to see the inside of the door; expecting to see a car battery and wires. If there's something there, it's hidden behind more gas canisters.

Something strikes me about the sail, but I can't put my finger on it. Full of holes, as I said, but there's more to it than that.

'How do I raise this thing?' I asked.

The man is watching us from the safety of the rib. 'Pull on that rope,' he replied. 'Don't raise it too much in this wind. We'll swing right round.'

Beams of light are illuminating the yacht from the jetty now. I turn to see several police officers watching us. Looks like Sharp is there too. Blue lights are coming along the seafront in the distance.

'I reckon I can open this door, if I pull hard enough,' said Mary, bracing herself.

'Don't touch it!'

I was unfurling the mainsail, just the top to reveal the sail number. Every yacht's got one. It had been back to front when it was rolled up, but now it's plain as day, the loose fabric fluttering in the breeze.

GBR0271X.

'That's HMS *Plym*'s number,' said Mary.

'Are there any hidden compartments on a yacht this size?' I asked.

'She's not big enough for that.' The voice is coming from the rib, so he's still there in the darkness. 'There might be a forward compartment, but there'll be another skylight behind you, if there is. I can't see from here. Under the bed is just about the only place she could be in there.'

I turn, look for a Perspex skylight, shine my torch down into the cabin.

There's a bed, no one lying on it. I try lifting the skylight, but it's locked from the inside.

'Have you got anything I can smash this with?'

'Use this.' An oar appears from the rib. Mary passes it to me.

I know what you're thinking. I'm thinking the same thing, common sense taking over in the nick of time.

Angela's not on board this yacht.

It's a booby trap. It'll make quite a bang when it goes up too.

I hand the oar back to Mary. 'We'll let the bomb squad handle it,' I said.

◆ ◆ ◆

'Where is he?' I asked when I stepped off the rib on to the jetty.

'Sitting in his car at Apex Park,' replied Sharp. 'He's smoking a cigar, apparently. Waiting for something, it looks like.'

'The bang. The yacht's full of gas bottles and cans of petrol. I couldn't see, but I'm guessing it'll go off when the door's opened. It'll go up like the *Plym*.'

'Apex Park's only about a mile in that direction.' Mary was pointing over the reed bed behind us. 'He'll see the explosion from there.'

'Are you sure, Bob?' asked Sharp.

I don't know why he asked me that, really. Perhaps it was to buy himself a bit of time to think. Anyway, I managed to stifle the obvious reply – *Of course I'm bloody well sure!* 'The sail number is zero-two-seven-one, the same as HMS *Plym*.'

Then he looked at me, his face blank. 'What d'you suggest we do?'

'Nothing to alert him we've found it,' I replied. 'I'm guessing he knows he was being followed, led us here deliberately, but we shouldn't confirm that for him. If there's no explosion, he'll give up and go home. In the meantime, we need the bomb squad and a thermal imaging camera, just to make sure Angela's not on board. I couldn't see her, but you never know. Once we've found her, they can tow it out into the bay and blow it up in a controlled explosion.'

'And how do we find her?'

'Keep the tail on him, hope for the best,' I said. Then I turned and walked up the jetty.

The keyholder was kind enough to open the clubhouse for us after that, made us all several coffees while we waited in the warm for the bomb squad to arrive. The naval team had been tasked, aptly enough, given that the device was on board a yacht, and it took them a couple of hours to arrive from Plymouth.

Hicks was still sitting in his car at Apex Park, so Sharp ordered no blue lights, directed them in via the Esplanade.

Tiredness and stress take a horrible toll. I sat watching Sharp, sitting in the huge windows at the front of the clubhouse, staring out across the estuary, picking at the skin at the base of his nails. It's easy to see how the case got the better of Eric Hall.

I remember the rising panic of the original search for Paul Bromfield, day after day. And now, here we are again. The only difference this time is we know who's done it. And I've got a plan. I said I'd got one. I'm guessing you want to know what it is, but you'll find out soon enough.

Just try to remember that I'm responsible for Angela. And I'm not a serving police officer anymore, don't have to read him his rights.

We were back on the jetty just after four, watching two naval bomb squad officers take the yacht club's rib across the river. The tide had turned now, the current ripping back out to sea, but the motor boat made short work of the crossing.

It had taken me five minutes or so to brief them, and the rib was full of equipment.

'What are they going to do?' asked Mary, appearing at my elbow.

'Thermal imaging camera first. Then they'll drill holes in the side, put little inspection cameras in to have a look around.'

'One spark—'

'It's a water-cooled drill, low speed.'

The bomb squad commander was standing at the end of the jetty, with Sharp, and I edged closer so I could hear the radio exchanges.

Nothing on the thermal imaging, which means one of two things. Angela's not on board, or she is, but she's stone cold.

Dead.

It was something that had occurred to me. Hicks has killed twice before. Once remotely, if you can call it that. Then Andrew Bucknall, a killing that was up close and personal. So, yes, he's capable of cold-blooded murder, make no mistake about it.

I don't.

We could hear the drill across the river, but only just. There was no way the sound would reach Hicks at Apex Park.

'It's a homemade device. Electric detonator, triggered by the door opening. There's a strong smell of petrol.'

'Any sign of the girl?'

'None, sir.'

'Is there any way you can look under the bed?'

'We can cut the skylight, go in.'

'Do it, Sam.'

'Yes, sir.'

'After that you'd better bale out. You've got twenty minutes before the tide strands you there all day.'

I wasn't the only one fidgeting, nervously. It was either that or we were all trying to keep warm on the jetty, shifting from one foot to the other, the water shimmering in the moonlight beneath our feet. We could hear the saw cutting the Perspex, see the torch lights across the river. Then a figure dropped down inside the forward cabin.

'Nothing, sir. There is storage under the bed, but it's empty.'

'All right. Get yourselves back over here now. We'll tow it out and blow it up a mile offshore when the police give us the go ahead. The next high tide's at two-thirty.'

Then Sharp's radio crackled into life. 'Hicks is on the move, sir. Looks like he's heading home.'

Sharp looked at me, sneered. 'Well, your little gamble didn't pay off, did it, Bob? He almost certainly knows we're on to him and he didn't lead us to the girl. So, now what?'

'Nothing's going to happen until tomorrow.'

'It bloody well is tomorrow,' snapped Sharp. 'The sun will be coming up in three hours.'

'I need to go home,' I said. 'Catch up on some sleep. I think we all do. If you wouldn't mind dropping me back to my car, Mary?'

'It was worth a try, Bob,' she said, to break the silence more than anything. 'We had to try something.'

She parked across the track twenty minutes later, watched me as I climbed out of the passenger seat.

'What time?' she asked.

'Ten at Bridgwater.'

'Fine.'

Then she turned her car in the lane and accelerated away. I listened to the rumble of her engine fading into the distance, standing there looking across the South Drain at the Edgar Lamb.

Lights were on upstairs, but then Hicks would have only just got home himself.

I opened the boot of my car, lifted the carpet, and took out the crowbar that I'd hidden behind the spare tyre. I'd thought it might come in handy one day.

I don't take any chances. Not anymore.

Like I said, I don't have to read him his rights.

Chapter Forty-Two

I tap on the windscreen of the Sierra parked along Station Road, the police officer in the passenger seat waking up with a start. The driver winds down his window.

'You're wanted back at Bridgwater. I'll take over.'

'Really?' The driver frowns, reaches for his radio.

I hold up the crowbar, make sure he gets a good look at it. 'Leave. Now.'

He turns the key, accelerates away, his lights coming on when he's over the bridge and further along the lane.

I reckon I've got twenty minutes. They'll think better of it when they get round the corner, radio Sharp, who'll drop everything and come running.

Twenty minutes should be enough.

If this was a Hollywood film, they'd use a baseball bat for this. I've got a cricket bat at home. It's a new Gray-Nicolls that I had signed by the Somerset squad of 1982, and it would be a shame to smudge the ink. Might be worth something, one day. The other problem with wood is that it leaves splinters. An iron bar is much safer, unless it's painted, of course. Then you risk leaving flakes of paint.

I learned something in my thirty years on the force.

So, a crowbar it is.

Gloves too, of course, although that's not just about fingerprints. There'll be lots of broken glass as well, I expect.

Not that I stand much of a chance of getting away with this. Can't say that matters at the moment. All I want is to know where to find Angela. I'll worry about the rest later.

The front door of the pub is glazed, an image of the old stationmaster etched into the glass. Edgar Lamb himself.

Hicks will know I'm coming after this, but then that's the idea.

The glass shatters with the first swing of the crowbar. Then I set about the lock; two swings at the wooden frame and I kick the door open.

The internal door isn't locked.

Now I'm in the bar, swinging the crowbar at the glasses on the counter – someone didn't do the washing up when they closed up last night. Won't need to do it now, either.

Now for the optics, behind the bar.

There's a door at the far end. I know it leads to the stairs up to the owner's accommodation. That's where he'll come from, so I'm keeping an eye on it as I work my way along. The optics, bottles on the shelf above, the mirror behind, fridges under the counter.

The door is opening slowly, the barrels of a shotgun appearing.

I've been expecting something like this and I'm ready for it. I know he's got a shotgun licence; clay pigeon shooting was the reason given.

I swing the crowbar at the barrels of the gun, two loud bangs and the table and chairs opposite are sent flying, peppered with shot. The gun falls to the floor, Hicks bending over to pick it up. I can see him through the frosted glass.

Oh no you don't.

I wrench open the door, swing the crowbar at his outstretched hand. There's a sickening crunch of bone, followed by a scream.

He falls backwards, sitting on the floor at the bottom of the stairs, clutching his right wrist to his chest.

I reach down, pick up the shotgun in my left hand, throw it across the pub.

'Where are the spare cartridges?'

Hicks grimaces, gestures to his left trouser pocket.

'Throw them to me.'

Too slow, so I swing the crowbar at the end of the banister, right above his head, the wood splintering with a crash.

'All right, all right!' He reaches into his pocket and tosses two red cartridges in my direction. I bend down, pick them up and put them in my pocket.

'Right, now where is she?'

'You'll never find her.' He sneers. 'She'll waste away just like my wife and son. Now, arrest me.'

'I'm not here to arrest you.'

I've never thought of myself as the intimidating type. I'm only five foot ten, and Hicks would tower over me if he wasn't on the floor. So, that's where he's going to stay.

I've never been particularly violent either. Let's just say this is not something that comes naturally to me, but Angela's life is at stake. And if Sharp arrests him, he'll say nothing; exercise his right to silence. Let her die.

Well, this is about her rights.

Look away now if you're squeamish.

I swing the crowbar at the side of Hicks's left knee. The Irish way. I know. I've seen it up close.

There's a sickening thud, a scream.

'Where is she?' My voice flat.

I have a horrible feeling I'm going to puke, but I can't let him see that.

He tries to bend his leg, lets out another scream.

I am way over the line now.

I aim the crowbar at his knee again, take a mock swing.

He's trying to pull himself up on what remains of the banister, gets himself sitting on the bottom step. His right wrist is still pressed to his chest, his left hand holding his knee. 'Let me get up. I'll tell you where she is, just for God's sake let me get up.' He leans forward, breathing hard, gasping. 'You've done well, Bob.' He's smiling through the pain. 'Twenty-four years I've waited for this moment.'

'What the fuck has Angela ever done to you?'

'She's a journalist, and they colluded to cover the whole thing up, didn't they?'

'No, they didn't. They were served with D-Notices; they couldn't print anything. And Angela wasn't even born when the bomb was tested.'

'They killed my wife and son.'

'Who did?'

'*They* did.'

'John Bromfield didn't. He was just following orders. And Paul Bromfield *certainly* didn't.'

'We tried to sue them, they said there was no connection to the bomb test. It was too much sun, they said. That might be true for skin cancer, but not a brain tumour. How does a one-year-old baby get glioblastoma, if not from nuclear radiation? You answer me that, Bob.' He's softening now, sadness taking over.

That's what he wants me to think, anyway.

'I can't. All I can tell you is that none of it is Angela's fault.'

'Then my wife got the same thing. She was over here on one of those extended visas, working her way around the country. Ended up here, behind the bar. Never left. Died in bed upstairs.' There are tears rolling down his cheeks now. 'She was twenty-nine years old, and I want everybody to know.'

'When you have your day in court, I suppose?'

'Exactly.'

'You'll get your day in court, on trial for the murder of Paul Bromfield. And then there's Andrew Bucknall.'

'You can guarantee that, can you?'

'What I can guarantee is you won't get your day in court unless you tell me where to find Angela, because I'll beat you to death with this iron bar.'

He's flexing his left leg, wincing. Obviously, I didn't hit it hard enough. 'Then you'll have your day in court for killing me. It'll all come out then.'

'I'll plead guilty. The hearing will be over in half an hour. No one will ever know the full story.'

He tries to pull himself up, collapses back onto the bottom step. 'The full story.' He's mumbling. 'Kids playing in a pond. They're all dead now. All of them. That's what this story is about.'

'No, it isn't. It's about a man taking his rage out on the wrong people.'

'You were supposed to find the boy.'

'Bollocks.'

Hicks shrugs. 'But the case went cold. That's when we tried to sue. The last straw was the Royal Commission. We'd fought for a public inquiry for years, but it wouldn't even hear evidence about what happened to the children at Amberley. Too far removed, they said. Then you come calling, Bob, and off we go again.'

'Paul Bromfield was nine years old. You could have rung. You didn't have to give your name.'

'His father was the captain of the ship, sitting there in my pub. We just couldn't believe . . .' He's shaking his head.

'What about Simon Horsey?'

'A trail for you to follow. And you did.'

'Why did Andrew Bucknall have to die?'

'He used to hang about up at the bunker, turned up one day when I was there planting the flowers. It was that article on the front page of the *Gazette*. We get it delivered early; it was still dark, so I drove over to his caravan, did what had to be done. Suddenly the flowers were the key to the whole thing, and he knew too much. Had to die. I felt bad about it. I really did, but I wasn't ready. I hadn't taken Angela yet.'

'But you didn't feel bad about Paul Bromfield?'

'It wasn't my responsibility. *They* did it when they detonated that bomb. And you lot, when you didn't find him.'

'What were you doing on the train that morning?'

He hesitates. 'I don't remember.'

'It was the nine-thirty, and you were travelling towards Edington Junction, so where had you been?'

'I must've been into Glastonbury for something.'

'At that time in the morning?'

'I really don't remember.'

'All right then, another question. What did you do when you got off the train with Paul? How did you get him to the bunker?'

'There was a car with the keys in it. I took it.'

'Where was it, this car?'

'In the car park of the Railway Tavern.'

'What sort of car was it?'

'I don't remember. It was white, I think.'

I nod. 'And you took him to the bunker because you knew no one would be going down there for ages.'

'Yes.'

'So, what have you done with Angela?'

He gives a cold laugh. 'You'll never find her.'

I've got the crowbar in my right hand, ready to swing it at his shin. I brace myself. 'One last chance.'

Suddenly, he lunges at me, knocks me backwards into the table and chairs that were scattered by the shotgun blast. Now we're fighting over the crowbar. He's holding the curved end with his left hand, trying to jerk it from my grasp.

I lash out with my right foot, kicking at the side of his left knee. He screams in pain.

Now he's hobbling towards the front door.

I follow, broken glass crunching beneath our feet.

Once out into the darkness he turns, making for his car. I can see him fumbling in his pocket for his keys, suddenly bathed in light.

Headlights have come on from somewhere. The vehicle is parked on the far side of the car park. I heard an engine running, idling, when I followed Hicks out of the pub; haven't had time to look for it. Now it's accelerating hard, wheels spinning on the gravel. It looks like a saloon of some sort. A Rover, possibly, but I'm blinded by the lights on full beam.

Hicks stops, turns. Too late, is hit by the car. He slams across the bonnet, his head smashing into the windscreen, shattering it, then he's lifted up and over the roof, landing in a heap behind it.

The car stops, engine revving.

Then the reversing lights come on.

I turn away, listen to the sickening thud as the car bounces over his body, before it turns and accelerates out of the car park, scattering gravel in its wake.

Chapter Forty-Three

Blood is seeping into the gravel underneath the twisted body of Frederick Hicks, taking with it my last hope of finding Angela alive.

There's no coming back from that. No chance he can tell me where she is now.

Light is streaming out of the windows and entrance porch of the pub, illuminating what's left of his body. There are tyre marks on his skull, the bones crushed under the weight of the car. Blood is oozing from his ears, nose and mouth, his mangled limbs at all sorts of sickening angles.

I can't look.

Sirens in the distance drag me back to the present, my first thoughts turning to self-preservation, I'm embarrassed to admit.

There's no way a pathologist will be able to tell which injuries I inflicted on him with the crowbar. Not that they slowed him down much.

There's a rhyne on the other side of the road. I walk fifty yards or so along, drop it into the water, hoping it'll look like it fell off a passing lorry. There's no blood on it, and no fingerprints, so I might get away with it.

That's if they find it, if they even look for it.

The sirens are getting closer now and I can see blue lights flashing in the trees lining the A39 up on the hill. They'll be turning left soon, dropping down.

I've got five minutes, maybe.

Something doesn't add up and I know what it is; think I do, anyway.

If I'd kidnapped a child, snatched him off a crowded train, I'd remember every detail. Wouldn't you? Even after all this time.

Every single detail, and yet there were convenient gaps in Hicks's memory.

I wonder why.

My first task is to get past Sharp. I'm no good to Angela locked up, am I?

Cars have screeched to a halt in the road, blocking the entrance to the pub car park. Sharp is first out of an unmarked car, striding across the gravel towards me.

'What the bloody hell's happened here, Bob?'

'He ran out of the pub, got hit by a car. It must've been waiting for him. The lights come on, I hear the engine screaming, and wallop. Then it reverses over him and is gone.'

'It wasn't you, was it?' He's staring at me, and I've a horrible feeling he really believes I might have done it.

'No, it fucking well wasn't. My car's on the track the other side of the drain. Check it if you don't believe me.' I take out my keys, lob them to him.

He passes them to a detective standing next to him. 'Check it.'

'It's the yellow Volvo estate,' I said.

'Tell me about this car,' Sharp demanded.

Paramedics are checking Hicks's body for vital signs. I should've done it, really, but you know what, fuck him. From where I'm standing, he got what he deserved. And Angela is my only concern now.

'It was a dark saloon of some sort. I didn't get the number, but it'll have front end damage and the windscreen shattered when it hit him.'

'Have you seen the car before?'

'No.'

That's a lie, but he doesn't need to know that. Not yet.

'What about the driver?'

'Didn't get a look at him.' I shake my head. 'He had a hood.'

That's a lie too. I saw him, plain as day. And he knows I saw him.

'You'd better come and have a look at this, guv.' The shout comes from inside the pub.

'You.' Sharp jabs his finger at me. 'With me, in here. Now.' I follow him into the bar. He's standing with his hands on his hips, taking in the scene of destruction. 'What the fuck happened here, Bob?'

'We had a discussion,' I replied. 'He confessed to the kidnap and murder of Paul Bromfield, the kidnap of Simon Horsey and the murder of Andrew Bucknall.'

'Did he tell you where the girl is?'

'No.'

'You fucked up then, didn't you?'

I did. And you and I both know it. There's still a chance, though. A small one.

There's a young detective standing next to me now, my car keys in his outstretched hand. 'His car's clear, guv. Not a mark on it.'

Sharp sighs, seems almost disappointed.

Git.

'What's all this broken glass?'

'He started smashing up his own pub when he realised I knew.'

'And the shotgun?' Sharp is looking at an officer holding it up by the barrels.

'He tried to shoot me. Missed. I took these from him when he tried to reload.' I reach into my pocket, take out the cartridges, drop them into an evidence bag being held up in front of me. 'Then he made a run for it. That's when he got hit by the car.'

'All right, Bob. I'll need a detailed witness statement from you, exactly what happened here; what he said, word for word.'

As if I didn't know that. It means I'm off the hook, though, for the time being at least.

Mary has arrived, standing back, trying to avoid eye contact with Sharp.

'You bloody well left him on his own, didn't you?' he said, glaring at her.

'He said he was going home to bed.'

I'm walking towards the stairs that lead up to the owner's accommodation, broken glass crunching under my feet.

'Where are you going now?'

'Have a look upstairs,' I replied. 'Have a word with the father-in-law, see if he really has got dementia.'

Sharp snaps his fingers at Mary. 'Go with him, and don't let him out of your sight this time.'

◆ ◆ ◆

There's a light on in every room, but they're all empty apart from one.

Clean and tidy, not what I'd expected at all. How d'you lead a normal life after what he's done?

After what happened to his family too, I suppose. If we're being fair about it.

I can't begin to imagine, but I like to think I wouldn't have reacted in the way he did – killing a child in the way he did.

Not to mention Andrew Bucknall.

The television is on in the living room, but it's only the Ceefax. He even did the washing up before he went out last night.

Pictures of his wife and son on the wall in the master bedroom, framed ones on the bedside table. His wife holding a baby, beaming at the camera.

I'm standing here, by his bed, looking at the photograph, trying to put myself in his position, trying to imagine how I'd feel if it had been Shirley and my firstborn, Christine.

I understand the anger, I really do, but he took it out on the wrong people in the wrong way. And that's unforgivable.

Then there's how I'd feel if it had been my daughter Christine, and my grandson.

His father-in-law's in the next room, so now's the time to find out if he really has got dementia.

Mary has opened the door of the spare bedroom. 'He's in here, Bob,' she said. 'His name's Terence Burnside. You need to see this.' She hands me a rolled-up piece of shiny fax paper. 'The Home Office faxed it over an hour ago. He was here in August 1962. Flew back to Australia on September eighth.'

The old man is slumped in an armchair. Corduroys, a check shirt and cardigan. There's a wool blanket on the floor in front of him, looks like it's slid off his legs.

I sit down on the end of the bed, right in front of him.

His skin is tanned, wrinkled, his eyes closed. He's drooling too.

'Mr Burnside?' Mary leans over, taps him on the forearm. No response, so she tries again. 'Mr Burnside?'

He opens his eyes slowly, stares at me, then Mary. 'Where's Fred?' His voice is weak.

'He's dead, Mr Burnside.' Matter of fact, ignoring the frown Mary gives me. 'I need to know what happened when he took the little boy off the train.'

'I wish he'd do more to help me.' He's staring at me, his face blank. 'Dead?'

‘He told me to ask you what happened to Paul Bromfield, said you’d tell me everything.’

He straightens, takes a moment to focus on me, looks me up and down. ‘He hadn’t planned it. He told him he’d get him an ice cream. Then he rang me from the phone box. I went and got them in his car, and he suggested we put the boy in the bunker till the fuss died down. He said the Observer lot never went down there, and it’d be fine.’ His eyes glaze over. ‘It was the man from the ship. Fred wanted him to suffer, that’s all. He said we’d hold the boy for a while, let him know how it felt, then let the child go. He said he was giving him food and water.’

‘Why did you help him?’

‘I had one dead daughter, my other daughter was dying, and my grandson was dead as well. Why wouldn’t I help him?’

‘What was Fred doing on the train?’

‘We were over from Australia, staying with them, had a row the night before – I don’t remember what about – he’d stormed out, went to stay in Glastonbury. I was going to find him, patch things up, say sorry.’ His hands are shaking. ‘I flew home a week later, rang Fred and he promised to release the boy. Promised me faithfully he’d release the boy.’

‘He didn’t though, did he?’

‘No.’ He’s rocking backwards and forwards in his chair now, the bones creaking in his hands as he squeezes his knuckles. ‘He said he wanted everyone to know what happened to his wife and son, but the police never came for him.’

‘He killed Paul Bromfield,’ I said.

‘I only found out later. I was so . . . sorry.’ Tears flowing freely now. ‘There’s been enough death. My wife died of a broken heart and look what it’s doing to me.’

He’s making the most of a lucid moment, and he knows what the dementia is taking from him.

My heart bleeds.

'He's killed someone else,' I said. 'He cut a man's throat in the peat fields. His name was Andrew Bucknall.'

'I don't know who this person is.'

His eyes are glazing over, and I can see I'm losing him. If he really has got dementia then lucid moments don't tend to last long. If he hasn't, then he's a bloody good actor.

'There's a missing journalist,' I said. 'He's taken her. A young girl.'

'He said a journalist would mean it got in the papers. I told him not to do it again, but he wouldn't listen. The Royal Commission last year was enough. The atomic tests had caused cancer, that's what it said. That was enough for me, and I told him.'

'Where is she?'

'I told him to stop. I wanted no more of it.'

'Her name is Angela,' I said. 'Did he tell you where she is?'

'Mr Burnside?' Mary is rubbing his forearm now, trying to keep him in the present. 'Where is Angela?'

'He used to talk to me, thinking I didn't understand what he was saying, that I'd forget.' He shrugs. 'I acted up for the doctors, pretended to be worse than I am, didn't want to have to go back to Australia. There's no one left for me there now.'

There's no one for you here, either.

I stand up. 'Where is Angela?'

'Something to do with balloons. He mentioned balloons.'

◆ ◆ ◆

I'm following Mary down the stairs, feeling conflicted.

What good's it going to do to prosecute the old man now? Chances are he'll be ruled unfit to plead anyway, end up being detained in a secure hospital for the rest of his life.

Is it really in the public interest?

It turns out to be an easy decision. Easy, when I think about how Paul Bromfield died. And if the old man ends his days being locked in a room, then so be it.

He may have dementia, but he'll know. In his lucid moments, he'll know.

I let Mary break the news to Sharp.

He looked at me. 'Where's the girl then?'

'The barrage balloon hangar over at Pawlett,' I replied. 'According to the old man.'

'We've searched the balloon hangar, guv,' said the young detective who'd checked my car.

'Not well enough, obviously,' I said.

Sharp looks at me, shakes his head. 'Go, Bob. Find her. Tear the fucking place apart if you have to.'

Chapter Forty-Four

Two uniformed officers are waiting for us when we arrive at the balloon hangar, parked across the high metal gates at the entrance to the compound.

You couldn't exactly miss the bloody thing. It's a giant shed, basically, built during the war and large enough to hold a barrage balloon. Must be all of eighty feet high, and the rusting corrugated iron sheeting is visible for miles around, some of the panels missing, whipped away by storms over the winter.

Some bright spark thought it was a good idea to make it a listed building. I pity the poor sod who's got to pay for it to be fixed.

'I didn't know they kept barrage balloons in sheds.' Mary is looking up from the passenger seat of my car.

'They didn't usually,' I replied. 'They used this one for testing devices to cut the wires. Planes would fly into them, try to cut the cables.'

'Oh, right.' She takes off her seatbelt, climbs out of my car. 'Hicks must've had a key.'

'There are some holes in the fencing around the far side,' offers one of the officers.

'And you checked this place?' I asked.

'Yes, sir.' He looks sheepish, nervous. 'There are various walkways and gantries inside, but she's not on any of them.'

'Let's have a look, shall we?'

I'm doing my best to stay patient. Hicks might've been lying, might've known his father-in-law would tell us. Might have moved her, even. I learned a long time ago to take nothing for granted.

The officer opens the padlock and the chain drops to the ground, the gate swinging open with a crash.

Two vast sliding doors tower over us as we walk across the crumbling concrete yard, weeds growing out of deep cracks.

The officer is sorting through a jumble of keys 'There's a side door.'

The sun is rising now, the first glow of dawn reflecting off the gable end of the hangar. The officer puts the key in the lock, turns it and wrenches open the door, the rusting metal squealing in protest.

'Who owns it?' I asked.

'Don't know, guv. I got the key off the bloke who runs the scrapyard round the side, but he just rents it.'

I noticed the cars piled up on the way in, brambles starting to hide them.

Strip lights are flickering into life now with that familiar clicking sound. Some of them anyway; a few tubes seem to have gone.

'There's an office in the far corner, but I checked that. She's definitely not in there.'

'Is there an inspection pit?'

'Don't know.'

I've brought a torch, just in case, and I'm weaving my way between old cars, the beam fixed on the ground in front of me. I'm looking for any sign of recent activity, scuffs, footprints in the dust. Mary follows, walking on the other side of the cars. There are several old Jaguars, a VW Beetle, a Dormobile, even an Aston Martin. Collectors' items one day, I suppose.

I know the good doctor said Angela wouldn't be underground. Actually, she said she *might not* be underground. Look for *some other aspect of Operation Hurricane.*

I did that and almost got myself blown to smithereens.

Angela will be underground, if only for the soundproofing it offers.

I can hear footsteps high above me now, look up to see a uniformed officer on the gantry overhead.

I try a shout, don't know why I hadn't thought of it before, really. 'Angela!'

Mary tries a shout too, our calls echoing around the void above the strip lights, pitch dark apart from the officer's torch.

Cars can be moved, I know that, and I'm squatting down, checking under each of them as I make my way along the line. There are no tyre tracks in the dust, though; no sign that tyre tracks have been swept away.

It takes us about twenty minutes to cover the whole floor area. Solid concrete, no inspection pit. I check the office too: empty.

The uniformed officers appear in front of us, looking relieved, if anything.

'See, guv. She's not here.'

'What about the air raid shelter?' I asked. 'Have you checked that?'

'What air raid shelter?'

'It's a military installation, built during the war. There'll be an air raid shelter.'

Blank looks.

'It'll be as far as they could get it away from the hangar, around the boundary fence, probably.'

'Follow me, guv.'

Around the side of the hangar a path weaves its way through the undergrowth towards the fence, chicken wire panels with barbed wire coils along the top. We turn sideways in places, brambles clawing at the sleeves of our coats, rain dripping off the branches of elderberry bushes above our heads.

'This is the gap in the fence, guv,' said the uniformed officer. 'We came along here before.'

All that means is that any footprints will have been lost under their boots.

'Are there any other paths?'

'Not that we could see. We walked right round the outside.'

Think, Bob, think.

I'm staring at the brambles when I notice the tangle in front of me is dead. All the rest have green shoots just starting to appear. I look down at the ground.

They've been cut.

Cut and put here to hide a path behind. I can see it now, a narrow path, footprints.

'Help me get this out of the way,' I said. I grab hold of the tangle of brambles, pull. The thorns are still sharp, cutting my hands to ribbons.

The uniformed officer is pulling too, dragging the brambles out through the gap in the fence.

'There's a path,' he said. 'Sorry, guv, we didn't see that.'

Mary looks at me, smiles.

Fifty yards through the undergrowth, trying not to obliterate the tracks in the mud.

And there it is.

A red brick entrance, steps down to a solid steel door.

A new padlock.

'We'll have that off in a jiffy,' said the officer. 'Warren, get that crowbar, mate. It was by the Aston.'

I bang on the door with my clenched fist. 'Angela?'

'About bloody time, Bob.' It's her voice, behind the steel door. 'Where the hell have you been?'

◆ ◆ ◆

The uniformed officer reappears carrying a crowbar and a sledgehammer that he's found in the hangar, and it takes them seconds to deal with the padlock, drag the heavy door open.

Then Angela appears, blinking furiously in the light.

'Are you all right?' I asked.

I was still grinning at her when her right hand connected with my cheek. A loud crack.

'That's for that bloody article.'

Then she throws her arms around my neck, hugs me, won't let go.

Mary glances at the uniformed officer, gestures to his radio. 'Better let everybody know,' she said.

Angela still hasn't let go.

'I knew you'd come,' she said. 'Did you get him?'

'He's dead.'

She's dishevelled, covered in dust, but otherwise seems to be in good health. Physically, anyway. Certainly, strong enough. My cheek is still stinging.

'Better get an ambulance,' I said.

'I don't need an ambulance.'

'You'll need to go home and get some sleep,' said Mary.

'Sleep? I've done nothing but sleep for the last three days.'

'It's day four,' I said.

'God, is it really?'

'What about water?' I asked.

'He left me with some bottles. I'm bloody starving, though. What time is it?'

'Just before eight, something like that,' I replied. 'In the morning.'

'You owe me breakfast. Then you can drop me at my office.' She holds up a bulging envelope. 'The world according to Frederick Hicks,' she said. 'His last will and testament.'

I reach out, try to snatch it.

'No bloody fear. He gave it to me. And it's going on the front page.'

Chapter Forty-Five

Hospital first.

Angela grumbled a bit, but that's just tough.

I left Mary to secure the crime scene, drove straight to Musgrove Park. They didn't take long with Angela; checked her over, gave her some electrolytes – sachets of stuff to dissolve in water – told her to drink plenty and eat bland food for a few days, little and often.

She didn't tell them about the bacon roll.

She looked all right, which was a surprise. A bit pale, perhaps, lost a bit of weight too, but it didn't seem to have slowed her down much.

I waited in the car for the tearful reunion with her parents. I'd rung them from the hospital, so they knew she was on her way, faces pressed to the glass in the front window when I parked across the bottom of the steps up to their front door.

Hugs on the garden path.

Then her father was tapping on the driver's window. I got out, rather than winding it down.

'You must come in, Bob,' he said, shaking my hand a little too vigorously, as it happened.

'I don't want to intrude,' I said.

I held firm, waited in the car for Angela to reappear, and it didn't take long. A shower, change of clothes, and she was soon running down the garden path, a piece of toast in each hand.

She'll go far, will Angela. Most people would have gone to pieces locked in that air raid shelter.

Not her.

Oddly enough, she said she never doubted for a minute I'd find her.

I bloody well did, particularly when Hicks died under the wheels of that dark saloon. Thought it best not to tell her, mind you.

I dropped her off at her office. It'll be a while before she gets her car back, but she told me not to worry, the *Gazette* have pool cars available, which is a shame because I rather liked the idea of her being immobile for a few days.

'Dad's going to pick me up from work,' she said, so I was relieved of chauffeur duty anyway.

Then it was over to Langport, a warehouse on the edge of the town. I waited for the clocks to stop chiming.

There was movement in the window of the ground floor flat. Jack Welshman must've seen me coming, opened the front door. Unshaven, a strong smell of whisky. Looked like he hadn't slept, but then I hadn't either so I wouldn't criticise a fellow for that.

He gave a sad smile. 'Did you get Hicks?' he asked.

'I didn't,' I replied. 'You did.'

He hesitated, took a deep breath. 'You saw me, then?'

I nodded, slowly.

'I did wonder. That bastard got what was coming to him.'

Can't argue with that.

'It said on the news you'd found the girl.'

'No thanks to you.'

'He told you where she was, surely?'

'No.'

'That bastard ruined my life,' hissed Welshman. 'I lost my career thanks to that case – my wife, my kids, my home. Everything. And he killed Eric.'

'Since when was this fucking case about you? That's the job.' I turned my back on him, stopped, looked over my shoulder. 'You've got twelve hours to do the right thing. They'll find you anyway, so handing yourself in will . . .' I let my voice tail off. 'You know the way it works, Jack. You don't need me to tell you.'

I walked off after that. Left him standing there.

Sobbing quietly.

◆ ◆ ◆

I'm standing on the jetty at Burnham-on-Sea now, looking out across the estuary. High tide's in half an hour, so it won't be long.

I arrived in time to see them towing the yacht out, GBR0271X just visible on the bit of the mainsail I'd unfurled, flapping gently in the breeze.

There's only one journalist here, with a photographer, several cameras with zoom lenses hanging around his neck. They're waiting further down the jetty.

She'd tried getting permission to go out with the bomb squad, then tried to find someone else to take her out there, but had been blocked.

There's an exclusion zone in place and no boats are being allowed out. Not even for journalists.

That's Angela for you.

They tried to work out how she'd found out about the bomb, but she just kept saying it was an 'anonymous tip off'.

I like to stay anonymous when I can.

Mary appears at my elbow. 'Thought I'd find you here, Bob,' she said. 'Jack Welshman just walked into Bridgwater police station, confessed to killing Hicks.'

'Did he.'

'You don't sound surprised.' Then she spots Angela. 'What the bloody hell's she doing here?'

'She'll tell you she's doing her job, I expect.'

'I won't ask how she found out about the bomb.'

'My guess is it's in Fred Hicks's statement.'

'It isn't. They've given us a copy,' replied Mary. 'Doesn't tell us anything we don't already know, though, to be honest.'

I'm half tempted to go home; not sure why I'm here at all, really. It's not as if I haven't seen explosions before.

'So, what happens now?' asked Mary. 'Back to the Cold Case Unit?'

'We'll see.'

A flash, followed by a huge ball of flame and thick black smoke billowing into the sky. Then the shockwave hits us with a bang.

'Blimey,' said Mary. 'Imagine what the Blue Danube must've been like.'

'I'd rather not.' I turn to walk back up the jetty.

'Where are you going now?'

'Home,' I said. 'There's the leftovers of a roast chicken waiting for me.'

Author's Note

I very much hope you enjoyed reading *Blast from the Past*.

Researching a crime novel set forty years ago (involving a cold case from over sixty years ago) makes the research even more challenging and I am indebted to a number of people who have been extraordinarily generous with their specialist knowledge. I would like to take this opportunity to offer them my sincere thanks.

To Lieutenant Commander Andrew McConochie RN Retired, who very kindly checked and corrected my naval references. I hope you are enjoying your retirement, Andy!

It turned out that my dear friend Rod Glanville's late father worked on the Somerset and Dorset Railway, so as well as being my harshest critic, Rod was able to offer first-hand experience of the steam trains, and the line that traversed the Levels. Thank you, Rod.

To David Hall and Clare Paul, who, as always, have shared their encyclopaedic knowledge of all things Somerset.

All mistakes are mine, of course, and mine alone, although I prefer to call them 'poetic licence'.

Pub names have been changed, for obvious reasons.

Steam railway enthusiasts will have spotted that I have taken a few liberties with the configuration of the excursion train from which poor little Paul Bromfield was snatched. The timetable too. I have also allowed for a little more steam and smoke swirling on the platform than might have been the case in reality!

I have moved the nuclear bunkers too. Oddly enough, they are situated right next to country roads, buried deep in the undergrowth these days, with motorists speeding by, blissfully unaware. I have moved them a little further away purely to make them feel more remote and sinister. For further information and exact locations, Subterranea Britannica is a useful resource. See subbrit.org.uk/locations/somerset/.

The single biggest liberty I have taken is turning the Somerset *County Gazette* into a daily paper when in real life it is a weekly, and has been since 1836. Needs must!

For further reading I would recommend *Operation Hurricane* by Paul Grace (Hachette Australia, 2023). The detail of the operation itself given in *Blast from the Past* is, I hope, correct. The holding tank for contaminated waste is true. That it overflowed when it rained is also true. The pond at Amberley is my embellishment.

I have been intending to feature the Somerset and Dorset Railway in a novel for some time and Bob investigating a cold case presented the ideal opportunity. I am pleased to report that I am too young to remember the old railway line, but walking it is fascinating, the section at Ashcott now part of the Ham Wall Nature Reserve. *Burnham to Evercreech Junction* by Vic Mitchell and Keith Smith (Middleton Press, 1989) is an invaluable guide for those interested.

I would like to thank my editorial team at Thomas & Mercer, Sammia Hamer and Ian Pindar, who remain as patient with me as ever!

Finally, I would like to extend my sincere thanks to the person who approached me at an author event two or three years ago and told me: 'The old nuclear bunker is still open at Pawlett. It would be a great place to hide a body.'

Damien Boyd

Devon, UK

July 2025

About the Author

Damien Boyd is a solicitor by training and draws on his extensive experience of criminal law, along with a spell in the Crown Prosecution Service, to write fast-paced crime thrillers featuring Detective Inspector Nick Dixon.

Follow the Author on Amazon

If you enjoyed this book, follow Damien Boyd on Amazon to be notified when the author releases a new book!
To do this, please follow these instructions:

Desktop:

1) Search for the author's name on Amazon or in the Amazon App.
2) Click on the author's name to arrive on their Amazon page.
3) Click the 'Follow' button.

Mobile and Tablet:

1) Search for the author's name on Amazon or in the Amazon App.
2) Click on one of the author's books.
3) Click on the author's name to arrive on their Amazon page.
4) Click the 'Follow' button.

Kindle eReader and Kindle App:

If you enjoyed this book on a Kindle eReader or in the Kindle App, you will find the author 'Follow' button after the last page.